The Specula

John Ste

Robert Barr

Alpha Editions

This edition published in 2024

ISBN : 9789361476082

Design and Setting By
Alpha Editions
www.alphaedis.com
Email - info@alphaedis.com

As per information held with us this book is in Public Domain.
This book is a reproduction of an important historical work. Alpha Editions uses the best technology to reproduce historical work in the same manner it was first published to preserve its original nature. Any marks or number seen are left intentionally to preserve its true form.

Contents

CHAPTER I—A NARROW ESCAPE

IT was a nasty night, with a drizzling rain nearly as thick as a fog—a rain which obscured the signals and left the rails so slippery that a quick stop was almost impossible—yet just the sort of night to make a quick stop imperative if disaster were to be averted.

Young John Steele, station-master, telegrapher, ticket-agent, and man-of-all-work in the lone shanty known on the railway map as Hitchen's Siding, ignored by all other maps, stood beside the telegraph instrument wondering whether the rain had affected the efficiency of the wires, or whether the train despatcher had gone crazy. Here was Number Sixteen, the freight from the west, coming in, and there were no orders for her. Number Three, known to the outside world as the "Pacific Express," the fastest train on the road, was already forty minutes overdue, tearing westward through the night somewhere, and John did not know where. All he knew was that she was trying to make up lost time as well as the greasy metals would allow, and here he stood without orders!

Once more he seized the key, and calling the despatched office in Warmington again demanded: "What orders for Sixteen?" Then he went outside, and on his own initiative kicked away the iron clutch that released the distant semaphore. The red star of danger glimmering through the drizzle to the east might hold the express if the driver saw it in time.

Number Sixteen had drawn up to the platform, and as her conductor came forward Steele ran to meet him, shouting: "Sidetrack your train, Flynn! Sidetrack her on the jump!"

"Where's my orders?" asked the conductor.

"There's no orders. *I* order you. Get her off the main line at once."

"*Your* orders! Well, for cold cheek——"

Steele lost none of the precious moments in argument, but, turning from the angry conductor, yelled to the engineer: "Whistle for the switch, and kick her back on to the siding. Number Three may be into you any moment."

No youth in Steele's position has the right to give a command to an engineer over the head of a conductor, neither should his orders to the conductor be oral—they must be documentary. Steele was shattering fixed rules of the road, and he knew it.

The conductor of a perishable goods train thinks himself nearly as important as if he ran an express, so Flynn was rightly indignant at this sudden assumption of unlawful authority by a no-account youth at a noaccount station. But a conductor is usually in a comparatively safe place, while the driver of an engine must bear the brunt of a head-on collision, so the grimy Morton at the throttle did not stand on etiquette, but blew the whistle for an open switch and backed his train into the siding. Steele watched the switch light turn to safety again, heaved a sigh of relief, then put his stalwart arms to the lever and slowly pulled off the danger signal to the east, and left the main line clear for the through express.

"What's all this sweat about?" cried Flynn. "Where's Number Three?"

"I don't know," replied John quietly.

"You don't know? Well, I'm blessed! I'll tell you one thing, my impetuous youngster. If Number Three has lost more time, and I'm ordered on to the next siding, you'll lose your job."

"I know it."

John turned in from the platform to the telegraph-room, and Flynn followed him. As they advanced the instrument began a wild rataplan, and Steele paused, raising his hand for silence. Even Flynn, who did not understand its language, felt that the machine was making a frantic, agonised appeal.

"Listen to that!" cried Steele, a note of triumph in his voice.

"What's it saying?" whispered the conductor, awed in spite of himself.

"'Sidetrack Sixteen! Sidetrack Sixteen! In God's name sidetrack Sixteen!' There's your orders at last, Flynn. It's lucky you didn't wait for them."

The final words were obliterated by a roar as of a descending avalanche, and the express tore past, ripping the night and the silence; fifty miles an hour at the least; the long line of curtained windows in the sleeping-cars shimmering in the station lights like a wavering biograph picture—there and away while you drew your breath. In the stillness that followed, the brass instrument kept up its useless, idiotic chatter. A heavy step sounded on the platform, and the engineer appeared at the door, his face ghastly in its pallor, the smudges on it giving a heightening effect of contrast.

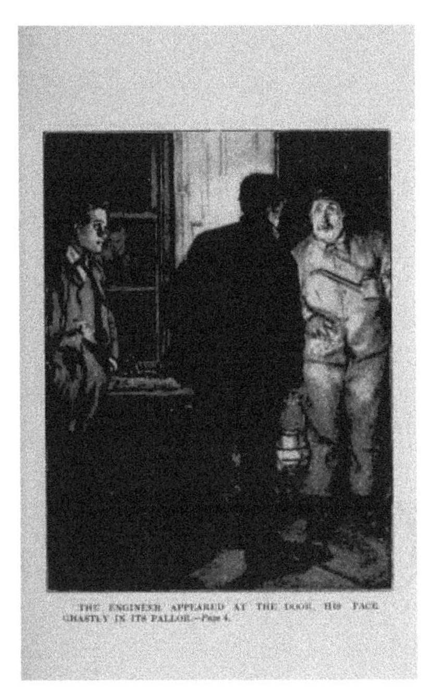

THE ENGINEER APPEARED AT THE DOOR, HIS FACE GHASTLY IN ITS PALLOR.—Page 4.

"God, Flynn," he gasped, "that was a close call."

The conductor nodded, and each man strode forward as if impelled by a single impulse to grasp hands with the youngster, who laughed nervously, saying:

"They're pretty anxious in the city. I must answer." Then he went to the instrument and sent the most undisciplined message that had ever gone over the wires from a subordinate to a superior.

CHAPTER II—PROMOTION

IN the train despatcher's office at Warmington, one hundred and twenty miles to the east of Hitchen's Siding, the force was hard at work under the electric light. Philip Manson, division superintendent, strolled in, although it was long past his office hours, for he was one of those indefatigable railroad men loth to take his fingers off the pulse of the great organisation he controlled, and no employee of the road could be certain of any hour, night or day, when Manson might not be standing unexpectedly beside him. As this silent man surveyed the busy room, listening to the click of the telegraphic sounders, which spoke to him as plainly as if human lips were uttering the language of the land, he was startled by a cry from Hammond, the train despatcher. Hammond sprang like a madman to the sender, and the key, at lightning speed, rattled forth—"Sidetrack Sixteen. Sidetrack Sixteen."

Instinctively the division superintendent knew what had happened. To the most accurate of men, faithful and exact through years of service, may come an unaccountable momentary lapse of vigilance. The train despatcher had forgotten Number Sixteen! Instantly the road spread itself out before the mind's eye of the superintendent. He knew every inch of it. The situation revealed itself to his mathematical brain as a well-known arrangement of men and pawns would display to an expert what could or could not be done on the chess-board. He knew where Number Three would lose further time on the up-grades, but now, alas! it was speeding along a flat country, where every minute meant a mile. Nevertheless, there was one chance in a thousand that the express had not yet reached Hitchen's, and his quick mind indicated the right thing to be done.

"Tell him to stop Number Three," he snapped forth.

The despatcher obeyed. Where disaster was a matter of moments, there was little use in awaiting the slow movements of a heavy freight-train when the express, a demon of destruction, was swooping down on the scene. There came no answer to the frenzied appeal. Every man in the room was on his feet, and each held his breath as if the crash and the shrieks could leap across one hundred and twenty miles and penetrate into that appalled office. Then the sounder began, leisurely and insolent:

"I sidetracked Sixteen on my own, and set the signal against Three until Sixteen was in. Are you people crazy, or merely plain drunk?"

The tension snapped like an overstrained wire. One man went into shriek after shriek of laughter; another laid his head on his desk and sobbed. Hammond staggered into a chair, and an assistant held a glass of water to his ashen lips. The division superintendent stood like a statue, a deep frown marking his displeasure at the flippant message that had come in upon such a tragic crisis. But the assurance that the express was safe cleared his brow.

"The man at the siding is named John Steele, isn't he?"

"Yes, sir."

"Send down a substitute to-morrow, and tell Steele to report to me."

"Yes, sir."

And this is how our young man came to be Philip Man-son's right-hand helper in the division superintendent's office of the Grand Union Station at Warmington City.

The Grand Union Station is a noble pile of red brick, rough and cut stone and terra-cotta, adorned by a massive corner tower holding aloft a great clock that gives the city standard time. The tower is the pride of Warmington—a pillar of red cloud by day and a pillar of fire by night, with the hours distinct a mile away. The tower may be taken as a monument to the power and wealth of the Rockervelts, although in larger cities they possessed still more imposing architecture to uphold their fame.

The Manateau Midland, which made this immense structure its eastern terminus, was merely a link in the Rockervelt chain of admirably equipped railways; but, as the title, Union, implied, other roads, mostly bankrupt lines or branches of the Midland, enjoyed running rights into the Grand Union Station.

The transferring of a country youth at an enhanced salary, from a lone pine shanty on the prairie to this palatial edifice in the city seemed to John like being translated bodily to heaven. Now he had his chance, and that was all he asked of fate. He delighted in railway work. The strident screech of the whistles, the harsh clanking of cars coming together, all the discordant sounds of the station-yard, were as orchestral music to him, and he never tired of the symphony. He speedily became the most useful man about the place, and was from the first the most popular. He had a habit of dashing here and there bare-headed, and to heat or cold was equally indifferent. There was not a trace of malice in the lad, and he was ever ready with a cheery word or a helping hand. He seemed able to do anything, from running an engine to tapping a wire, and was willing in an emergency to work night and day, without a grumble, till he dropped from fatigue. Silent Philip Man-son watched Steele's progress with unspoken approval, and loved him not the less that for all the lad's witty exuberance not a word had ever passed his lips about that sinister blunder at Hitchen's Siding. Those things are not to be spoken of, and even the general manager knew nothing of the crisis. The train despatcher had retired, nerve-broken, and the newspapers never guessed why.

But there was one man who did not like John, and that was no less important a personage than the general manager himself. His huge room in the lower part of the tower was as sumptuously furnished as an eastern palace. T. Acton Blair, general manager of the Manateau Midland, was supposed to be related to the Rockervelt family, but this was perhaps a fallacy put forth to account for the placing of such a palpably incompetent man in so responsible a position. He was a bald-headed, corpulent personage, pompous and ponderous, slow moving and slow speaking, saying perfectly obvious things in a deep, impressive voice, as if he were uttering the wisdom of ages. His subordinate, Philip Manson, as everybody knew, was responsible for the efficiency of the road; and when he wanted a project carried out, he always pretended it was Blair's original idea, so the general manager got the credit if it was a success, and Manson shouldered the blame if it was not.

One morning, as Philip Manson was about to leave the general manager's room, after the customary daily interview with his chief, the latter said: "By the way, Manson, who is that individual who rushes about these offices at all hours, as if he thought he were running the whole Rockervelt system?"

"I suspect you refer to John Steele, one of my assistants, sir."

"I don't like him, Manson; he seems obtrusive."

"I assure you, sir, he is a most capable man."

"Yes, yes, I dare say; but, as I have often told you, the success of our organisation is in method, not in haste."

"Quite so, sir."

"That person always gives me the idea that something is wrong—that a fire has broken out, or a man has been run over. I don't like it. His clothes are untidy and seem to have been made for some one else. I shouldn't like Mr. Rockervelt to see that we have such an unkempt person on our clerical staff."

"I'll speak to him, sir; I admit his manner does not do him justice."

When Manson next encountered John alone, he spoke with more than his usual severity.

"Steele, I wish you would pay some attention to your clothes. Get a new business suit and take care of it. Remember you are in the city of Warmington, and not at Hitchen's Siding."

"Yes, sir," said John contritely, looking down with new dismay at his grease-stained trousers.

"I wish also you would abandon your habit of running all over the place without a hat."

"I'll do it, sir."

The catastrophe came with appalling suddenness. The Pacific Express Steele had saved, but himself he could not save.

Tearing down the long corridor at breakneck speed, he turned a corner and ran bang into the imposing front of the general manager. That dignified potentate staggered back against the wall gasping, while his glossy silk hat rolled to the floor. John, brought up as suddenly as if he had collided with a haystack, groaned in terror, snatched the tall hat from the floor, brushed it, and handed it to the speechless magnate.

"I'm very, *very* sorry, sir," he ventured. But Mr. Acton Blair made no reply. Leaving the culprit standing there, he put on his hat and strode majestically to the division superintendent's room.

"Manson!" he panted, dropping into a chair, "discharge that lunatic at once!"

The division superintendent was too straightforward a man to pretend ignorance regarding Blair's meaning. His face hardened into an expression of obstinacy that amazed his chief.

"The Rockervelt system is deeply indebted to Mr. Steele—a debt it can never repay. He saved Number Three last November from what would have been the most disastrous accident of the year."

"Why was I never told of this?"

"For three reasons, sir. First, the fewer people that know of such escapes, the better; second, Hammond, who was responsible, voluntarily resigned on plea of ill-health; third, Hammond was your nephew."

Mr. T. Acton Blair rose to his feet with that majesty of bulk which pertains to corpulent men. It was an action which usually overawed a subordinate.

"I think you are making a mistake, sir, regarding our relative positions. I am general manager of the Manateau Midland, and as such have a right to be informed of every important event pertaining to the road."

"Your definition of the situation is correct. Both you and Mr. Rockervelt should have been told of the narrow escape of the express."

There was a glitter as of steel in the keen eyes of the superintendent, while the inflated manner of the manager underwent a visible change, like a distended balloon pricked by a pin. Mr. Blair knew well the danger to himself and his vaunted position if the event under discussion came to the knowledge of the great autocrat in New York, so he tried to give his surrender the air of a masterly retreat.

"Well, well, Mr. Manson, I don't know but you were right. The less such things are talked of, the better. They have a habit of getting into the papers, and undermining public confidence, and we should all try to avoid such publicity. Yes, you did quite right, so we will let it go at that."

"And how about Mr. Steele?"

"After all, Manson, he is in your department, and you may do as you please. I should rather see him go, but I don't insist upon it. Good afternoon, Mr. Manson." The great man took his departure ponderously, leaving Manson somewhat nonplussed. As soon as the door to the corridor closed behind Blair, the door to Manson's secretary's room, which had been ajar during this conversation, flew open, and the impetuous Steele came rushing in.

"Excuse me, Mr. Manson," he cried, "but I was waiting to see you, and I could not help hearing part of what you and Mr. Blair said. I did not intend to listen; but if I had shut the door it would have attracted attention, so I didn't know what to do. I suppose he told you we had a head-on collision, round a curve, with no signals out."

The young man tried to carry it off jauntily with a half nervous laugh, but Manson's face was sober and unresponsive.

"It was all my fault, and you had warned me before," continued Steele breathlessly. "Now you stood up to the old man for me, and made him back water; but I'm not going to have you get into trouble because of me. I've discharged John Steele. I'm going in now to Mr. Blair, and I'll apologise and resign. I'll tell him you warned me to quit rushing round, and that I didn't quit. I'm sorry I telescoped him, but not half so sorry as that I've disappointed you."

"Nonsense!" said Manson severely. "Go back to your desk; and let this rest for a day or two. I'll see the manager about it later on." He noticed the moisture in the younger man's eyes, and the quiver of his nether lip, so he spoke coldly. Emotion has no place in the railway business.

"No, sir, I'd never feel comfortable again. There's lots of work waiting for me, and it won't have to wait long. I'm going for it as I went for Mr. Blair's waistcoat. But I want to tell you, Mr. Manson, that—that all the boys know you're a brick, who'll stand by them if they—if they do the square thing."

And as if his disaster had not been caused by his precipitance, the youth bolted headlong from the room before Manson could frame a reply.

The division superintendent put on his hat and left the room less hurriedly than John had done. He made his way to that sumptuous edifice known as the University Club. The social organisation which it housed had long numbered Manson as a member, but he was a most infrequent visitor. He walked direct to the cosiest corner of the large reading-room, and there, in a luxurious arm-chair, found, as he had expected, the Hon. Duffield Rogers, an aged gentleman with a gray beard on his chin and a humourous twinkle in his eye. Mr. Rogers was a millionaire over and over again, yet he was president of the poorest railway in the State, known as the Burdock Route, whose eastern terminus was in the Grand Union which Manson had just left. Rogers occupied a largely ornamental position on the Burdock, as he did in the arm-chair of the club. He was surrounded by a disarray of newspapers on the floor, and allowed the one he was holding to fall on the pile as he looked up with a smile on seeing Manson approach.

"Hallo, Manson! Is the Midland going to pay a dividend, that you've got an afternoon off?"

"What do *you* know about dividends?" asked Manson, with a laugh. He seemed a much more jocular person at the club than in the railway-office, and he was not above giving a sly dig at the Burdock Route, which had never paid a dividend since it was opened.

"Oh! I read about 'em in the papers," replied the Hon. Duffield serenely. "How's that old stick-in-the-mud Blair? I'm going to ask the committee of this club to expel him. He has the cheek to swell around here, in *my* presence, and pretend he knows something about railroading. I'd stand that from you, but not from T. Acton Blair. He forgets I'm president of a road, while he's only a general manager. I tell him I rank with Rockervelt, and not with mere G. M's."

The old millionaire laughed so heartily at his own remarks that some of the *habitués* of the reading-room looked sternly at the framed placard above the mantelshelf which displayed in large black letters the word "Silence." Manson drew up a chair beside the old man and said earnestly:

"I came in to see you on business, Mr. Rogers. There is a young fellow in my office who will develop into one of the best railroad men of our time. I want you to find a place for him on your line."

"Oh! we're not taking on any new men. Just the reverse. We laid off the general manager and about fifteen lesser officials a month ago, and we don't miss 'em in the least. I've been trying to resign for the past year, but they won't let me, because I don't ask any salary."

"This man will be worth double his money anywhere you place him."

"I am not saying anything against your man except that we don't want him. The Burdock's practically bankrupt—*you* know that."

"Still, John Steele, the young fellow I'm speaking of, won't want much money, and he understands railroading down to the ground."

"If he is a valuable man, why are you so anxious to get rid of him?" asked the wily president, with a smile.

"I'm not. I'd rather part with all the rest of my staff than with Steele; but Mr. Blair has taken a dislike to him, and——"

"Enough said," broke in the president of the Burdock. "That dislike, coupled with your own preference, makes the best recommendation any man could ask. How much are you paying Steele?"

"Ten dollars a week."

The old man mused for a few moments, then chuckled aloud in apparent enjoyment.

"I'll give him fifteen," he said. "Will that satisfy him?"

"It will more than satisfy him."

"But I pay the amount on one condition."

"What is that, Mr. Rogers?"

"The condition is that he accepts and fills the position of general manager of the Burdock Route."

"General manager!" echoed Manson, "I'm talking seriously, Mr. Rogers."

"So am I, Manson, so am I. And don't you see what a good bargain I'm driving? You say Steele is first class. All right; I know you wouldn't vouch for him unless that were so. Very well. I get a general manager for fifteen dollars a week; cheapest in the country, and doubtless the best. I confess, however, my chief delight in offering him the position is the hope of seeing old Blair's face when he first meets in conference the youth he has dismissed, his equal in rank if not in salary. It will be a study in physiognomy."

If the staid Philip Manson thought that Steele's native modesty would prevent him from accepting the management of the Burdock Route, he was much mistaken. When Manson related quietly the result of his interview with the Hon. Duffield Rogers, the youth amazed him by leaping nearly to the ceiling and giving utterance to a whoop more like the war-cry of a red Indian than the exclamation of a Scottish Highlander. Then he blushed and apologised for his excitement, abashed by Manson's disapproving eyes.

"I tell you what it is, Mr. Manson, I'll make the roadbed of the old Burdock as good as you've made the Midland, and I'll——"

"Tut, tut!" said Manson, in his most unenthusiastic tone; "you can do nothing without money, and the Burdock's practically bankrupt. Be thankful if you receive your fifteen a week with reasonable regularity. Now, here is a letter to the Hon. Duffield Rogers. Give it to the doorman at the club, and Mr. Rogers will invite you in. You will find the president a humourous man and you have a touch of the same quality yourself; but repress it and treat him with the greatest respect, for humourists get along better with dull people like myself than with one another. Although you are leaving the jurisdiction of Mr. Blair, do not forget what I told you about paying attention to your clothes. You will be meeting important men whom you may have to persuade, and it is better to face them well groomed; a prepossessing appearance counts in business. Prepossession is nine points in the game. Here is the letter, so be off." The division superintendent rose and extended his hand. "And now, my boy, God bless you!"

The tone of the benediction sounded almost gruff, but there was a perceptible quaver underneath it, and after one firm clasp of the hand the divisional superintendent sat down at his desk with the resolute air of a man determined to get on with his work. As for John, he could not trust his voice, either for thanks or farewell; so he left the room with impetuous abruptness, and would have forgotten his hat if he had not happened to hold it in his hand.

To the ordinary man the Burdock Route was a badly kept streak of defective rails, rough as a corduroy road. To John Steele it was a glorious path to Paradise; an air line of tremendous possibilities. He went up and down its length, not in a private car, but on ordinary locals and freight trains. He became personally acquainted with every section foreman and with nearly every labourer between Warmington and Portandit, the western terminus. He found them, as a usual thing, sullen and inert; he left them jolly and enthusiastic, almost believing in the future of the road.

He proved an unerring judge of character. The useless men were laid off, while the competent were encouraged and promoted. He could handle a shovel with the best of them, or drive in a spike without missing a blow. In a year he had the Burdock Route as level as a billiard-table without extra expenditure of money, and travelers were beginning to note the improvement, so that receipts increased. He induced the Pullman Company to put an up-to-date sleeper on the night trains, east and west, and withdraw their antiquated cars hitherto in use.

But there was one thing Steele was not able to accomplish. He could not persuade the venerable president of the road to regard it as anything but a huge joke. The Hon. Duffield Rogers absolutely refused to leave his comfortable chair in the club and take a trip over the Burdock. The president delighted in Steele's company, and got him made a member of the club, setting him down as a graduate of the Wahoo University, which was supposed to exist somewhere in the remote West. Rogers was a privileged member and a founder of the club, so the committee did not scrutinise his recommendation too closely.

"It's no use, John," he would say, when his fervent assistant urged him to come and see what had been done on the Burdock. "Life is hard enough at best without my spending any part of it in a beastly place like Portandit. I hear you have done wonders with the road, but you can't accomplish anything really worth while with a route that has no terminus on the Atlantic. As long as you have to hand over your Eastern traffic to the Rock-ervelts at Warmington, and take what Western freight they care to allow you, you are in the clutch of the Rock-ervelts, and they can freeze you out whenever they like.=

```You may grade, you may ballast your road, if you will,

```But the shadow of Rockervelt's over you still."=

Thus Steele always received his discouragement from his own chief, and with most people this would ultimately have dampened enthusiasm; but John was ever optimistic and a believer in his work. One day he rushed into the club, his hat on the back of his head, and his eyes ablaze with excitement.

"Mr. Rogers, I've solved the problem at last!" he cried. "I tell you, well make the Burdock the greatest line in this country."

He shoved aside the heaps of magazines from the reading-room table and spread out a map on its surface. The Hon. Duffield rose slowly to his feet and stood beside the eager young man. A kindly, indulgent smile played about the lips of the aged president.

"Now see here!" shouted Steele (they were alone together in the room, and the "Silence" placard made no protest). "There's Beechville, on the Burdock Route, and here's Collins' Centre, on the C. P. & N. Between these two points are sixty-three miles of prairie country, as level as a floor. It will be the cheapest bit of road to build in America; no embankments, no cuttings, no grade at all. Why, just dump the rails down, and they'd form a line of themselves! Once the Burdock taps the C. P. & N., there is our route clear through to tide-water, independent of the Rockervelt System."

Steele, his face aglow, looked up at the veteran, but the indulgent smile had taken on a cynical touch. Mr. Rogers placed his hand on John's shoulder in kindly fashion and said slowly:

"If that were possible it would have been done long since. You could not get your charter. Rockervelt would buy the Legislature, and we in the West haven't money enough to outbid him."

Steele's clenched fist came down on the map with a force that made the stout table quiver.

"But I've *got* the charter!" he roared, in a voice that made the doorman outside think there was trouble in the reading-room. The Hon. Duffield Rogers sank once more into his arm-chair and gazed at John.

"*You've got the charter?*" he echoed quietly.

"Certainly, and it didn't cost me a cent. The Governor signed it yesterday."

"Out of the mouths of babes and sucklings—" murmured the old man, who had years of experience behind him in the bribing of law-makers. "In Heaven's name, how did you manage it?"

"I went to the capital, became acquainted with the legislators—splendid fellows, all of them—personal friends of mine now; I showed them how such a link would benefit the State, and the bill went through like *that*." John snapped his fingers.

"Well, I'm blessed!" ejaculated the old-time purchaser of valuable franchises.

"Now, Mr. Rogers, you understand financiering, and know all the capitalists. I understand the railway business. You raise the money, I'll build the road, and we'll be into New York with a whoop."

For one brief instant Steele thought he had conquered.

Like an old war-horse at the sound of the bugle, Rogers stiffened his muscles for the fight. The light of battle flamed in his eye as the memory of the conquest of millions returned to him. But presently he leaned back in his chair with a sigh, and the light flickered out.

"Ah, John!" he whispered plaintively, "I wish I had met you thirty years ago; but alas! you weren't born then. What a team we would have made! But I'm too old and, besides, your scheme wouldn't work. I might get up the money, and I might not. The very name of the Burdock is a hoodoo. But even if the money were subscribed and the link built, we would merely be confronted by a railroad war. The Rockervelts would cut rates, and the longest purse is bound to win, which means we should go to the wall."

Steele sat down with his face in his hands, thoroughly discouraged for the first time in his life. He felt a boyish desire to cry, and a mannish desire to curse, but did neither. The old gentleman rambled on amiably: "You are a ten-thousand dollar man, John, but your line of progress is on some road with a future. Follow my advice and take your charter to that old thief Rocker-velt himself. There lies your market."

"How can I do that," growled John from between his fingers, "when I am an employee of the Burdock?"

"Technically so am I; therefore, as your chief, I advise you to see Rockervelt."

"All right!" cried Steele, springing to his feet as if his minute of deep despondency had been time thrown away that could not be spared. He shook hands cordially with the president, and returned his genial smile.

---

# CHAPTER III—-WAYLAYING A MAGNATE

ON the steps of the club he was surprised to meet Philip Manson, who, he knew, rarely honoured that institution with his presence.

"I was just going up to see you, Mr. Manson. I want you to do me a favour. I'm off to New York, and I'd like a letter of introduction to Mr. Rockervelt."

The brow of the division superintendent knitted slightly, and he did not answer so readily as the other expected.

"Well, it's like this, Steele," he said at last: "I am merely a small official, and Mr. Rockervelt is an important man who knows his own importance. Etiquette prescribes that I should give you a letter to the general manager, who is the proper person to introduce you to Mr. Rockervelt. So, you see——"

"Oh, very well," exclaimed Steele, sorry he had asked. This rebuff, following so closely on the heels of his disappointment, clouded his usual good nature. He was about to go on, when Manson detained him, grasping the lapel of his coat.

"Don't be offended, John; and I'll tell you something no one else knows. I'm going to quit the railway business."

"What!" shouted Steele, all his old affection for the man surging up within him as he now noted the trouble in his face. Manson quit the railway business! It was as if he had calmly announced his intention to commit suicide.

"That old fool Blair has been making trouble for you?" he cried.

"Oh, no! That is to say, there always has been a slight tension, and it doesn't grow better. I've made a little money—real estate has risen, you know, and that sort of thing—and I've been working hard, so I intend to resign. I take it you have some scheme to propose to Mr. Rockervelt?"

"Yes, I have."

"Very well. Your scheme, if it is a good one, will prove your best introduction. He's an accessible man; but plunge right to the point when you meet him. He likes directness. And, by the way, he will be in Warmington on Wednesday morning. The big conference of railway presidents begins Thursday afternoon at Portandit, and he will be there, of course. We attach his private car to Number Three, Wednesday night, and your best time to see him might be in his car during the four miles he's running to the Junction. The express waits for him at the Junction. You haven't much time, but it will prove all the time he'll want to allow you if your project doesn't appeal to him."

"Say!" cried Steele, a thrill with the portent of a sudden idea, "couldn't you persuade Rockervelt to hitch his car to the Burdock 'Thunderbolt'? I'll run him through to Portandit, and save him that dreary daylight trip from Tobasco."

Manson shook his head.

"No; Mr. Rockervelt would not go over any other road than his own. I could not propose such a thing, and Mr. Blair would not."

Steele walked down to the Grand Union Station deep in thought. He had determined to take Rockervelt's private car from its place with one of his own pony engines and attach it to his own express, and he was formulating his plans. Once away from the Junction, the Government itself could not stop him. And now we need a railway map to explain the situation. From Warmington to Portandit or to Tobasco is a long night's ride. The "Thunderbolt" leaves the Junction on the Burdock Route at 8 p.m. The "Pacific Express," on the Midland, departs at 8.20; one train from the south side of the station, the other from the north.

At ten minutes to eight Philip Manson received a telephone message asking him to remain within call. A short time after, when the men were coupling the private car to the west-bound train, Steele rushed in to the telephone cabin and shouted:

"That you, Mr. Manson?"

"Yes; who are you?"

"Steele. I've just coupled Rockervelt's car to the 'Thunderbolt.' Release Number Three, for she will wait in vain. Telegraph all those people that Rockervelt was to meet at Tobasco to-morrow morning to take the midnight train for Portandit and meet him there."

"Steele, are you out of your senses?"

"No. It's all as I say. Nothing can stop us."

"I haven't the list of the men that——"

"Then call up Blair. He's in his private car on Number Three, which of course you know. You must get the list."

"John Steele, I implore you to stop before it is too late. This is an outrage. It's kidnapping—brigand's work. You are breaking laws that will——"

"I know, I know. Good night, Mr. Manson."

"Just one moment, John, I've something important to tell you. Mr. Rockervelt telegraphed to me——"

But the young man was proof against all blandishments, determined to go his own way, so he rang off before his friend could finish the sentence.

Steele rushed out to the platform, nodded to the waiting conductor, swung himself on the Pullman car, the conductor swung his lantern, and the "Thunderbolt" swung out into the night.

When the deft and silent negro had cleared away the breakfast dishes next morning and removed the tablecloth, Mr. Rockervelt leaned back in his chair and lit a cigar. There was much to think of, and he was thinking much. The car rolled along with gratifying smoothness, and the great man paid no attention to the scenery, otherwise he might have been startled, for he knew well the environment of his own line. As for the negro, all roads were alike to him, and he attended solely and silently to his master's comfort. He hovered about for a few moments, then said deferentially:

"Day's a gennelman, sah, in de sleepah ahead's been asking for you, sah, two or three times dis mawning, sah. He'd like to have some conversation with you, sah, if you's disengaged."

"Who is he?"

"Here's he's cawd, sah."

Mr. Rockervelt glanced at the card, murmuring: "John Steele, General Manager, Burdock Route. That's strange." Then aloud: "Show Mr. Steele in, Peter." The magnate did not rise as John bowed to him, but waved his hand toward a chair, a silent invitation of which his visitor did not avail himself. He recognized the great man at once from the many portraits he had seen of him.

"I hope you have slept well, Mr. Rockervelt," began the new-comer.

"Excellently."

"And I trust you found the road-bed in good order." Mr. Rockervelt raised his eyebrows and looked with some surprise at the polite inquirer before him.

"My own bed and the road-bed left nothing to be desired, since you are so kind as to ask."

"I am delighted to hear you say so, sir," cried John with enthusiasm. His host began to fear some demented person had got into his car, and he glanced over his shoulder for Peter, who was not visible.

"Why should you be delighted to hear me praise my own road?" he asked in tones that gave no hint of his uneasiness.

"Well, sir, to tell you the truth, I wished a few minutes' talk with you, and that's not as easy come by as you may think. You are not on your own road, but on the Burdock Route, now rapidly approaching Portandit. I took the liberty last night of attaching your car to this train, sir, instead of to your own Number Three."

Rockervelt sat up in alarm, glanced out of the windows, first on one side, then on the other. Bringing back his gaze to the man before him, hot anger added colour to the usual floridness of his countenance.

"You took the liberty, did you? Well, let me tell you, sir, it is a liberty you will bitterly regret."

"I am sorry to hear you say that, sir," replied John humbly.

"The liberty! Curse it, sir! you have disarranged all my plans. There are three men in Tobasco whom it is imperative I should meet this forenoon before the convention opens."

"Quite so, sir. I had them telegraphed to take the Midnight and meet you at Portandit instead. They'll be waiting for you when you get in, sir."

"The devil you did!" gasped Rockervelt, sinking back in his chair.

"You see, sir, it's an uneasy conference you would have had on that rocky road to Dublin, the T. and P. A long forenoon's ride, sir, with a line as rough as a rail fence. It would be like coming down the Soo Rapids, only you wouldn't travel so quickly. You are too good a railroad man, sir, not to hate a day journey, and I counted on that."

"It's a minor matter, but you happen to be right."

"I have a carriage waiting for you, sir. You can drive to your hotel at your ease, hold the conference in your room, and drop in to the convention whenever it pleases you, sir."

"Have you also arranged my return to New York, Mr. Steele? By what route do you intend to send me back?" John laughed that cheerful, infectious laugh of his. He realised that the danger point was passed.

"I hope you will get safe back to New York whatever route you take, sir."

"Thank you. How long have you been general manager of this road?"

"About two years, sir."

"Where did you learn the business?"

"In the greatest railroad school of this world, sir—the Rockervelt System."

The faint shadow of a smile passed over the face of Mr. Rockervelt for the first time during the interview.

"That I take as a handsome return for my testimonial to your road-bed. Why did you leave us?"

"I failed to please Mr. Blair, sir."

"In whose department were you?"

"In the division superintendent's."

"Did you please Philip Manson?"

"I think I did, sir."

"Um! Well, now, you did not waylay me for the purposes of pleasant conversation. I don't like to see good men leave us; and if your object in kidnapping me was to come back to us, I may at once admit I am willing to entertain a proposal."

"No, sir. That was not my object, although I make bold to say that an offer from Mr. Rockervelt would exact respect from the greatest in the land, and I'm no exception to my betters. What I wanted, sir, was to persuade you to cast your eye over this map. The red line represents sixty-three miles of level country, and——"

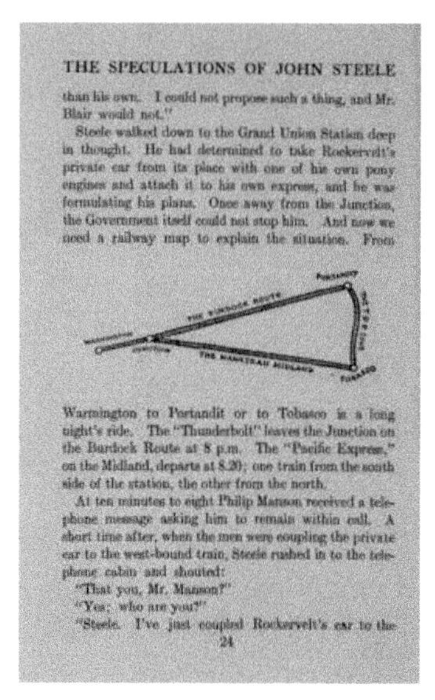

THE SPECULATIONS OF JOHN STEELE

than his own. I could not propose such a thing, and Mr. Blair would not."

Steele walked down to the Grand Union Station deep in thought. He had determined to take Rockervelt's private car from its place with one of his own pony engines and attach it to his own express, and he was formulating his plans. Once away from the Junction, the Government itself could not stop him. And now we need a railway map to explain the situation. From

Warmington to Portandit or to Tobasco is a long night's ride. The "Thunderbolt" leaves the Junction on the Burdock Route at 8 p.m. The "Pacific Express," on the Midland, departs at 8.20; one train from the south side of the station, the other from the north.

At ten minutes to eight Philip Manson received a telephone message asking him to remain within call. A short time after, when the men were coupling the private car to the west-bound train, Steele rushed in to the telephone cabin and shouted:

"That you, Mr. Manson?"

"Yes; who are you?"

"Steele. I've just coupled Rockervelt's car to the

24

"I see; if a railway were built along that red line, your road would have access to New York independent of me. Well, young man, don't let that red line worry you. I could not allow you to get a charter."

"You're quick to see the possibilities, sir."

"Yes, but here are no probabilities."

"I'm not so sure of that, sir. Like the other fellow's fifteen dollars, I've got the charter in my inside pocket."

"Do you mind showing it to me?" asked Rockervelt, unconsciously finishing the line of the song referred to. John handed him the documents, and the great man scrutinised them with the quick care of an expert; then he folded them up again, but did not offer to return them. He gazed out upon the flying landscape for a few moments while Steele stood expectant.

"How did you overcome Blair's opposition?" he inquired at last.

"There was no opposition."

The president frowned, and a glint of anger appeared in the cold, calculating eyes.

"I expect Blair to watch the Legislature as well as the railway."

"He watches neither, sir."

Rockervelt glanced sharply at the confident young man who thus dared to asperse one of the minor gods of the Rockervelt System.

"Then who looks after the Midland?"

"Philip Manson, and does it quietly and well."

"Where did you get the money to put this through? A syndicate?"

"No; I didn't need any money. All I needed was that one of your general managers, should be sound asleep, and time to make personal friends of the members of the House."

"I see you are prejudiced against Mr. Blair."

"I am, sir."

Rockervelt pulled himself together as one who has had enough of badinage and now prepares for business. His impassive face hardened, and the onlooker saw before him the man who had ruthlessly crushed opposition, regardless of consequences.

"Now, young man," he began, in a voice that cut like a knife, "do you know the value of these documents?"

"Yes, sir; they're not worth a damn!"

"What!" cried Rockervelt, suddenly sitting bolt upright. "I thought you had kidnapped me to hold me up, as is the genial Western fashion. Don't you want to sell this charter?"

"No, sir. I offered the charter to the Hon. Duffield Rogers, president of the Burdock, as was my duty, but he said you could beat any combination that might be formed in the long run."

"Yes, or in the short run. Sensible man, Rogers. Well, sir, you do not expect an exorbitant price for a worthless charter?"

"I want no price at all. The charter is yours. But I'd like to offer you a hint as well as the charter, and the advice is to make Philip Manson manager of the Midland."

"I see; and what for yourself?"

"Only bear me in mind when you have a vacancy for a well-paid official down east."

The young man had been standing during this long colloquy, but now Mr. Rockervelt asked him to be seated, and there being a suggestion of command as well as of request in his tone, John Steele, drew up a chair to the table that divided them.

"You have quite definitely made up your mind, I take it, that T. Acton Blair is unfit for the position of general manager of the Manateau Midland," said the chief with quiet irony.

"Yes, I have," replied Steele, defiantly, "and so has everybody else who knows him."

"And yet you admit the Midland is a well-managed road?"

"Certainly, but that is because of Philip Manson."

"Quite so. 'The page slew the boar; the peer had the gloire,' as the old poet said, and the peer, too, has the bigger salary, as a modern writer might remark. You never heard any reason given, I suppose, why Blair holds a better position than Manson?"

"Oh, yes, I did," cried the impetuous young man, "it is said that Mr. Blair is a relative of your own."

The expression of displeasure that clouded the face of the railway prince gave instant intimation to Steele that his reply had been tactless.

"I imagine you have a great deal to learn, Mr. Steele, and I predict before you are as old as Mr. Blair you will receive some sharp lessons in diplomacy. You have shown yourself competent to smooth out the roughnesses that formerly characterised the Burdock route, but those same capabilities may not be equal to removing obstacles in your own path of life. The Midland is a well-managed road, and you say the credit belongs to Manson. Very good. I put Manson in his place, and so my purposes are fulfilled. If I made him general manager, as you suggest, he might or might not be a success, yet we are both agreed that he is a success in his present position. Now you, I see by this card, are general manager of the Burdock route. Does the Burdock, therefore, take a high place in the railway system of America?"

"It does not," candidly admitted John Steele. "Why?"

"Because there is no money behind it."

"Exactly. My excellent friend, the Honorable Duffield Rogers, has plenty of money, but he knows enough to take care of it. He doesn't waste any of his wealth in trying to make the Burdock route all that his capable general manager may wish it to be. So you see, Mr. Steele, finance has to be considered as well as good road mending. In that department T. Acton Blair occupies a high position among the railway men of the West. If you ever accumulate a little money, and doubt my statement, venture your cash in a contest where Blair is your opponent, and, I venture to say, you'll regret it. On the other hand, if you should happen to become a friend of Mr. Blair, and he cared to give you a tip or two in higher finance, you may grow rich in following his lead. In this very matter of the charter there is a possibility that you have entirely underestimated the general manager of the Midland. It is on the cards that he agrees with you and me regarding the worthlessness of the charter."

"I'll swear he knew nothing about it," persisted Steele, knowing as soon as the sentence was uttered that again he had let his tongue run away with his judgment.

"Perhaps he did, and perhaps he didn't. I strongly suspect he knew all about it, and hoped you would entangle old Rogers into a railway war, in which case I venture to assert, Blair would have crushed both you and your chief. Of course you tried to get Rogers to take up the struggle?"

"Yes, I did."

"And he very politely, but quite definitely, refused?"

"That also is true."

"Well, you see, Mr. Steele," said Rockervelt, with something almost approaching a laugh, "there is more wisdom in grey hairs than most young persons are willing to admit. Would you be surprised if I told you that I have determined to ignore your advice, and so will not remove Mr. Blair from his position?"

"I am not in the least surprised, now that I know your opinion of him."

"Maybe then I can astonish you by admitting that I intend to remove your friend, Mr. Manson, from the situation he so worthily fills."

"To place him in a better position, I hope?"

"Oh, yes. I have been in need of him for some time in our New York office. I should have taken him long ago, if I'd had the right man to put in his place. The other day I received Philip Manson's resignation, and without either accepting or declining it, I telegraphed him to let me know whom he suggested as his substitute. Yesterday I received his reply, and although I have been unable to follow the advice you have tendered me so far, I may accept it regarding the new candidate."

With this Mr. Rockervelt pressed an electric button, and an alert young man answered his call.

"Meldrum, bring me that last letter of Manson's about the division superintendency of the Midland."

The secretary returned a moment later with the document, which he handed to Rockervelt, who tossed it across the table towards Steele. The letter read:

*Dear Sir:*

*In my opinion the best man to appoint as division superintendent of the Manateau Midland is John Steele, at present general manager of the Burdock route. He was formerly employed on the Midland in various capacities, and was promoted entirely through efficiency. Although the position he occupies on the Burdock is nominally higher than that left vacant by my resignation, yet I think Mr. Steele would be content with less honour and more money.*

*Yours faithfully,*

*Philip Manson.*

As Steele looked up from the reading of this letter Rockervelt said sharply:

"*I* think you are the man referred to by Manson?"

"Yes, sir."

"It is rather strange that you should have taken all the trouble to attach my car to your train when I had left word with Manson to get into communication with you, and arrange an interview between you and me at Portandit."

"I was merely anticipating your wishes, Mr. Rockervelt. It is lucky I rang off Philip Manson last night so abruptly at the telephone, for I imagine this is what he was about to tell me."

"How much are they giving you on the Burdock route?" asked Rockervelt abruptly.

"Fifteen dollars a week."

Instead of expressing his surprise at the smallness of the amount, Rockervelt merely said:

"Do you get your money?"

"Oh, I see to that," replied Steele with a laugh; "I am general manager, you know."

"What salary do you want to take Philip Manson's place?"

John Steele cast down his eyes, and meditated in silence for a few moments.

"Would fifty dollars a week be too much?" he asked in a tremor.

"It's rather a jump," said Rockervelt calmly, "but I think the organisation can stand it, if it is satisfactory to you."

"It is more than satisfactory to me," replied Steele, earnestly. He was to learn later that modesty was its own reward. He could as easily have had double the money, and perhaps more. Multi-millionaire as he was, however, Rockervelt was not the man to throw away needless cash.

"We will take that as settled," he said, and this ended the interview.

# CHAPTER IV—A CONSPIRACY

THE greatest blessing that Providence can bestow upon a young man is self-knowledge. Success comes to those who know their own powers while it is yet day. To learn for the first time at eighty that you have immense capabilities in any given direction is futile. To possess that knowledge at twenty is better than to own a gold mine. It is the old adage exemplified: "If age but could; if youth but knew."

Steele's two years' management of the Burdock route should have given him confidence, but his bargain with Rockervelt showed it had not done so. If he had been shrewd enough to allow Rockervelt himself to name the compensation that should have gone with his new position, he would have made a much better financial deal than that which he accomplished. If he had then added a little shrewd bargaining, he might have bettered himself still further, but John Steele had endured an early life of poverty, and the salary he now received seemed to him munificent.

The same qualities of under-estimation which caused Rockervelt to chuckle with satisfaction at a sharp bargain driven interfered with the young man's success as new division superintendent of the Midland. When he was duly installed, his immediate chief, T. Acton Blair, quaked. Blair was well acquainted with the ruthlessness of Rockervelt, and he trembled for his own position. He wondered how much Rockervelt knew. Was he aware of Blair's years of tyranny over the capable Philip Manson? Did he know how nearly the premier train of the road had come to being wrecked through the incompetence of a relative of his own, whom he had forced into the train despatched office in spite of the protests of Philip Manson? Now Manson was gone to New York, promoted to a position of greater power and influence than any he had hitherto held, and instead of Blair's being allowed to place some favourite in the vacant office, Rockervelt himself had intervened to appoint the very man who had saved the Pacific Express: a man whom Blair had practically dismissed two years before. If Blair possessed, as Rockervelt alleged, an acute brain in other directions than that of practical railway management, this brain was deeply perturbed when its owner, with over-done warmth, welcomed the new division superintendent of the Midland on his return to the great company. Innocent John Steele accepted this cordiality at its face value, and his own kind heart prompted him to let bygones be bygones, and to make the new condition of things as pleasant as possible for his nominal chief. At first this bewildered Blair; then he came to the conclusion it was merely deep craft on the part of the young man, and finally he reached the fact that Steele was quite honestly endeavouring to do his duty, and trying to please his superiors, a fact which a more alert mind would have assimilated months before. When, after weeks of doubt and fear, Blair at last realised that John Steele had in reality buried the tomahawk; that he had no knife concealed up his sleeve; that he was honest, straightforward and capable as his predecessor had been, the general manager felt like a man who had been taken advantage of. Instead of being thankful that his former fear was groundless, his resentment burned all the brighter, and he brought his genius for intrigue into play, determining to trip up the young man on the first favourable opportunity. But while he waited for that opportunity, he resumed the old tactics which had been so successful in pushing Philip Manson to a resignation, and proceeded to make John Steele's place as uncomfortable for him as possible. There is no tyranny like the tyranny of a coward, and before John Steele had been six months in his new position, he learned what it was to live under the heel of a despot.

Nor did he enjoy the consolation which must have sustained Philip Manson, who possessed the enthusiastic loyalty of his subordinates. Manson was a born master, who had risen step by step into the position of division superintendent. Added to this, he was quiet, taciturn and unemotional. John Steele, on the other hand, was the embodiment of good-fellowship; talkative, humourous, genial; who believed every one around him as honest and whole-hearted as himself. But there were those beneath him who had regarded themselves quite properly in the line of promotion, and whose ambitions had been stirred when it became known that Philip Manson was about to retire. Then, to their chagrin and dismay, an outsider had been chosen for the place who, two years before, was little better than an office boy among them, and their friendliness for him at that time had been merely a tribute to his unfailing good nature; his willingness to help. This universal liking, however, was perhaps unconsciously tinged with contempt. Their feeling was rather admiration for a joyous soul than respect for a young fellow of talent. No one had an inkling of Steele's real merit except Philip Manson, and this silent man never volunteered information. When Blair wished Manson summarily to dismiss Steele, he got information he had not expected about the latter. When Rockervelt telegraphed regarding Manson's successor, he also received information, but Manson made no confidant of any of his subordinates, and perhaps if one of them had been shrewd enough to guess how good a man Steele was, that person might have been thought worthy of the recommendation which the former division superintendent had bestowed upon Steele.

When an insider is promoted, he not only steps into the vacant place, but the one beneath him advances to the position he formerly held, and so it goes down along the line, until the lowest grade is reached. Each man gets his little move upward, and universal joy is the result. But when an outsider is brought in, he stops the move as effectually as a jammed log arrests the progress of all the timber further up the stream. Although the genial John met smiling faces among his subordinates, there was nevertheless envy and hatred behind the smiles. Things began to go wrong; he could not give his orders explicitly enough to be sure that they would be understood. He met no open opposition, but the most annoying things happened in spite of all his precautions. A little harshness and injustice here would have acted as a tonic upon the whole clan. If he had flung out of the office the first man who misapprehended an order, whether that man were guilty or not, his path would have been smoother from that time forward; but here his own proneness to blame himself rather than to censure others was his worst enemy, and the office became honeycombed with negligence, apathy, incompetence and sullen insubordination. There was no sympathy to be expected from T. Acton Blair; in fact, the stout man saw with secret satisfaction that the division superintendent was not getting on. He would condole with Rockervelt on this regrettable failure next time he met him, instilling the poison very subtly, and assuming a tone of deep regret and disappointment. Meanwhile, his whole attitude towards the young man had changed. He was querulous and fault-finding; he magnified the failures, and slighted the successes. John Steele found himself between the upper and nether millstones that were grinding his nerves to rags. Day and night he worked like a Trojan to bring the necessary order out of the chaos that had somehow come to enshroud him, and underneath was the gnawing distrust of his own endowment properly to fill the place to which he had been appointed. He was working to the very limit of his powers, and preparing for himself an inevitable breakdown. He supplemented every one, instead of making every one supplement him. It never occurred to him that the chaos against which he contended was deliberate, for a railway business differs from any other on earth, in that carelessness or neglect is juggling with men's lives. A mistake comparatively innocent in any other branch of commercial activity may mean the massacre of a score of men and women on a railway. Many a night he sat disconsolate in his office when every one else had gone, and yearned for half an hour's talk with Philip Manson. The whole difficulty was not one which he could commit to writing, and even if he attempted that, he might fail in making Manson understand the situation; a situation so completely the reverse of that which had obtained during Manson's own reign. At last he determined to take a few days off, visit New York, and consult with his former chief. This brought about his first open conflict with T. Acton Blair, and then he weakly succumbed.

"Mr. Blair," he said one day, after the formal morning's interview was at an end, "I'm going to take a run down to New York."

"Oh, are you?" replied Blair. "For what purpose, may I ask?"

"I wish to talk with Philip Manson."

"About what?"

"Well, about a great many things; about the general situation here, for instance."

"Offhand, I should say I am the proper person to consult on such a subject," said Blair, with some acidity.

"Of course," replied Steele, mildly, "but you see, Man-son was my predecessor. He has probably been through what I am going through now, and I should like a few hints from him."

"Who is to fill your place while you are away?"

"Johnson could do that."

"Do you think he is competent?"

"Oh, quite competent."

"Then can you explain why Mr. Rockervelt put you in the place of Manson, if Johnson was capable of filling it?"

"You had better ask that question of Mr. Rockervelt," suggested Steele, his temper rising.

"I shall certainly do so if you leave your post. You are either necessary here or you are not. If you begin to suspect that you are not the man for the position, then you should resign."

"I am the man for the position, Mr. Blair; still, even the best of men, which I do not pretend to be, needs a little advice now and then, and I intend to seek it from Philip Manson."

"A man who knows his business neither seeks nor acts on advice. If you go to New York you go in spite of my prohibition, and I shall take your departure as an act of resignation, and proceed accordingly. I am either general manager of this road or I am not."

Now this latter phrase was one which Blair was exceedingly fond of using, and it had done duty several times during Philip Manson's *régime*, who had invariably shown Mr. Blair in exceedingly few words that, when it came to the point, he was not the autocrat he pretended to be. Manson would have made an excellent poker-player. He could have been beaten by better cards, but never by a bluff, and Blair's pet phrase was pure bluff.

"Oh, very well," said John Steele, rising and leaving the table, while his opponent raked in the chips. Steele did not know he had reached the climax where a determined answer would have given him the game, nor did he realise how disastrous was his defeat. A poltroon is a bad man to run away from.

John Steele retreated to his own room, and a sweet smile overspread the chubby face of the corpulent man he had left victorious. A week later came the second encounter, which although it carried a second apparent defeat for John Steele, proved, nevertheless, to be the most important turning point of his life.

The division superintendent entered the general manager's room with a telegram in his hand. Blair, looking up, noticed the agitation of his manner, and the paleness of his face.

"Mr. Blair, I have just received a telegram which says that my uncle is dying. I wish to go to him, and intend to leave by to-night's train. He lives in the north of Michigan. I have therefore come to let you know that I shall be absent for a few days, perhaps."

Blair continued to gaze at him with a winning smile on his cherubic face.

"Would it not be a simpler matter, Mr. Steele, if you were to write to Philip Manson, and ask him to take a trip to his old home? You are a member of his club, I understand, and could quite readily hold your conference there if either of you did not care to discuss the state of affairs in this office."

"I don't understand what you mean, Mr. Blair."

"Oh, yes, you do. The dying uncle device, or the funeral of a relative device, have all been tried upon me before. I am proof against such schemes, and really, Mr. Steele, I paid you the compliment of believing you to be more original."

"Do you think I am lying to you?" asked John indignantly, taking a step nearer the general manager's table.

"We don't call it lying, Mr. Steele; we may term it diplomacy, or what you like. A week ago you requested leave of absence to consult Philip Manson. I refused my permission. Now you come to me with the story of a dying relative. I am bound to believe you, although I made a friendly suggestion a moment since which apparently you do not intend to accept, so we will get back to the original situation. Your uncle is very ill, and I am very sorry. There are doubtless at this moment many excellent persons in extremity, yet nevertheless the trains of the Midland must run, and even if Mr. Rock-ervelt or myself were removed to a better land, not a wheel would cease turning on our account. Therefore, hoping you will accept the expression of my deep sympathy, which I hereby tender to you, I must nevertheless refuse to allow the office of division superintendent to remain vacant for one hour."

"But this is the only relative I have in the world," protested John, earnestly. "Here is the telegram I have received. Read it for yourself."

Mr. Blair, still smiling, waved his stout hand gently to and fro, but refused even to glance at the paper laid before him.

"I do not doubt in the least that the despatch comes from Michigan. I can even guess that it is worded in the most urgent terms, and that the signature is perfectly genuine. Nevertheless, Mr. Steele, it is better we should understand each other. As I told you a week ago, if you leave your position without my permission you will find that position permanently filled on your return. This is a free country, and you are entitled to go or stay as you please. If you hand me in your resignation, as your predecessor did, I shall say to you as I said to him, 'Go, and prosperity be with you,' but while you are a member of my staff, you are under my orders. Do I make myself sufficiently plain?"

"Yes, you do," replied John Steele, picking up his telegram and leaving the room.

Once more at his own desk he sat there for a long time with his head in his hands. At first it was his determination to resign forthwith. The situation was growing as intolerable for him as it had been for his predecessor, but the longer he thought over what had happened the more he realised the impossibility of surrender. If he resigned now, he left the Rockervelt system a failure. He would be compelled to begin at the foot of the ladder again, handicapped by practical dismissal; to strive as an unsuccessful man, his years of experience counting for nothing. But even if that consideration did not harden his resolution to remain where he was, the thought of his uncle would alone have been sufficient to turn the balance. Bitterly he accused himself of his neglect of the old man who, as he had just said, was his only relative on earth. While he was escaping from the hopeless poverty in which they had both lived, the struggle for existence had become so interesting that it had obliterated the fact that Dugald Steele was still where he had left him, and not a penny of money had the young man ever forwarded to him. Up to the time his salary was made fifty dollars a week he had not only saved no money but had run into debt. These obligations were now liquidated, and he had a few hundreds in the bank; the nucleus, he hoped, of more to follow. The old man had brought him up, after a fashion, allowing him to go to school during the winter months, but every waking hour the uncle forced the nephew to work almost beyond the limit of his youthful powers, and at last had driven him forth with blows and cursings during one of those periodical fits of temper which had made Dugald Steele a terror to the neighbourhood. One letter, indeed, John had written to his old home, when he got his situation at Hitchen's Siding, but that had remained unanswered, and he had taken it for granted that his uncle's anger was permanent. Nevertheless, the telegram showed that the uncle had kept the letter, or remembered the address, for the despatch had been sent to Hitchen's Siding, and from there forwarded to John Steele's office in Warmington.

However, there was little profit in bemoaning a state of things he could not remedy. It was certain that Blair would carry out his threat, if Steele left his place without permission, so there was nothing for it but to sit tight.

With a deep sigh the young man pulled himself together, drew toward him a sheet of paper and wrote a letter that proved to be more important than its wording would have led a casual reader to suspect.

---

## CHAPTER V—A FAVOURITE OF FORTUNE

DUGALD STEELE cordially hated his neighbours, and evinced little hesitation in telling them so, whenever opportunity offered. He lived apparently in the depths of extreme poverty, occupying a dilapidated wooden, unpainted house at the northern outskirts of the village of Stumpville, Michigan. He kept no servant, but cooked his own meals, and if any trespassers dared to set foot on his property, he threatened them with a shotgun. He was a cantankerous, crabbed old Scotsman, snarling like an unowned dog, and going about in shabbier clothes than the most ragged tramp that had ever honoured Stumpville with his fleeting presence.

Dugald and his younger brother Neil, the latter then newly married, came out of the highlands of Scotland to the lowlands of Michigan. It was not that the life in the American backwoods was harder than life in the northern part of Scotland, but the hardships were different, and they affected the health of the young wife; she died because of a falling tree—a tree she had never seen, and whose final crash she had not heard. Her husband was felling oaks in the forest, and one of them lodged in the branches of another, resting there at an angle of forty-five degrees. Neil, unaccustomed to forestry in its gigantic American form, not knowing the danger he ran, set himself to chop down the impediment, when the half-fallen tree suddenly completed its descent and crushed him, face downward and lifeless, into the forest mould. To the elder brother fell the grim task of chopping through the fallen timber and rolling the log from off the dead man. The wife died from the shock, and their little boy was left to the care of his taciturn uncle.

No one is alive who knew Dugald Steele in his youth, and so none can tell what early experiences may have warped his character. Perhaps the stinging poverty of those days gave him an exaggerated idea of the necessity of hoarding money; perhaps the tragic death of his brother, whose rude coffin he made with his own hands from slabs of the tree that killed him, crushed out his natural affections instead of ripening them; but, be that as it may, he was, during the latter part of his life, a hard man, whom no tale of pathos could move into the expenditure of a penny; a gnarled, cross-grained, twisted specimen of humanity from whom all emotion, except that of hatred, seemed to have departed.

When he died a will was found leaving all his property to a neighbouring town simply, as he said in the document, written by his own hand to save a lawyer's fee, that he might wreak posthumous revenge upon his neighbours, who would understand, now that it was too late, what they had missed by not being decent to him. But this will was invalidated by a later one, which shows how a man with a kind heart may sometimes do well for himself when he little understands what he is about.

Nemesis comes to all of us, and it is strange that it should have rested on old Dugald, as the result of the hard, honest work in his young days. Seeing no smoke from his chimney, a kindly woman neighbour, with fear and trembling, penetrated to his dwelling, and found him knotted on the floor with rheumatism, snarling and waspish as ever, but helpless. The woman ran for assistance, and he was lifted into his bed, where he lay when the doctor came, while the old man protested that he had no money to pay him, and would not pay him if he had. The doctor, however, did the best he could for him, and told the neighbours that the old man was stricken with his last illness, which indeed proved to be the case. The doctor said to his patient that if he had any relatives he wished to see he had better send for them, offering to write if the old man gave him an address. All his life Dugald Steele had distrusted medical advice, but it is likely that on this occasion something within him corroborated the verdict which had been passed upon him. He lay there for a long time in silence, the doctor waiting, and at last said, in a hoarse whisper, that he would like his nephew to know he was ill, giving the address as John Steele, Hitchen's Siding; but, he added, with a return of his cantankerousness, that the doctor was to tell his nephew he need not come unless he wanted to. The doctor at his own cost sent a telegram, and late that night received a long answering despatch from John Steele which deplored the impossibility of the sender's going to Stumpville at that time, begged that no expense should be spared in getting the old man what comforts he needed, and concluded by saying that a check for a hundred dollars had been posted to the physician for the purpose indicated.

The young man knew his uncle well enough to be aware that if he sent the money direct to him, that miserly person would hoard it, rather than spend a penny on whatever necessities he required. He also knew the delight his uncle experienced in handling money, so when he sent the letter he enclosed two crisp new ten-dollar bills.

*My Dear Uncle,—he wrote,—I am deeply grieved to hear from the doctor of your illness and sincerely hope it is not serious. I would come to you at once if I could, but, alas, there is over me a severe taskmaster who refuses me even a day's leave, yet my position here is so good that I dare not jeopardise it by absenting myself without permission, for if I lose my job I lose also the chance of assisting you. Please accept the twenty dollars which I send you, and get for yourself whatever you may need. Procure the best physician in the place, and a nurse. I will send you more money right along, and if it is not enough, refer creditors to my employers, and they will, I think, guarantee that I can pay any debt you may incur. Please do not stint yourself, but order what you want, or whatever the physician thinks you should have, and do not imagine that the spending of money will leave me short, for I have several hundred dollars in a bank, and will send it to you as you require it. So, dear uncle, keep up a good heart and take every care of yourself.—Your loving Nephew.*

The woman sitting at the bed-head read this letter to the old man, wondering if he was paying attention, for his eyes were closed. Presently she saw a tear trickle down his withered cheek and she thought his heart was softening, but the first remark he made did not seem to verify that conclusion.

"Give me the money," he demanded in a harsh whisper.

The bills were handed to him, and his long, yellow fingers, like talons, closed avariciously upon them; lingeringly dwelling on their smooth texture, thumb and finger rubbed them up and down. His next remark was more encouraging.

"Read the letter again," he said, and the woman did so, although anger was in her heart that affection should be wasted upon one so unworthy. There was a long silence after she had finished the second reading, and at last she asked him:

"Shall I send for another doctor?"

"No," growled the old man, "doctors can do me no good. Go and tell Lawyer Strathmore I want to see him. Tell him I have just received twenty dollars, else he won't come."

The lawyer came on the strength of the woman's assurance that the money had arrived, and on his return to his office his partner said: "Well, what struck the old Highlander? Wanted to make his will, I suppose. I hope he hasn't left his ancient suit of clothes to me."

"Oh, he's gone clean crazy," replied Strathmore, "but I secured ten dollars all right enough, so it doesn't matter. He seems to think he owns Michigan. Two hundred thousand dollars Michigan Central Railway stock are deposited in the vaults of the Wayne County Savings Bank. Seventy-nine thousand dollars Northern Pacific stock deposited somewhere else. Cash in the bank over thirty thousand dollars—amounting all in all to something like three hundred thousand dollars, which is left to a nephew of his, a railway man on the Manateau Midland."

"By Jove, Strathmore," cried the partner, who had been a newspaper man in his youth and saw a sensation in this, "I wouldn't take my oath that it isn't all right. He's just the sort of a dilapidated old miser who would turn out to be a rich man."

"Impossible," said Strathmore.

"Improbable, perhaps, but a telegram to Detroit would soon let us know."

And it did let them know. The inhabitants of Stumpville learned next morning that an old man had died in one of their most ruinous shanties who could have bought and sold each of them, and all of them combined.

When the telegram came announcing his uncle's death John Steele rose from his desk, locked the door, and paced up and down the room with bent head. He had not expected this outcome, for although his uncle was old, he had weathered so many gales, it had not occurred to the young man that there must come one storm which would lay the gnarled old oak level with the ground. Unavailingly did he regret that a consideration for his own position had kept him from the bedside. With a sigh he stopped his walk, pulled himself together, sat down at his desk, and wrote a brief note to Blair, saying he had just received a telegram informing him of the death of his uncle; that he intended to start by the next train for Michigan, and would put Johnson temporarily in his place. He might be gone as long as three days, but anything addressed to Stumpville would find him. Pinning the telegram to this, and folding up the documents, he sealed them into an envelope addressed to T. Acton Blair, and sent the letter by a messenger to the general manager's room. He knew that official was in his office, but until the time John took his train there came no response to his note. He called in Johnson, and briefly placed him in transient command. The young man received his appointment with a smug satisfaction that he found it impossible quite to conceal, and although his departing chief noticed this, he made no comment upon it.

During his journey to Stumpville John Steele meditated upon his plan of campaign. The sense of injustice he had felt ever since Blair refused him permission to visit his uncle was now crystallised into a determination to use the iron gauntlet rather than the velvet glove in future. Naturally he was of a conciliatory disposition, but the exercise of forbearance had resulted in failure and disorganisation. The next move lay with the general manager. If Blair persisted in dismissing him, he would appeal to Cæsar, for Cæsar himself had placed him in the position he held.

Arriving at Stumpville, he went direct to the telegraph office, and found awaiting him a despatch which, he was well aware without opening it, came from the general manager; no one else knew his address. The fact that he telegraphed instead of sending a messenger to his room in the same building, which he had had ample time to do, seemed to Steele the first sign of weakness. Blair wished to settle this matter at long range. Tearing open the envelope he read: "I am amazed that you should have left your post without at least personal consultation with me. I have made your appointment of Johnson permanent, but will hold his former office open for you unless you decline to accept it."

Steele smiled grimly as he read these words. They showed that Blair had not the courage definitely to dismiss him. The general manager was afraid to burn his bridges behind him, hoping possibly that Steele would telegraph his resignation or his indignant refusal of the subordinate position.

Before leaving the city, John Steele had withdrawn from the bank several hundred dollars in order that he might pay any debts his uncle had contracted, and in order also that his funeral should be as imposing as if the old man had been the leading citizen of the place. Then to his amazement he learned that Dugald Steele had made him comparatively a rich man, but this independence made no difference in Steele's projects for the future. He liked work for its own sake, and he was particularly attached to the duty which chance and good fortune had assigned to him. He was not going to allow that task to be interfered with by a pompous wind-bag like T. Acton Blair, and much less so by a gang of undisciplined subordinates who needed to hear the crack of the whip over their heads.

On the journey back to the city, however, a germ of thought formed in his mind, for the present to lie dormant, but in the future to develop into marvellous things, watered by circumstance, fertilised by disaster. Pondering on the strange, almost repulsive character of the old miser who was gone, it occurred to John Steele that mere hoarding could never have produced the sum of money he had accumulated. In his uncle's mental equipment there must have been a shrewd understanding of the world's affairs, of which he secretly took advantage to his own enrichment. Quite unsuspected by his neighbours this recluse had played a game of finance that proved marvellously successful. This could not have been done in Stumpville. Dugald Steele had evidently worked through a broker in some large city, and John Steele began to wonder if he, too, had inherited this seventh sense of money-making which has produced those bulky unearned fortunes for which America is celebrated or notorious.

John resolved to watch the markets in future and learn some of the rules of the game; then he would venture in a small way, so that it did not matter whether he won or lost, and thus put his suspected hereditary abilities to the test. He was very sure from what he remembered of his uncle that the cautious old man had never plunged blindly into speculation. Unless he was very much mistaken, there had been nothing of the gambler about Dugald Steele. He surely amassed his wealth because of a well-informed belief in the continued progress of his adopted country, placing his money here and there where he believed it would secure the advantage of a rise in values.

Thus the glow lamp of sweet reasonableness shed its mild rays upon the entrance of a path new to John Steele; a path which offered alluring vistas, but led into a wild and dangerous country—the path of speculation.

When Steele opened the door of the division superintendent's room, Johnson, seated in the division superintendent's chair, whirled round abruptly with the frown of high authority on his brow, apparently annoyed that any one should have taken the liberty of entering without knocking.

"Ah, Steele, it's you, is it?" cried Johnson airily, neglecting to prefix the word "Mr." which he would have used a week before. "How-d'e-do, how-d'e-do? When did you get back?"

"My train arrived just three minutes ago," replied John Steele calmly. He closed the door behind him, and stood there, while Johnson remained seated, palpably uneasy, evidently determined to carry off the situation with an air of bonhomie. Mentally he had no doubt rehearsed it several times during the past few days, but the man now confronting him was not the anxious, worried individual who had left the chair he continued to sit in, or the genial, good-humoured youth of former years. For the first time in their intercourse Johnson saw before him the stern demeanour of one in authority, and inwardly he quaked, though outwardly he endeavoured to maintain the guise of airy indifference which appeared fitting for the encounter.

"You received Mr. Blair's telegram, I suppose?" said Johnson at last, becoming more and more embarrassed by the frigid silence. Somehow the crisis was not evolving exactly as he had pictured it. He was *de facto* division superintendent, yet somehow this new, quiet man before him did not appear to recognise his elevation.

"Everything has gone right since I left, I take it; otherwise I should have heard from you," remarked Steele, ignoring the question just put to him.

"Oh, yes," said Johnson, "everything has gone smoothly. Look here, Steele," cried Johnson in a burst of candour, "why didn't you reply to the old man's telegram? You know how touchy he is on questions of discipline. He very generously offered you the position I held, and you didn't even take the trouble to acknowledge his kindness. I can assure you, John, it has been all I could do to keep the old man from promoting Car-ruthers into my place, but I succeeded in persuading Mr. Blair to take no further steps until you returned. I said I was sure you would have some satisfactory explanation to offer."

"You were quite right; I have. And now, Mr. Johnson, you will reap the reward of your own kindness. The place you have so generously kept open for me I take pleasure in bestowing upon you; but in return for the counsel you have been good enough to give me, I warn you that unless I get a little better service than has been rendered for some months past you will not hold the position."

Johnson threw back his head and laughed loudly.

"Steele, my dear boy, that's a good bluff, but it won't work. I have been made division superintendent by the general manager of this road. Mr. Blair and myself have both been very patient over your unauthorised desertion of your post, but I tell you frankly that my patience is at an end. I offer you the position which I formerly held. If you do not at once accept it, I shall call Car-ruthers in and give him the vacant place."

"Do," said John Steele.

Johnson's hand hovered over the electric button, but he forbore to press it, looking anxiously toward the impassive man who had made such a curt reply to his threat.

"I dislike exceedingly to call Carruthers. I want to give you every chance, Steele."

"That is very good of you, but don't hesitate on my account. I may say, however, that if you touch that button, or issue any further orders in this room, you will automatically have dismissed yourself from the service of the Midland Road."

"Oh, that's it, is it? You're going to show fight, are you? I'll very quickly convince you that you haven't the slightest chance of winning. I have behind me the general manager of this road, and he has the owners of the system behind *him*. If you bring on an unnecessary contest, in which you have no possibility of victory, I shall then not allow you to be employed on this line, even in the meanest capacity."

"I quite understand, Mr. Johnson, that either you or I must leave. Now, press the button, and make your promotion without further talk."

All this time Johnson's hand had been hesitating over the ivory knob. It trembled slightly, but at last it took the plunge, and made the signal. Presently there came a knock at the door, and James Carruthers entered, glancing uncertainly from Steele to Johnson, apparently undecided whom he should first address. Johnson's voice was extremely urbane, and it brought joy to the heart of his former colleague.

"Carruthers," he said, "you will now take my place in the other room, and with your new position I am happy to say there will be an addition to your salary."

"Thank you, Mr. Johnson," replied Carruthers, very humbly, meanwhile glancing timidly at the silent man standing there. Perhaps James Carruthers would have been more certain of his promotion had John Steele made the announcement. The latter's kind heart was not proof against this mute appeal, and a smile came to his lips as he said: "Have no fear, Carruthers. It gives me great pleasure to sanction your appointment. Now, just step around to Mr. Blair's room, and ask him to come here for a moment."

"You will do nothing of the sort, Carruthers," cried Johnson truculently, springing to his feet with clenched fist. It was neck or nothing now, and he knew it. "I am division superintendent, and in this room you take orders from no one but me."

Poor Carruthers stood with his hand on the door knob, wishing himself safely back in his own room, while Johnson took a determined step toward him, seeing the youth's hesitation, and resolved to overcome it in his own favour. Then a quite unimportant incident happened which caused him to face the other way, and to feel that somehow he had lost a point in the game. Without any hurry John Steele had seated himself in the division superintendent's chair. Steele, momentarily ignoring both commander and commanded, rang a bell at the private telephone which communicated with the general manager's room, and placed the receiver at his ear.

"Is that you, Mr. Blair? This is John Steele. I have just returned, and I want you to step round to my room, as I wish to make a rather important communication."

There was a momentary pause, and so intensely still did the room become that the two men standing there looking at John Steele could hear the indefinite murmur of the voice coming over the telephone.

"No," said Steele firmly, "the conference must take place in this room, and it must take place now. Otherwise the complaint I have to make against you will go by telegraph direct to Mr. Rockervelt, and I shall leave by to-night's train for New York."

Again there was a pause, and a ghostly suggestion of a whisper. Then Steele said: "Oh, I am not on the war-path at all. In fact, such is my deep respect for yourself that it rests entirely with you to say whether there will *be* a war-path or not. Personally I see no necessity for it. Just step round, and we'll talk it over in the most amicable way. Yes, Johnson's here." With that Steele hung up his receiver, swung round on the swivel chair, the usual winning smile on his lips as he met the gaze of two very anxious young men. His voice, however, was sharp enough when he spoke.

"Carruthers, clear out," whereupon Carruthers opened the door and disappeared as if by magic.

"Johnson, sit down. You are just about to learn a lesson on the value of all this backing of which you have been boasting."

Before Johnson could either accede to the request or disobey it the door opened and the stout gentleman entered. There was a severe frown on his brow intended to denote resolute strength, but an expression of uncertainty in his lower face which hinted at weakness.

Steele waved his hand amiably toward a deep leather-covered easy chair, and into its luxurious folds the fat man sank, drawing forth a handkerchief, which he passed across his brow, and somehow the action appeared to obliterate the frown.

"You said in your telegram, Mr. Blair, that I was in fault because I left without personally consulting with you, but I think you will forgive my error when you remember that having applied for permission to leave when my uncle was dying, and being refused, it would have been futile for me to appear before you with proof of his death and a further request for leave of absence. You would have been bound in consistency to refuse, while I was equally determined to attend my uncle's funeral. If you disbelieved my words when I told you he was dying, you could not have so stultified yourself as to credit the news of his death."

"I did not disbelieve your word," protested Blair, timorously.

"I understood you to do so. If you did not, then your action was at once cruel and tyrannical. However, that is past and done with, so we will say no more about it, unless you choose that it should come up later on. Now, I may inform you that my late uncle has left me a legacy that approximates three hundred thousand dollars. As the interest on this, even at one per cent, is more than I receive as division superintendent of the Midland, you will easily understand that I do not retain my position merely from mercenary motives. I am to-day in a position of independence which makes the outcome of any struggle we may engage in a matter of perfect indifference to me."

"I am happy," said Blair, again mopping his brow, "to be the first of your old colleagues to congratulate you on your improved prospects. John Jacob Astor once said that a poor man with a hundred thousand dollars might make a fortune in this country. Although times have changed since then, still, a poor man with three times that amount has numerous opportunities denied to more poverty-stricken individuals. As for the struggle you speak of, I really see nothing on earth that either of us would gain by engaging in it."

"*I* am quite at one with you there, sir, and indeed you will find me the least belligerent of individuals if I but get my own way, which I intend to insist on hereafter, so far as my immediate department is concerned. While I have no fear of the struggle I suggested, neither have I any desire to engage in it. You see, Mr. Blair, you would be too severely handicapped from the start to give you a chance. Your task would be to show that Mr. Rockervelt is a fool, while all I should need to do would be to prove that he is the wisest of men. You are too shrewd a judge of human nature to doubt the outcome of such a contest. Mr. Rockervelt prides himself on two things. First, the unerringness of his judgment regarding men; second, the excellence of his various roads, and he reaches the second by means of the first. Now, he placed me in this chair. If he had wished you to choose the occupant, he would have delegated that duty to you. If he had desired the estimable Mr. Johnson here, he would not have had the slightest hesitation in enlisting Mr. Johnson's co-operation. Now, if you stood to gain anything by forcing a hopeless issue I could comprehend your attitude, but anything you wish you can have through good will, so where is the use of coercion or of a fight?"

"I assure you, my dear Mr. Steele, that I have no desire whatever to bring on a fight. I have said so all along."

"Very well, Mr. Blair, there's no more to be said, and I predict you will find me the most deferential, accommodating subordinate that ever worked in your office."

"But where do I come in?" ejaculated the panic-stricken Johnson, whose face had become paler and paler as this colloquy went on.

"My dear sir, you *don't* come in," said John Steele urbanely. "I told you that at the beginning, when I counselled you not to enter a contest where you were bound to be the loser. I commend to you in future the sensible attitude assumed by Mr. Blair."

"Mr. Blair," persisted Johnson, "you appointed me division superintendent, and assured me you would stand by that appointment."

"Oh, well," explained Blair, "you see how it is yourself. I did so under an entire misapprehension. I thought that Mr. Steele had openly defied my authority, which I now understand was not the case. Am I right in that, Mr. Steele?"

"Perfectly right, sir. I had no desire to impugn your authority, and I apologise for my abrupt action, which certainly bore that complexion."

"There, Johnson," said Blair, almost pleadingly, "you must see that puts a different face on the matter entirely."

It certainly put a different face on Johnson, who stood there with dropped jaw, gazing pitifully at his backboneless chief.

"I am very sorry there has been any misunderstanding," said Blair soothingly. "Such, of course, occurs in all offices, but luckily discipline is so perfect here that a few words will adjust things in their right proportion to each other. You have done very well, Mr. Johnson, during your short occupancy of this room, and when you resume your old place you may be certain that both Mr. Steele and myself will remember you when a chance for promotion occurs."

"I regret to say," remarked Steele casually, before Johnson had an opportunity of speaking, "that Mr. Johnson's last act during his temporary occupancy of this chair was to promote Carruthers into his vacant place, and this promotion I myself confirmed. I recommend Mr. Johnson to take a vacation for a month, and if during that period he secures another situation, I shall be happy to recommend him, and probably you, Mr. Blair, would not object to do the same."

"Certainly not, certainly not," muttered Blair hastily. "If, at the end of a month," continued John Steele, "you have not suited yourself, Mr. Johnson, you may return to me, and I'll see what I can do for you. I am going to rearrange my staff, and give most of its members a step upward. Some of them, however, will take a step downward, and some will be promoted over the heads of their seniors. All this will require a little thought and manipulation, but, as Mr. Blair truly says, discipline is everything, and I am determined to carry out his wishes in that respect."

"Well, Mr. Steele," said the general manager, rising with a deep sigh of satisfaction, as if everything had gone exactly as he planned it, "anything I can do to help on the good work will not be stinted. Call upon me when in any difficulty, Mr. Steele, and be assured of my most whole-hearted support," and with that the great man held out his hand, which Steele, springing to his feet, clasped cordially. Without a glance at the crest-fallen Johnson, T. Acton Blair strode majestically from the room.

John Steele turned to his desk.

"May I have a word with you, Mr. Steele?" asked Johnson.

"Yes, this day month," said John Steele without looking up.

---

# CHAPTER VI
# "THERE'S NOTHING HALF SO SWEET IN LIFE"

JOHN STEELE now entered upon a period of his life which was most interesting and enjoyable. The numerous petty and annoying incidents which had heretofore been the cause of friction between himself and his numerous subordinates disappeared as the mist fades before the rising sun, and he found himself at the head of as willing and energetic a staff as any man could wish to have co-operate with him. With his chief even the most captious of men could have no fault to find, and Steele was far from being captious. T. Acton Blair seemed a changed man. No one could be more genial and considerate. He even drifted into the habit of calling his division superintendent "John." Their business conferences were of an exceedingly friendly and amiable character, and yet John frequently censured himself when he detected deep down in his own nature remnants of distrust still lingering regarding his urbane superior. Once when Blair was gone rather longer than usual on a visit to New York, some inquiries that came through caused him to surmise that Blair was undermining him at headquarters, but on Blair's return John felt rather ashamed of himself. That good man had indeed mentioned him to the powers that be, but the mention had been entirely to his advantage, with the result that John got ten dollars a week added to his salary, quite unsolicited. Blair almost apologised for his action, saying by way of excuse that the road was really getting so prosperous, and had been so free from disaster ever since Steele had joined it, that Rockervelt was pluming himself on having chosen the right man once again.

"By the way," said Blair casually, "Mr. Rockervelt informed me he had read in the newspapers of your windfall. He asked me in what your money was invested, but I was unable to tell him."

"Most of it is in railway stocks," replied Steele.

"Ah, that would have interested him. Are any of the Rockervelt stocks in your safe deposit vault?"

John laughed.

"No, I don't think I possess a single share, even in the Manateau Midland. Perhaps it wouldn't be a bad idea to make a transfer."

"Oh, I don't know," replied Blair, impartially. "Unless a man is a professional speculator he generally loses in transferring his stock from one interest to another. The broker usually gets a slice when this happens. Still, I am sure Mr. Rockervelt would be rather pleased to hear that you own stock in the Midland. He encourages that sort of thing, especially among his higher officials, imagining quite rightly, perhaps, that they are just a leetle more careful if they are part owners of the road they operate. I think it's a very good idea, myself; still, at the present moment all the Rockervelt lines are booming, and I don't know any investment I could more cordially recommend. Still, I'm prejudiced in the matter, so don't let what I say influence you in the least. But if you should buy a block of Midland, for instance, I wish you'd let me know, so that when I am next in New York I can answer Mr. Rockervelt's former question. It certainly wouldn't do you any harm with Rockervelt, and there's no better security on the market."

The newspapers had made much of John Steele's luck in falling heir to a considerable sum of money. The circumstances and unexpected nature of the legacy gave the item a semi-sensational value which was not neglected by the reporters, and even if the amount was in many cases exaggerated, the reputation of being a wealthy man revealed an entirely new world to the young superintendent—the world of social life. He was taken up by society with a warmth that was peculiarly gratifying to so modest a man as John Steele, and for this taking-up T. Acton Blair was largely responsible. On two or three occasions he invited John to dinner, where the young man met many delightful people. He now saw a side of Blair that had heretofore been entirely hidden from him, and, in spite of Rockervelt's former warning, quite unsuspected. Blair as a host was one of the most charming of men; debonair and polite as a Frenchman; a very prince of good fellows. His house was a veritable palace, and when first John was ushered into the midst of its magnificence, it seemed scarcely credible that a young nobody like himself, but a few years past occupying a miserable position on the railway in the prairies, should actually have browbeaten and defeated the owner of all this wealth.

Blair evinced no rancour over this defeat, and Steele esteemed him a human nettle, dangerous only when timorously handled. Steele was too shrewd a man not to have recognised that he had discovered the weak spot in Blairs armour, which was a fixed aversion against being brought into conflict of any kind with the great Rockervelt, and this knowledge gave the young man assurance that his position on the staff of the gigantic corporation was more stable than he had hitherto regarded it. He now saw Blair as a genial, easy-going man, who always took the line of the least resistance, avoiding unnecessary trouble, which was wise in one-so well to do in the world's goods, and as John himself was imbued with the most kindly feelings toward even his enemies, he had the gratification now of beholding his future extend before him like a well-ordered railway line: a clear right-of-way, and no signals against him.

One morning Mr. Blair entered the division superintendent's room, accompanied by a man so much like himself that he might almost be taken for his younger brother.

"Mr. Steele," cried the general manager, in his most amiable manner, "I wish to introduce you to Colonel Beck, an officer of the company, who keeps us all out of prison. Colonel Beck is Mr. Rockervelt's chief legal adviser, who knows so much about the law that he can enable any one with money to evade it. Colonel Beck, this is Mr. John Steele, our youngest, and I believe I may add, our most capable division superintendent."

The Colonel laughed pleasantly as he shook hands with the young man.

"Mr. Blair gives you a better character than he bestows upon me," said the lawyer, with a good-natured twinkle of the eye. "If there is one characteristic more distinctive than another in the Rockervelt system, it is the unvarying respect it holds for the law."

"Oh, that's true enough," rejoined Blair. "Why shouldn't we respect the laws when the Colonel here makes most of them pertaining to railways?"

"Are you then a member of the Legislature?" asked John innocently.

Both of the fat men laughed, and Colonel Beck replied: "No, I am not so restricted as all that. A member of the Legislature possesses one vote. In the secret sanctity of this room, now that my friend Blair has given a hint in that direction, I may say I control many votes in the various Legislatures, and perhaps a few in the National Capitol as well. Still, that's all among ourselves, Mr. Steele, and, getting to safer ground, I may add that I esteem this meeting a pleasure, for you are one of the few men I have heard Mr. Rockervelt speak highly of, and when Mr. Rockervelt praises a man I like to know that man and make him my friend if possible, for he is sure to go far. I think," continued the Colonel, turning toward Blair, "that Mr. Rockervelt said the superintendent here was rather a considerable shareholder in the Midland."

"Mr. Rockervelt was a trifle premature if he said that," replied the general manager. "He spoke to me about it last time I was in New York, but I was unable at the time to give him definite information."

"He is not in the least premature," Steele intervened quietly. "Since our conversation a while ago, Mr. Blair, I have sold out all my Michigan Central Stock with some of my Northern Pacific, and have invested in Manateau Midland."

"Ah, then you are one of us," cried Beck, with enthusiasm; "I wish I had known you before you made the transfer, because I could have introduced you to brokers who would have done the job at the same rate they transact business for us, which I may add is a considerable shade lower than the general public pay. In future if you have any dealings on the market, I shall be glad to give you the benefit of both advice and introduction, which may result in your saving money."

"I am an investor, rather than a speculator," replied John, "and more anxious to get good securities than exorbitant dividends."

"A very wise rule of conduct," said the Colonel, nodding his head sagely several times; then, abruptly changing the subject, he once more expressed his pleasure at making the acquaintance of John Steele.

"I live part of the year in New York, and part in this city," continued the Colonel, "for I am a native here. I arrived a week ago, and to-morrow night we give a little house-warming which I should be glad, Mr. Steele, if you would attend. Not a great crush, you know; a homely gathering rather than a fashionable function, but you shall meet very choice people there, eh, Blair? You'll corroborate me in that, I'm sure?"

"Yes, Colonel," responded Blair, "you are altogether too modest. Your dinners might well form a model to Lucullus, and I can assure Mr. Steele that he will meet people whom it may be a great advantage for him to know. Now, there's a handsome, unsolicited testimonial."

"No, by Jove, it was solicited, wasn't it?" cried the genial Colonel, rubbing his hands together. "Well, Mr. Steele, may I depend on you? You will forgive the shortness of the notice, because of the shortness of our acquaintance."

John Steele accepted the invitation with a cordiality equal to that with which it was tendered.

The prediction of both the stout gentlemen that John Steele would meet interesting people whom he should be glad to know was more than fulfilled, although his joy of new acquaintance was concentrated on one person.

Miss Sadie Beck was the most beautiful girl Steele had ever seen. Her face was sweet and innocent; her complexion of purest ivory tinted with dawn, the colours that go with hair of Californian gold, profuse and waving; the whole entrancing picture being lighted up by eyes as blue as a June sky.

The portals of the Beck mansion proved to be the gates of Eden, with Eve awaiting him within the Paradise. John, hitherto all unused to the society of women, found himself in the presence of Sadie Beck thrilled with emotions of which he knew nothing, and life quite unexpectedly presented possibilities that dazzled him.

Colonel Beck was a widower, and the only child of his only brother was mistress of his household. The Colonel had been too busy a man to think of marrying again after his wife had died, but circumstances solved the problem which his own immersion in great affairs prevented him from grappling with. His elder brother had been as unsuccessful in business as Colonel Beck was the reverse, and dying, he left his daughter to the care of her wealthy uncle, who had given her the most fashionable education money could procure, and then had installed her as the fascinating hostess of his home, a position which she amiably filled to the delight of his guests, and to the complacent satisfaction of himself.

The effect of this new-born friendship upon John Steele was instantaneous and permanent. All the counsels which Philip Manson had formerly tendered to him, urging a greater care in his personal appearance, and a stricter attention to the niceties of dress had made but ephemeral impression upon the object of Manson's solicitations; but now, without a word being spoken, John became almost a modern dandy. The hairdresser's constant attention worked wonders with his head covering, and the most expensive tailors found him an exacting customer.

John discovered suddenly that the onerous duties of division superintendent required a far wider outlook than he had so far bestowed upon them. He must know the law pertaining to his profession, and therefore he found frequent consultations necessary with the adviser to the corporation, and that urbane gentleman did his best to enlighten so diligent a student. Frequently, as was bound to happen with a man on whose shoulders rested a portion at least of the legal business pertaining to a wide-spreading railway system, Colonel Beck was occupied in his own study, compelled to refuse himself to any visitor, and great as should have been the disappointment of so earnest a pupil, John, nevertheless, could scarcely conceal his delight that the niece rather than the uncle should be his entertainer upon these occasions. The elderly lady who acted as chaperone in the Beck household was a placid nonentity, whom even a less strenuous person than John Steele might easily have ignored. She always contented herself with reading the latest book or magazine in a corner under the shaded electric light, while Sadie sat at the piano at the further end of the large room, and played most divinely certain soft, clinging, sentimental harmonies which might be carried on in conjunction with whispered conversation.

Sadie was a deservedly popular young lady, and often, to his chagrin, John found others in the drawing-room, claiming a share of her attention, and to do Miss Beck justice, she bestowed her favours with impartial charm upon all alike, although as time went on John Steele flattered himself that there was reserved for him a tone slightly more confidential than any of the others received. If the old Colonel saw what was going forward, almost, as one might say, before his eyes, he made no sign, and certainly treated the young division superintendent with an even cordiality that would have proved flattering to a man of much higher standing in the company's service than was John Steele.

During this interesting period of his existence the young man lived in an intoxicating, rose-hued atmosphere. "Lucky in love, unlucky in war" was proving itself false in his instance. Never before had he been so successful in his business; never so popular with superiors and subordinates alike. Difficulties appeared only to vanish before the magic wave of his hand. His suggestions were adopted, his plans prospered, and perhaps most inspiring of all, his sagacity and his energy met unasked appreciation. His salary was raised to a hundred dollars a week, and Blair, when he announced the fact, referred almost apologetically to the ever-increasing prosperity of the road, due largely, he was good enough to say, to the efficiency of the division superintendent.

And yet there was one pebble in his shoe. With increase of means, curiously enough, there came the increased knowledge that intrinsically he was a poor man. The property which a few months before had seemed wealth, now appeared what Blair had actually suggested it to be, merely the nucleus around which an energetic man might accumulate a fortune. He was in the social class of the millionaires, but not in their financial class. No matter what dividends were paid on two or three hundred thousand dollars' worth of railway stock, that income, added to his salary of five thousand a year, would never support a palace such as Blair lived in, or even a mansion similar to the one inhabited by Colonel Beck. Sadie, with the demeanour of a queen, needed also the income of a queen. John had no delusions on that score, and furthermore, being proud, he could not ask her to step down, but to step up. The germ that had remained dormant in his mind since his uncle's death now developed into the belief that he might become as prosperous in speculation as he proved to be in all other walks in life. Often in after years he remembered the coincident conjunction of necessity, development and opportunity. Any two of the trinity would have been inactive without the presence of the third, but the trio travelling by different highways met at the crossroad, and then important things happened.

One eventful evening he dressed for dinner and dined early at the club; then he strolled up the avenue to the residence of Colonel Beck. Ushered into the drawingroom he found Sadie standing by the open piano, idly touching the upper keys with the tips of her fingers, standing there as if she were waiting for him, yet he knew she was waiting for some one else, for her opera cloak hung over the back of a chair beside her, and she was arrayed superbly for dinner, ball or reception. Never afterward could John give to himself any lucid description of what she wore, except that she looked like a radiant angel garbed in white. Her raiment was diaphanously, airily beautiful. Her gleaming, snowy shoulders, superb neck, and crown of golden hair made up a vision almost unearthly in its loveliness, which at once entranced and startled the young man. She turned toward him that superbly poised head, with the arched brows of surprise at his entrance mellowed by a seductive smile of a welcome not to be misunderstood. John himself was one of those well-set-up young men who look their best in evening dress, and as he came rapidly forward down the long room the girl could see the soul shining in his eyes, and the sight brought added colour to her own fair cheeks.

"Sadie," he cried, taking both her hands in his, although she offered him only one, "if but a painter could place on canvas even a hundredth part of your adorable beauty to-night, his fame would ring down the ages."

The girl laughed.

"Is it so striking as all that? Then I am sorry I can give you but fifteen minutes of it, for my uncle is taking me out to dinner, and man-like he is late, having just arrived home and gone upstairs to dress."

"Fifteen minutes! What is it the poet says of fifteen minutes as compared with a cycle of Cathay? Fifteen minutes, Sadie, with you, is worth an eternity with any one else on earth. Why, bless my soul, the Declaration of Independence was signed in ten!"

Again the girl laughed, trying, not very strenuously, to disengage her hands.

"Do you wish me to sign a declaration of independence?" she asked.

"Yes, a declaration of independence from all the world except me."

"In other words, a declaration of dependence on you rather than independence of the rest?" she corrected.

"Sadie, I've adored you ever since I met you. The picture on canvas that I spoke of is impossible, for there is not genius enough existent to do it justice. But there is a picture I ask you to look at," and he swung her round almost rudely until she saw the reflection of two young people holding each other's hands in the tall pier-glass.

"If you appreciate that Princess as she deserves, you will wonder at the conceit of the man standing beside her, that he dares to ask for the original."

Sadie looked at her counterpart with a certain complacency, for doubtless she was a girl who had received many proposals, and was not to be swept from her feet even by one so impetuous as this. But that she was gratified by the young man's earnestness, one needed but a glance at her sparkling eyes and rosy cheeks to see. She turned from the glass to him.

"Is it the girl from New York or the gown from Paris you so warmly admire?"

"Answer me, Sadie, answer me," he cried.

"Hush, hush," she whispered, "I hear my uncle coming," and now she struggled in earnest to release herself, but strenuously he held her firm.

"Answer yes or no."

"Which word will release me most speedily?" she demanded.

"The first."

"Then it must be yes. A fine masterful lover you are!" she cried with pretended indignation, as she whisked herself free from him.

It was a maid who came in, and taking up the white cloak, she adjusted it over the fair shoulders of her young mistress. A moment later the Colonel, rubicund and beaming, entered the drawing-room.

"Ah, Steele, is that you?" he saluted his visitor, shaking hands in the most friendly manner; "has my niece told you that we must enact the inhospitable savage tonight, and turn you forth in a cold and pitiless world?"

"Yes, Colonel," laughed John, who was in such a state of joyous exaltation that he would have laughed, no matter what his host had said, "yes, and I must confess that it is like being turned from Paradise."

The Colonel, smiling, allowed his eyes to pass from the exuberant young man to the downcast face of his niece, who seemed absorbed in the rearrangement of her white cloak. If the Colonel suspected anything, he said nothing that might give a hint of his surmise.

"Do you know that Mr. Rockervelt is in town?" he asked.

"No," replied the young man, in some astonishment.

"He arrived here by the noon train," continued the Colonel, "and all this afternoon we have been in close session at Blair's house. Mr. Rockervelt spoke of you, and said he was sorry he could not see you this trip. We are dining with him to-night at Blair's, but ladies being present, no business will be talked. Mr. Rockervelt leaves by special at ten o'clock."

"Rather a short stay," commented Steele.

"Short, but important," replied the Colonel, as he led the way to the door.

John Steele had the advantage of escorting Miss Sadie to her carriage, and the felicity of pressing her hand before he made way for the Colonel to enter. He stood there for a moment, watching the receding back of the carriage, and then walked uncertainly down the avenue, treading not upon hard flagstones, but on clouds, his mind far aloft in the realms of romance, while his body bumped heedlessly against innocent passers-by, or those who hoped to be passers-by *until* he ran into them, interrupting their course and causing one stranger to remark that it was a pity to see a young man so drunk this early in the evening.

---

# CHAPTER VII—THE FIRST CAST OF THE DICE

NEXT morning John Steele was startled to receive a rather peremptory message from Colonel Beck requesting him to call at once at his residence. The young man instantly obeyed, and mounted the steps with some trepidation, wondering whether Sadie had made a confidant of her uncle, and fearing that the uncle's designs for his niece excluded a division superintendent from any discussion regarding her future. He was shown into the Colonel's study, a large room on the first floor at the back of the house. The Colonel greeted him with what might be termed absent-minded friendliness. He was evidently perturbed about something, and after requesting his caller to sit down, himself paced up and down the room two or three times with a shade of perplexity on his brow. At last he threw himself into his office chair, and sitting back, interlocked his hands behind his head, and bent his looks upon the visitor he had summoned.

"I thought it best, Mr. Steele, to ask you to come here, as what I have to say is extremely private, and I wish to incur no interruptions, and to obviate the possibility of eavesdroppers."

"Yes?" interpolated John, thinking this opening must certainly pertain to the episode of the previous evening in the room beneath.

"You said to me once," went on the Colonel, "that you were an investor, not a speculator."

"Yes," repeated his listener.

"Has it ever occurred to you that a man may be both, or rather, that he may indulge in all the advantages of successful speculation without any of the risks that occur through playing in the open market?"

"If such a thing could be done," said John with a smile, "it would be the very heaven of financiering."

"Such a thing not only can be done, but it *is* done, every day. It is the outsider who speculates, and who must incur the uncertainties which accompany speculation. Those on the inside do not speculate, but operate in a security as absolute as that of a bank which receives a certain amount from a depositor. Now, I told you last night that although Mr. Rockervelt's visit was brief, it was important. Its importance lies in this. The financial year now drawing to a close—the financial year, I mean, so far as the Rockervelt system is concerned—has been far and away the most prosperous in its existence. Manateau Midland stock to-day stands at 162 1/2, which is much under its intrinsic worth. But before I proceed with this exposition of values, I should like to ask you a question or two. Am I right in surmising that you owe your position entirely to Mr. Rockervelt?"

"Yes, to him through Philip Manson's recommendation."

"Ah, Philip Manson! I believe he is one of Mr. Rockervelt's favourites, too. He was your predecessor, wasn't he?"

"Yes. Mr. Rockervelt took him to New York, and put me in his place here."

"The chances are, then, that Mr. Manson will get his tip straight from Mr. Rockervelt himself, and, if he takes advantage of his knowledge, will doubtless operate through our brokers in New York. Well, the position is just this, Mr. Steele: Times have been good, and I tell you in confidence, what perhaps you have already guessed, that never has the Rockervelt system enjoyed a more prosperous year. The various roads, thanks to efficient men like yourself, have been remarkably free from disaster, and in truth during the twelve months now closing there has been no serious accident at all. In spite of our determination to let the actual state of affairs be known only to those on the inside, among whom Mr. Rockervelt, without saying it in so many words, evidently reckons yourself, the general public has arrived at some inkling of the facts. Stock which a month ago could be got for a hundred and fifty-two sells to-day at over a hundred and sixty. Still, the public has no real idea of how prosperous we have been, and I venture to predict that our next declaration of dividends, which is less than a month away now, will come as a complete surprise, and those who previously possessed inside knowledge will benefit accordingly. Of course, your duties heretofore have not brought you into contact with the finance of a huge corporation like the Rockervelt system, so I may tell you that after the annual meeting is held and a good dividend is declared the real owners of the railway, such as Mr. Rockervelt and his colleagues, sell their stock to the general public, buying it back during the ensuing year at a lower figure, in time for the next election of officers. We are now all loaded up with as much as we can carry, and it has been agreed that the time is ripe for the introduction of a very select few, like Manson, yourself and one or two more, into the inner circle. We take into our confidence only those who are actively engaged in the management and working of the various roads; men on whom we depend for our continued success. Now, our brokers have just been in communication with a man who wishes to sell stock to the amount of something like half a million, and I have asked them not to part with it or to seek a customer until I had communicated with you."

"Colonel," said the young man, his face aglow with excitement at the chance offered to him, "that is very kind of you, but you see, my money, or at least most of it, is already in Midland stock to the amount of between two hundred and three hundred thousand dollars."

"Yes, I was aware of that, but our brokers will arrange everything for you. If, instead of buying the stock outright—and by the way, what did you pay for it?"

"I got it at a trifle less than a hundred and fifty."

"Why, there you are. Suppose you had, instead of buying it outright, taken an option, say, on a million, you would already have made a hundred thousand dollars on the rise. Our brokers will arrange the financial details and you can secure the stock you now possess and the half million block as well, with ample margin to spare. Then, when you have taken your profits, you can do as you please: reinvest if you like, or wait until the inevitable reaction comes and buy in at a lower figure a much larger amount than you now possess."

"All right, Colonel, I'll do it. In fact, I leave the matter entirely in your hands to arrange with the brokers."

"Thanks. I don't attempt to conceal from you that it is a great opportunity, and I need not ask you to hold in strict confidence all I have told you, for we don't care to see the price go much higher until after the dividend is declared. There's just one request I must make which perhaps you will have no hesitation in granting. We should like to secure the voting proxy of this stock against the general meeting, to be used in the Rockervelt interest."

"Oh, certainly," cried John, delighted.

The Colonel selected some blank forms from the receptacle on his table before him, rapidly filled them in, and passed them across for John to sign, which he did almost without glancing at them, Colonel Beck in somewhat legal language pointing out the purport of each instrument.

"Well, that's all right," said the Colonel, as he gathered up the signed papers. "I'll see the brokers at once, and get the deal put through."

As John Steele came downstairs, he realised that these were business hours, but considered himself justified for the first time in his life in filching a few moments from them. He determined to see Sadie, and learn whether or not it was her wish he should at once communicate with her uncle on a matter which did not concern the buying or selling of stock.

Sadie received him in a morning room that was partly library. Her first utterance rang with a tone of imperiousness that was new to him.

"Why have you been shut up with my uncle so long in his study this morning?"

"Because he sent for me."

"Why did he send for you?"

"To make some arrangements about the future." Sadie's blue eyes were scintillating with excitement or anger; the young man could not quite tell which. "What arrangements?" she demanded.

"Well, our conference was strictly confidential, and your uncle asked me not to mention the subject to any one."

The girl almost stamped her foot.

"You know very well what I mean," she said. "Did he send for you because of—because of—last night?"

"No, Sadie, he didn't. To tell the truth, when I received his message this morning I thought perhaps he suspected something last night, and wished to question me, and I assure you I felt very uneasy meeting him before speaking first with you and learning your views upon the matter. However, his conversation was entirely about the railway business, and some new features of it, which arose through Mr. Rockervelt's visit yesterday."

"Then you said nothing to him about last evening."

"No, Sadie, I could not take such a liberty without your permission."

"Ah," sighed the girl, with evident relief, "you did give me a fright when I learned you had gone to my uncle's room so early in the morning, and when you stayed so long."

"Don't you want me to speak of our engagement, then?"

"There is no engagement. You were so boisterous standing there by the piano that I had to say 'Yes' to release myself, otherwise my uncle would have come in upon a fine tableau."

"I hope you are not going back upon that 'Yes,'" said the young man earnestly.

For a few moments the girl did not answer. She seemed in an uncertain temper that morning, and rather inclined to pout, yet to the ardent young man she appeared more entrancing than ever.

"I am going neither back nor forward," she said at last. "I desire to remain just where I am. I am not sure of myself. I think you took an unfair advantage of my dilemma last evening with your obstreperousness; and there are many reasons why I should not wish to be bound by the answer you forced me to give."

"You shall not be bound," replied John very seriously; "everything must be exactly as you wish it to be. You, doubtless, have been and will be sought by lovers richer than I, but you will never find one more devoted to you."

"Oh, I wasn't thinking of riches," explained the girl petulantly; then after a pause she added: "though I may as well confess I am quite unsuited to be a poor man's wife. The cottage with roses clambering over it looks very beautiful in a painting, and a description of it reads well in a magazine story, but when I was a small girl, I endured the reality of poverty and I don't want any more of it. I suppose you think that very sordid?"

"No," rejoined John Steele gravely, "I think it very sensible."

"I should loathe a house in the suburbs with two servants, or its alternative, the middle-class hotel or superior boarding-house down town. My education and my bringing-up haven't fitted me for these delights."

"You incur no danger from a cheap house in the suburbs or its alternative. I am at present earning five thousand dollars a year, and am only on the threshold of my profession. I own absolute cash-producing property to the extent of about three hundred thousand dollars, and if you will consent to our engagement being made public when I am a millionaire, I guarantee that the announcement will take place before two months are past." Up to this point the girl's eyes had been fixed on the floor; now she raised them level with his, and he saw that all resentment had fled from them, leaving in its stead a sparkle of mischief and merriment.

"Why," she laughed, "one would think that the financial conversation upstairs with the uncle was resumed in the morning room with the niece. I suppose these monetary revelations arise because of the business suit you are wearing in this hard morning light; but I think I like you much better, John, in evening clothes, under the radiance of shaded lamps. I am sure neither of us thought of money last night, and I certainly did not this morning until you began talking about it."

She held her hand out to him, and he took it with enthusiasm.

"I do not wish anything said of our engagement at the present moment," she went on. "There is nothing very terrible about such a proviso, is there? I have many friends in this city, and I don't wish them all set gossipping, as will be the case if any announcement is made. We will let the '*yes*' stand where it did, but you must give me a little time quietly to learn how my uncle may regard the news. You will come here, I hope, just as if nothing had happened, and if I receive you as crossly as I did just now, I give you leave to scold me. Is that a bargain?" she concluded brightly, smiling up at him, and giving him freely what he had taken the night before, her two hands in his.

"It is a bargain," said John with content, drawing her suddenly toward him and kissing her, an act to which she submitted half with reluctance, half with acquiescence.

And so for a month everything went on as before, except that John was perhaps the most frequent visitor at the Beck household. He thought more of his love than of his money, as it is right and proper a young man should, for youth is the time of optimism, and everything was progressing smoothly.

A week before the general meeting Blair departed for New York, and before he left he appointed Steele acting general manager *pro tem.*, which had the effect of making John the busiest man in the city, giving him little opportunity to think of either femininity or finance. Colonel Beck accompanied Blair to the metropolis, but had returned the day before the annual meeting was held. There were large interests in the West, he said, which would require his unremitting attention during the next few days, and this proved a true prediction.

On the evening of the day of the general meeting Steele left his office late, intending to snatch a hasty meal at the club and return to his work. He found the streets in unusual commotion; newsboys were rushing frantically here and there yelling at the top of their voices: "Great panic in New York."

Steele bought a paper, and the glance he bestowed upon the black headlines rooted him to the pavement.

"Financial Thunderbolt," he read. "No dividend for Rockervelt shareholders. Panic on the Stock Exchange this afternoon. Heavy drop in all securities. Rockervelt stocks leading the rout. Are we on the verge of a crisis? Fall of twenty-eight points in Rockervelt holdings when the Stock Exchange closed. Fears for tomorrow."

"Twenty-eight points," muttered the grave young man to himself. "That means a loss to me of nearly two hundred thousand dollars!"

Without reading further particulars, Steele thrust the paper into his pocket, and continued his journey to the club. His mind was in a whirl, but clenching his teeth, he strove to rearrange his thoughts and settle upon a course of action. It was too late that day to do anything. If he had only known of this disaster as soon as it occurred; if he had had word as early as was possible after the passing of the dividend, he might have got out without a loss of more than thirty or forty thousand dollars perhaps. What an innocent lamb he had been; almost begging to be shorn. Not a single precaution had he taken. It needed but a word to Philip Manson in New York, and a telegram would have apprised him at once of what had happened in the general meeting; yet here he had remained buried up to the eyes in the business of this corporation, which had evidently been engaged in a gigantic game of thimble-rigging; working like a fool while all the world knew of the topical item except himself. The reason of this complete absorption in duty suddenly struck him like a blow in the face, and he stood still at the thought of it. Blair had put upon his shoulders the burden of general manager without relieving him of the task of division superintendent, and he had been struggling to fulfil adequately the obligations of both offices. Had Blair done this for a purpose? One suspicion led to another. Might not the whole net in which he found himself enmeshed be of the general manager's weaving? If so, Blair had found him an easy victim.

His meal at the club, instead of being snatched as he had intended, was a most leisurely one, but his appetite was gone and he ate little. He did not go back to his office, but walked up the avenue to Colonel Beck's house, only to find that the Colonel and his niece had gone out for the evening.

John Steele was at his broker's office the moment it was opened. A crowd was collected before the place, but only those were allowed in who had dealings with the firm.

"I was just about to telegraph you," said the junior partner, who received Steele in his private office. "I rather expected you in yesterday, but as we had no instructions we held on."

"Why didn't you telegraph me yesterday?"

"Why?" asked the broker, justly indignant at such a childish suggestion. "You left no instructions, and as every ticker in town announced the news, I did not think it necessary. The fact is that as soon as the announcement came we were so busy here that no one in the office had time to turn round. The crash was so unsuspected we were not prepared."

"It seems to me," said John bitterly, "that a firm like yours, intimately connected with the Rockervelt interests, should have had some idea of what was coming."

"Oh, well, so far as that goes," said the junior partner airily, "I might be equally justified in saying that an official like yourself, holding an important position on the Rockervelt staff, would have been much more likely to get the straight tip than we."

"Oh, I got a tip all right enough," replied John, grimly, "but it seems to have been a crooked rather than a straight one."

"Ah, well," said the broker, with the easy nonchalance of one whose withers are unwrung, "these mistakes happen now and then. The outlook in New York this morning is very-gloomy. Of course things may rally before noon, but we can't count on that. I was going to telegraph you that we must have margin put up; not less than twenty-one thousand dollars, and even that will only give you three points lee-way when your present margin is absorbed."

"Do you think twenty-one thousand would save me?"

"Who can tell?" answered the junior partner with a shrug of his shoulders. "It all depends. If you can inform me what Mr. Rockervelt will do during the next two hours, I can predict what will happen with the stock. I expected he would support it, but apparently he is letting it go smash."

"Why shouldn't he? He is the cause of it all," said John. "I know the road earned a dividend, even if Rockervelt didn't declare one."

"Well, there you are," said the broker. "The public always loses its head at a time like this. Rockervelt stocks are now away below their intrinsic value, but that fact won't prevent their going lower if the panic continues."

"What would you advise me to do?" asked Steele.

"I don't give advice; I take instructions. We'll hang on just as long as we can, but if the decline continues, we must sell your block before it gets below the margin."

"I hold three times twenty-one thousand, face value in Northern Pacific Stock. Can you tell me if there is any chance of raising twenty-one thousand dollars on it?"

The broker shook his head.

"You might have done that two days ago, but now? with gilt-edged stock like Rockervelt's on the toboggan how can you expect to raise a loan on Northern Pacifics? I don't believe any one would venture a thousand dollars on that security to-day. Those who have money are sitting on it, waiting for the clouds to roll by. This may be merely a little financial flutter and a quick recovery, or it may prove the beginning of a commercial crisis that will last for two or three years."

"Yet these devils in New York heedlessly run the whole country into such a risk to make a few more dirty dollars for themselves, who are already millionaires."

The veins in Steele's forehead were swelling, and his hair bristled with indignation, but the broker merely threw back his head and laughed.

"Satan reproving sin!" he cried. "What were you doing, a man with a quarter of a million or so, but trying to add a few dollars, dirty or clean, to that amount."

"True, true," said John, calming down suddenly, "you are in the right. Well, good morning; I see there's a host waiting for you, and as you have no advice to give, and no money to lend, I'll see what I can do outside." He walked to the nearest telegraph station, and sent a message to Philip Manson in New York:

"*Can you telegraph me twenty-one thousand dollars? Will forward as security sixty thousand par-value Northern Pacific.*"

This handed over, he returned to his office, opened the safe, took out the Northern Pacific securities, and placed them on his desk. For an hour and a half he was busy giving directions to this man or that, then a telegram was brought in to him from Philip Manson.

"Very sorry, but have lost everything I possessed in yesterday's panic."

"Poor old Manson," mused Steele sadly. "So he was caught in the trap too. Well, after all, when an old and experienced man is nipped, there is some excuse for myself." He thrust the securities in his pocket, put on his hat, and paid a visit to Colonel Beck. That benign gentleman received him with beaming effusion.

"Ah, Mr. Steele, I am so sorry we were out when you called last evening. It was a little dinner to which I had accepted an invitation more than a week ago, little dreaming that such a financial storm was about to break over our heads. Sit down, Steele, sit down. What can I do for you?"

"You can lend me twenty-one thousand dollars."

The smile faded from the cherubic face of the Colonel, and a shade of melancholy took its place.

"You mean, then, that your margins have all but disappeared?"

"That is exactly what I mean."

"Would twenty-one thousand save you?"

"You can tell that better than I, Colonel, being more in the confidence of the Rockervelts. I offer you as security nearly three times the amount in Northern Pacific stock."

The Colonel slowly shook his head.

"I shouldn't ask for security at all, Mr. Steele, if I had the ready money, but this unexpected crisis has tied up all the funds at my disposal."

"Unexpected! Do you mean to tell me you did not know the dividend was to be passed?"

Colonel Beck placed the tips of his fingers together, and gazed across the apex before him at the young man, more in sorrow than in anger.

"My dear Mr. Steele, I have no doubt you heard the news before I did. As I told you in this very room, large dividends had been earned, and of course I came to the conclusion that they would be declared. Then you say, quite justly, if a dividend was earned, why was it not declared? The reason is a most convincing one, and I am expecting every moment Mr. Rockervelt to give it to the public. When he does so, people will learn how senseless is the panic which has ensued over what is, after all, an exceedingly simple matter; one of those exigencies of business which are constantly occurring.

"While I was in New York I was consulted about the case; indeed the main lines of the deal were settled, although the method of payment was left open. You may be aware that Mr. Rockervelt is aiming at the Pacific coast, and gradually extending his lines to the west. Very well. About a week ago he got a private offer of the L. S. & D. Road, for which at the present moment he has no use, but which in a few years' time, when he makes certain connections, will be a most valuable link in his chain to California. Now, Mr. Rockervelt seeks advice, and listens to it, but no man can tell whether he will follow that advice or not. The information I have received from New York is to the effect that at the last moment Mr. Rockervelt made up his mind that instead of declaring a large dividend, as he might have done, he would put the amount in the L. S. & D. Road. Of course, he could have explained this at the meeting, but he did not do so, and there I think he was wrong. However, as you know, he works along his own lines, and perhaps his announcement might have raised difficulties before all the papers were signed. I imagine this is why he has made no statement. The truth is that just after the meeting he left in his private car for the West, intending to go over the L. S. & D. Road, but I am sure that when he realises the effect of his reticence on the business affairs of the country, he will be prompt to make his explanation, and save any further depreciation of securities. His manifesto will doubtless appear in to-night's papers, or in the morning sheets at the latest."

"I'm afraid that won't help me, Colonel Beck, and as you are yourself unable to accommodate me with the money for a few days, I suppose it would be useless to ask if any of your wealthy friends would accept my securities and hand me over the money."

"I fear not, I fear not," said the Colonel, with an air of inexpressible sadness. "At times like these every one pulls tight the purse-strings. If I went to the richest friend I have and asked to be accommodated with a loan, telling him the true story of the passing of this dividend, I am very sure I should not be believed." John rose to his feet, a wry smile on his lips.

"It is rather deplorable, Colonel Beck," he said quietly, "that people should so distrust their fellow men, and even though you say so, I find it impossible to believe that any one should suspect you of setting a trap."

"Ah, well," sighed the Colonel, "we must take life as we find it, you know, and not as we would have it. Time sets all things right, and I am old enough to be philosophical. Must you go? Well, drop in when you can, and if the financial tension relaxes, I may be able to be of some assistance."

John went downstairs and, as on a former occasion, expressing a wish to see the young lady of the house, was conducted into the morning room, where she greeted him, as it seemed to his now over-sensitive nerves, somewhat distantly.

"Sadie," he said, "I told you in this room that I was worth three hundred thousand dollars; that I was earning a salary of five thousand dollars a year, and that within two months I expected to be a millionaire. I must now inform you that all my money has been swept away, that I am about to resign my five thousand a year, and that I shall probably never be more of a millionaire than I am at the present moment."

"Oh, I'm so sorry," said the girl, with the breathless haste of one who is confronted by a condition, and does not know the exact words that fit it.

"I am sorry too," said John simply.

He stood there for a full minute, and there was silence between them, until at last the girl appeared to force herself to speak.

"Still, you are young, Mr. Steele, and this is a country of great opportunities, is it not?"

"I think it is," said John, with a grin; "yes, it is generally understood to be a land of excellent chances, and, as you say, I am young, much younger than when I was in this room last time. I knew as a general proposition I was young, but I had no idea I was the infant I have found myself to be."

As he spoke the girl drew herself up, and tried to assume an air of haughty indignation.

"If you are laughing at me," she said, "I think it is very unkind."

"I give you my word, Miss Beck, that I do not feel much like laughing, and least of all at you. I merely came in to bid you good-bye."

He held out his hand, and she took it gingerly, at arm's length, as it were.

"Good-bye," she said, "and I wish you luck."

"Thank you," replied John simply.

---

# CHAPTER VIII—AN IMPENDING CHANGE

TO borrow money at any time is difficult; to borrow during a panic is impossible. John Steele spent the first half of the second day of the crisis in attempting the impossible. Every man to whom he applied seemed to be in the same position as himself. All stocks had come down in sympathy with the Rockervelt slump, and it seemed as if every person supposed to be rich was then engaged in a frantic endeavour to prevent ruin by putting up all the ready money in hand, or else trying, like John himself, to borrow.

About half past twelve he gave up the quest, and made a second call on his brokers. It was the junior partner again who received him.

"Ah, Mr. Steele," cried the broker, "here you are, eh? They say all things come to him who waits."

"That isn't true in my case," replied John. "I've been waiting all day for money and couldn't get it. It didn't come."

"Well, I've been waiting for you," rejoined the broker. "I have had messengers after you all over town. Called at your rooms, at your office, at your club; found any number of people who had just seen you, but not one of the searchers caught sight of *you*."

"What's the news?" asked John, without much hope.

"We hung on to your stock till ten minutes to twelve, and then we had to let it go. We were lucky enough to get a purchaser for the whole block at a price that just cleared us, but I can tell you I spent a bad quarter of an hour before I got into touch with him."

"When you say cleared, I suppose you mean that I'm entirely wiped out, but you got from under without loss."

"I don't know a better way of putting it than that," replied the broker.

"I didn't think there was a man in town with ready money enough to make such a purchase to-day. I wish I had managed to encounter him. Perhaps I might have detached twenty-one thousand dollars from him."

"It is very likely, for he is a friend of yours, and from your own office. He said there was no secret about it; so I may as well tell you the purchaser is Mr. Blair, general manager of the Midland."

"Oh, he's back from New York, is he?"

"Yes, he returned this morning; haven't you seen him? Haven't you been at your office at all today?"

"No, I've been calling on friends and acquaintances. I suppose the stock is going up now?"

"Well, such a large purchase had first the effect of putting the brakes on its downhill course, and now it has recovered two points. Then the news from New York is encouraging. It seems that the Rockervelt forces, both in New York and Chicago, are buying all that is offered. You see, Mr. Rockervelt himself left for the West just before the scare, and I imagine he didn't realise how serious it was."

"Quite so. I heard he had gone West. Pity there are no telegraph wires to the West, isn't it?"

The broker laughed.

"Oh, I guess Mr. Rockervelt is as foxy as they make 'em. I don't suppose he's lost anything over this shake-up, and perhaps he thought it was a good time to squeeze a little of the dampness out of the stock. I expect a very rapid recovery. The country is prosperous, and from the way things look this last hour or two we've been going through a little squall, but not entering upon a financial crisis."

"That's a blessing," said John with a sigh; "still, the squall has upset my canoe, even if the big liners ride through it. Good-bye."

Once outside, instead of feeling depressed, as he had expected, John experienced an unaccountable thrill of elation. The disaster was complete; complete beyond recall; complete in spite of anything he did or did not do. The very finality of the catastrophe seemed to lift a weight that had been oppressing him for a night and a day. He remembered that he had had practically no dinner the evening before, and no breakfast that morning, and now a fierce and healthy hunger which seemed to have been biding its time sprang upon him. A glance at his watch showed that it was nearly two o'clock. He walked rapidly to the University Club, noted for its excellent cuisine, and wrote on an order card the menu of a sumptuous meal. A deferential servitor approached silently to his elbow.

"Mr. Steele, No. 1623 wants you on the telephone."

"All right, ring him up, and tell him I'll be there in a moment, and if he is impatient, inform him I am at present engaged on the important choice between camembert and brie."

Sending his order upstairs, he went into the little telephone cabin. He knew the number meant the general manager's office.

"Hello, is that you, Blair?—Yes, this is Steele.—What's that?—Oh, no, now that you mention it, I haven't been there last night or this morning. How's the old road running?—What? It isn't doing so well outside.—Oh, if it comes to that, I've been general manager and division superintendent for the past week, so surely you can act Pooh Bah for a day. To tell the truth, it seemed to me that a road whose stock was falling so rapidly wasn't worth general managering or division superintending.—Levity? Bless you, no! I'm the most serious man in town.—Oh, I'm sorry you think my remarks flippant. Have you had lunch? I've just ordered a meal for a millionaire; come down and have a bite with me.—Oh, had it, eh? You're an early bird. I've ordered a late bird grilled upstairs. Sure you won't drop round, and have a cup of coffee and a liqueur?—Yes, I see, you're quite right. Somebody must attend to business.—Well, I'll drop round on you at four o'clock. Good-bye."

John Steele allowed himself a good hour and three-quarters for his luncheon, then he strolled down to the Grand Union Station, and, exactly as the big bell in the tower tolled four he walked into the general manager's room.

Mr. Blair was seated at his broad table, and as he looked up his chubby face was a study in various emotions. Superficially it wore the conventional, official frown which a great man may call to his aid when a subordinate's conduct has been such as to merit disapproval. The severity of the frown, however, was chastened by the expression of the just man, who, although righteously offended, is nevertheless prepared to listen to an explanation, and perhaps accept an apology. The lips were prepared to censure, or even, in a last resort, to condemn, although, if the case merited leniency, one would not be surprised to hear them admonish and advise. It was the face of a simple and honest man, willing to forgive, yet not afraid to punish.

The eyes, however, rather gave the situation away. In them twinkled triumph and glee, and lurking in their depths was a background of malice and hatred.

"Mr. Steele, I was amazed to find on my return from New York that you had absented yourself without permission from your duties," began Mr. Blair, in a sincere more-in-sorrow-than-in-anger tone.

"Oh, that's all right," said John airily. "I was general manager *pro tem.*, you see, and a general manager may do what he pleases. But I was division superintendent also, so I asked the general manager for an hour or two off, and permission was granted me."

"As you know, Mr. Steele, I am the most forbearing of men, but such a tone as you have adopted will not do. As I told you over the telephone I was surprised at the flippant manner you thought fit to adopt, but I expected a satisfactory explanation when we met face to face."

"If that is the case, sir, I shall be so sorry to disappoint you. The satisfactory explanation I beg to offer for my absence is that I was busily engaged in gambling."

"Gambling!" cried Mr. Blair in astonishment; "this is shocking. It is my opinion that a man cannot be an efficient servant of a great railway and a speculator at the same time."

"I quite agree with you, Mr. Blair, and we are two shining examples of the truth of your aphorism. You are the most inefficient railway servant I ever met, and at the same time the most successful gambler. I am an excellent railway man and the most idiotic speculator there is in the country at the present moment. What's the use of wasting that sanctimonious 'holier-than-thou' look of yours? You know, and I know, that you don't care a hang about my being away a day. What you want me here for is to gloat over me. You've got my three hundred thousand dollars as slick as any bunco man ever achieved a much smaller sum over a green farm hand from the country. I'm here, not to receive any censure or to make any apology, but so that you may enjoy the effects of my humiliation and defeat. I am the last person in the world to deprive another of innocent amusement. Here I am, therefore. I have just come out of the tail end of the threshing machine, and have brought the remnants for your inspection. What do you think of them?"

"I am exceedingly sorry to hear that you have been unfortunate in your financial transactions."

"Of course you are. Thanks ever so much."

"Did you succeed in raising twenty-one thousand on your Northern Pacific stock?"

"No, I have it with me yet. That N. P. stock sticks to me closer than any friend I have in town. You don't want to buy it by any chance?"

"No," said Blair smoothly. "I have quite recently made a very large investment in Midland shares, re-buying a block that I was fortunate enough to sell at its highest point, and have therefore no desire to acquire further securities at the present moment."

"You're just in the same fix as all the rest of my acquaintances, Mr. Blair, so your refusal does not disappoint me."

"You lost also the thirty thousand you had in the Bank at Detroit?"

This was said very quietly, and for a moment amazed the listener by the accurate knowledge the elder man possessed of his affairs. The next instant John Steele gave utterance to a shriek of laughter, smiting his thigh with his open palm as if he had just heard the best joke in the world. The young man strode up and down the room giving way to shout after shout of hilarity, while the elder, all trace of humbug vanishing from his face, rose to his feet in alarm, believing that misfortune had turned the other's brain, and fearing a transformation into a sudden savagery that might make his isolated position one of danger. His eyes rested longingly on the door, while his hand nervously sought the electric button. John, seeing these premonitions of interruption, controlled himself with an effort, and stammered: "Sit down, Blair; it's all right. Don't get frightened. I'll explain in a minute. You see, it was this way," said John, coming up in front of the table again, and resolutely crushing down his bubbling tendency to merriment; "that thirty thousand was deposited in the Detroit bank by my late uncle. I possess my own little bank account here, which I have been adding to week by week. Consequently, I never needed to draw a check upon Detroit. Now, the funny thing is that I have been searching this town from cellar to garret that I might borrow twenty-one thousand dollars, and all the while I could have drawn my own check for the amount, and had nine thousand odd left over."

"Do you mean to say, then," said Blair, visibly disappointed, "that you didn't put in the thirty thousand as margin?"

"I did not. Do you feel you ought to have a check for that thirty thousand? You remind me of the hotel keeper at a summer resort down East, whose customer said: 'You have made a mistake in my bill,' and when the proprietor denied that there could be any error, the guest explained: 'Oh, there must be, for I have still ten dollars left.' The beautiful part of it is, Blair, that if I had thought of my thirty thousand I would have put it in; so I am mighty glad I didn't think of it, for it would not have saved me. I was looking over the figures of the decline on the tape at the club, and found that the stuff reached its lowest point at about half-past eleven, and that point would have not only wiped out my thirty thousand, but another thirty thousand as well. The brokers told me they had hung on till ten minutes to twelve, but they evidently knew their customer, and got out on the rise. I am afraid, Blair, that even brokers are not truthful men. It's a wonder that staunch, true hearts like you and me can make a living in this deceitful world. Well, Mr. Blair, I have come to bid you good-bye, and I venture to predict that I'll have more fun out of that thirty thousand dollars than I had out of the three hundred thousand. Wealth isn't everything here below. Meanwhile keep on living a virtuous life, and you will reap your reward by and by. Never become discouraged in well-doing. Ta-ta."

With that John Steele took his departure from the Grand Union Station, packed up his traps, and took train for Detroit, where he lifted his money from the bank, and left on the night express for New York.

Here he rented Drawer 907 in the Broadway Safe Deposit Vaults, and in this drawer he placed his Northern Pacific stock and locked it up. He next turned his money, all but a thousand dollars, into a letter of credit on Europe; then bought a first-class ticket to France on the biggest boat sailing that week. He determined to burn his bridges behind him before he called on his old friend Philip Manson, for he knew instinctively that Manson would strongly disapprove of the course he had laid out for himself, and, remembering his great esteem and affection for Manson, he was not sure enough of himself to venture within the circle of his influence without some extraneous aid to hold him to his purpose.

It was nearing twelve o'clock when he went up in one of the half-dozen elevators of the huge Rockervelt building, and was ushered into Philip Manson's room.

"Hello, Mr. Manson, how are you?" he cried cheerily, as his former chief rose to greet him. Although he called the much more important general manager plain "Blair," he never was able to drop the prefix "Mr." from Man-son's name. His respect for his solemn friend was as deep as his affection, and the strong regard manifested itself unconsciously in this manner. Manson's appearance gave no indication that he had passed through a crisis which had ruined him. He was the same quiet, reserved man he had always been, and a touch of grey at the temples was all the change John noticed as having taken place since he saw him last. The stern face relaxed into a bright expression of welcome as he shook hands with the young man from the West.

"I am very glad to see you," said Manson. "Did you get my letter?"

"No, I left Warmington the day I telegraphed you."

"Ah, well, it doesn't matter. It was merely about your telegram I wrote. I am very sorry indeed that it proved impossible for me to send you the money, and I merely wrote a fuller explanation than my telegram contained."

"You got caught in the crash, then?" said Steele.

"Yes, everything I possessed was swept away. It serves me right for doing what I never did in my life before, which is to dabble in stocks. Was I right in supposing from your telegram that you also had become involved?"

"Yes, and if you had sent me the money it would have been lost; so you see, you don't need to regret that you didn't have it. The funny thing is that

I had myself thirty thousand dollars in the Detroit Bank, which, in the excitement of the day, slipped my memory as effectually as if it had been only thirty cents."

"And did you save it?" asked Manson, with as near an approach to eagerness as he could show.

"Oh, yes, but the saving was an act of Providence, as we always try to make out our accidents are, and not through any sanity on my part. How did you come to put everything in stocks? I thought you never gambled?"

"I didn't, up till about a week ago. Colonel Beck gave me the straight tip, which I understood came direct from Mr. Rockervelt, and I was foolish enough to act upon it."

"He did the same kind office for me, but he's merely a stool-pigeon for old Blair. Blair was the man behind the gun."

"We have no proof of that," said Manson, judicially.

"*I* have proof. Blair didn't hesitate to confess as much after he had raked in my money. Blair's one of those oily hypocrites who smile and smile, and remain the villain. He never forgives, though he may appear to do so."

"You were always inclined to be prejudiced against Mr. Blair, John," said Manson meditatively. "Still, there's little use in talking of what is past. I suppose you read Mr. Rockervelt's statement in the papers?"

"Admirable piece of virtuous indignation, isn't it? What a beautiful sermon against all speculation! And yet it is stated very freely that those on the inside have made millions by selling the road and buying it back again. I wonder what fool it was that said you couldn't have your cake and eat it too."

"Well, let's think no more about it. When are you going back West, John?"

"I leave to-morrow, at noon, but I don't go West; I go East."

"East?"

"Yes, I sail on the first out-going liner to-morrow, and hope to drop off in France."

"Why, you've never given up your situation, have you?"

"Oh, yes, it was impossible for me to remain. I'm done with railroading."

"Nonsense. What's your purpose?"

"Mr. Manson, I don't exactly know. Reason tells me that I'm no worse off than I was the day my uncle died, when I had little thought of coming into any money I didn't earn. Indeed, I am very much better off. My salary has been doubled. I have thirty thousand dollars in cash, and a bundle of Northern Pacific securities which has just been placed in the Broadway Safe Deposit. I don't understand myself in the least. Reason tells me that I ought to get angry and slaughter somebody, yet I feel no resentment. I am hurt, rather, that I was sand-bagged in the house of my friends. Still, even that fact doesn't appear to affect me much. Nevertheless, there's a change. I suspect it's the beginning of dry-rot. I fear that from being a useful man I have become a useless one. The utter folly of hard work, faithful service, reasonable honesty, and all that, has been brought home to me."

"Nonsense, nonsense, John," expostulated Manson.

"I am not theorising, Mr. Manson, but am merely trying to explain something to you which I do not myself understand. My uncle managed to get together a certain amount of money during thirty-five years. I lost that money in as many hours. If I worked honestly like a beaver for the next ten, fifteen or twenty years, it is unlikely I could save that much; yet my dear friend Blair, during, say, half an hour's silent meditation, evolves a plan, perfectly legal, by which the money is transferred from my bank account to his—transferred beyond possibility of recall. You will say perhaps, as my broker said, that I am just as bad as he is. I expected to place some one else's money in my bank account, beyond recall, and didn't succeed. Therefore I make a row. But the truth is, I am not making a row. I admit all any critic may say of my folly, but I realise that being an honest, hard-working efficient man doesn't pay in this country. At least, it pays only in allowing you to scrape together a modest competency, which may be quite lawfully filched from you in ten minutes. You will add I am a fool to throw over my shoulder a situation worth five thousand a year. You may even mention the hundred thousand young fellows of my age who would jump at my chance. I admit all that; I admit I'm a fool; I admit anything. I am the most open-minded person on earth at the present moment, and the least argumentative. I am like a boat that has been tied to a pier until somebody has cut the rope, sending it adrift. If you ask the boat where it's going, it doesn't know. I don't know what I'm going to do. I am only aware that I've got close on thirty thousand dollars in a letter of credit. I can have a high old time on that money for a year in Paris. I can have an hilarious time on it for two years in various capitals. I can study in Germany with the greatest luxury for five or ten years on that amount, or I can live thirty years in Europe in some quiet out-of-the-way place and be sure I shan't die of starvation. I'm all at sea, like the boat I was speaking of. I thought I knew John Steele pretty well, but I find I don't know him at all. All his ideas of morality, energy, industry, have turned somersaults. I am going over to Europe, where it's quiet, to get acquainted with the new John Steele."

Philip Manson had been regarding him with almost painful concentration while he spoke, and when the harangue was finished he said, soothingly, persuasively, looking at John: "Come with me up to the Adirondacks and enjoy a week's fishing, or to Maine, and put in two weeks, or to Canada, and stay three weeks."

Steele laughed heartily.

"Oh, yes, I know. Why don't you advise me to go to some sanitarium and consult a physician on mental aberration? I want to fish, but it is to fish out the secrets of John Steele. By this time to-morrow I shall be kissing the tips of my fingers to the statue of Liberty."

"John," said Manson, solemnly, "you are taking a false step. If you go to Europe in this frame of mind you are making a grave mistake which may not be easily remedied. Opportunities come once, twice, thrice, but they don't come always, and if they find a man persistently not at home, they pass on. In a year or two this little set-back you have experienced will have almost completely passed away from your mind. Look at me. I am a much older man than you. I have lost everything I succeeded in accumulating, yet I set my face toward re-earning it. You are on the threshold of a great success; you have in you the making of a first-class general manager. Now, I can well understand that you don't care to be in an office that contains Mr. Blair. I cannot say I blame you for that, but Mr. Rockervelt will be back here the day after to-morrow. You wait till he comes; I'll go in and see him, and I am sure you will be offered a position that will give you ample scope for the powers we both know you to possess."

Steele shook his head slowly.

"I have told you, and evidently you don't believe it, that I have no desire to develop any powers of usefulness I may possess. I suppose I am in the state of mind that makes a labouring man become a tramp. You are a stalwart oak of the forest, Mr. Manson, and the gale that has merely ruffled your branches has uprooted the sapling."

"Nonsense, John; it has simply given the sapling a bit of a twist."

"That may be so. It is quite possible that by the time I touch at Southampton or Cherbourg I may be yearning for that stolid old statue of Liberty again, and perhaps I shall take the next steamer back. In that case Mr. Rockervelt will have had the disadvantage of endeavouring to run his system without me for three weeks or thereabouts, and so we will deal with him more effectually than we would the day after to-morrow, when he doesn't know what a vacuum my absence has caused."

"Don't try to be cynical, John. It doesn't sound convincing from the lips of so sensible and capable a young fellow as you are."

"On the other hand," John went on unheeding, "it may be that I have taken to the road; that I am in reality the tramp I feel myself to be. Perhaps there has been a mistake in the outset, and Europe is really my country, not America. My father was born over there, and who knows but that thousands of years of ancestry are calling to me. That is a question Europe will settle. I half suspect that I shall feel so out of it after a month over there that you'll find me again coming up this express elevator before you realise I've been away. Any how, my steamer ticket is in my pocket, and I am off to Cherbourg or wherever they like to land me, in the morning. And now, Mr. Manson, you know this wicked city better than I do. Let's get out to some good eating house and enjoy a substantial meal. What's the best restaurant in town? It isn't every day a capitalist asks you to lunch with him. I'm the prodigal son, so we'll reverse the ancient parable and kill the fatted calf before I start on my travels."

---

# CHAPTER IX—LOVE'S SPECTRE

JOHN STEELE sat at one of the little round tables in the Café Germania, where a customer may have brown Munich beer in a big stone mug with a white metal lid. The *café* was very full, so also were some of the *habitués*; and on a raised platform at the corner were seated the members of a Viennese band, giving forth music in the smoke-beclouded room. Steele was waiting for a friend, and had turned a chair face forward against the little table, that a place might be ready for him when he arrived. With his fountain-pen the young man had just written a cable despatch, in answer to a transatlantic message that lay before him, mutilated somewhat in its English, as is the habit of Italian telegraph offices, but still understandable, which was lucky, for more often than not a telegram in a foreign language comes out second best after an encounter with the system of Italy.

A breezy individual made his way through the smoke and the throng to the vacant chair, tipped it back and sat down in it. "I'm late, as usual, John," he said, "but that is one of my official prerogatives. So I won't apologise, but will make it up in beer, now that I am here."

"There is little use of being United States Consul at Naples if you can't do as you like, Jimmy. There isn't any too much money in the office, so one must seek compensation in other directions."

"Do as I like? That's exactly what I can't do. I'll be hanged if every citizen of the great Republic that blows in on me in Naples doesn't seem to imagine I'm a sort of man-of-all-work for him. And I'm expected to be polite, and to fetch and carry for all concerned. Truth to tell, Steele, I'm tired of it; I've a notion to chuck the whole outfit and go back. Now, to-night, I was kept at my office long after business hours by a persistent man who would not take 'No' for an answer—actually thought I was lying to him, and had the cheek to intimate as much."

"And were you?"

"Certainly I was; but it was not etiquette for him to throw out any hints about my lack of veracity. It was all on your account, and I'd indulge in any amount of fiction to oblige a friend. He wanted your address, and wanted it badly; but I didn't know that you were anxious to see him, so I prevaricated and told him that if he came in to-morrow morning I'd see if I could get it for him."

"That's singular. No one has been looking for me for years past. I thought and hoped I had been forgotten over in the States. What was his name?"

"Here is his card. Colonel Beck, of New York."

"Colonel Beck! Thunder!"

"Know him? Don't wish to see him, I take it."

"No, I don't, and I'm much obliged to you, Stokes, for holding him off. How long is he going to stay in Naples?"

"Said he was going to stay till he found you."

"In that case I'll strike for Calabria or Sicily or somewhere; get among the real brigands and avoid this pirate. He used to be a legal adviser to the Rockervelts and probably is yet. Supposed to be rich through fleecing innocent lambs like myself. The shorn lamb, however, avoids the wolf, so I'm off to-morrow morning."

"What's the use of leaving now if your fleece is gone? He can't hurt you. Did he shear you in days gone past?"

"It's a long story. What strikes me, however, is the coincidence of old Beck turning up at this moment. There is, in fact, a coincidence within a coincidence. Read that cablegram."

Steele shoved over to his friend the message he had received that day from New York. The Consul wrinkled his brows over the Italian-English of the despatch, and made out its purport to be as follows:

*John Steele, Naples.*

*Have you block Northern Pacific? If so, send me particulars and full powers to deal. Act at once. Stock booming, but expect a crash shortly. Come over yourself if you can, immediately. The block will make you rich if realised without delay.*

*Manson.*

"Who is Manson?" asked the Consul.

"Philip Manson was my chief on the Manateau Midland Railway before he went east to New York. I succeeded him on the Midland. He and I lost about all we possessed in the Rockervelt panic a few years ago. I was what you would call a 'quitter' and came to Europe. Manson was a 'holdfast' and so he is still in New York."

"Then why not go right over and see him, instead of taking that trip to Calabria?"

"Well, to tell the truth, I do feel a yearning for the States, but I think I'll wait until I hear how this deal turns out. Read my answer to his cablegram," and the young man handed to his friend the document he had written before the other came in.

*Stock in Broadway Safe Deposit vaults. Drawer nine hundred seven. Mailed you ten days ago key and legal papers. Make what you can, and we will share even.*

*Steele.*

"Oh, I was wondering where I had seen the name Man-son before!" cried the Consul. "Were those papers you signed in my office a week or two since the documents referred to?"

"Yes."

"That's very strange. You sent them across ten days before you got the request for them."

"Exactly. Those shares had rested for years in the Safe Deposit Vaults. Manson had never referred to them in his letters to me and I had never referred to them in my letters to him, yet I suddenly made up my mind to throw them on the market."

"Why, that almost makes a person believe there is something in this thought-wave theory—telepathy, or whatever they call it."

"I am afraid it has a much more prosaic origin. A fortnight since you told me there had been a tremendous rise in Northern Pacific stock. That set me thinking, and I remembered I had a number of shares hidden away in Drawer 907. The stock was of no use to me, so I thought I might as well discover how badly some other fellow wanted it. Thus I threw the onus of selling on my friend Manson."

"You must have a good deal of confidence in him to give him a free hand like that. What's to hinder him from bolting with the money?"

"Nothing at all, except that he won't do it."

"I love to meet this charming belief in one's fellow man these cynical times, but I thought you said you lost money with him. Was he your partner?"

"No. The losing of the money was through no fault of his. He had nothing to do with my speculation. We were merely in the same boat, that's all. Nipped by the same pair of pinchers."

"So that was what disgusted you with America. I am disappointed with your story. Wasn't there a woman concerned at all?"

"No."

"Where does our friend Colonel Beck come in?"

"Beck comes in owing to the fact that he persuaded me to undertake the speculation by which I lost several hundred thousand. He gave me false information, and I believe he knew it to be false."

"Any proof?"

"No. Circumstantial evidence, that's all. I believed him to be my friend, and in fact acted the tenderfoot to perfection. I was even green enough to go to him when the crisis came, believing that a loan of twenty thousand or thereabout would save me, but he refused to let me have the money, although I offered this same stock I am cabling about as security."

"Perhaps he didn't have the money, like the man who neglected to buy Chicago."

"He said his ready money had been swept away by the panic, which I doubt. I have never seen him since, and somehow have no particular desire to meet him now."

"I appreciate your feeling in the matter. By the way, Steele, there was a very pretty girl with Colonel Beck—a *very* pretty girl, and charmingly attired. She did not say a word all the time the Colonel was talking, but she looked unutterable things and was deeply interested in our conversation. I thought she was a trifle disappointed when I told the Colonel I didn't know where you were. I supposed she was the Colonel's daughter."

"The chances are," mused Steele, "that the young lady is Miss Sadie Beck, niece of the old gentleman. She was rather a handsome girl when I knew her."

"Ah!" drawled the Consul, "then there is no particular reason why she should be anxious regarding your whereabouts?"

"None that I am aware of."

"I see. Well, are you going back to America after all?"

"I haven't quite made up my mind what I shall do, Jimmy, except that I shall call at your office in the morning, and there mature my plans, with your assistance."

"If you call at my office, you are more than likely to run against Colonel Beck. I expect him there bright and early."

"By Jove! I had forgotten about the Colonel. Still, there is no hurry. I can drop in later, when the Colonel has moved on."

All arrangements, however, bow to Chance, and Chance now intervened to upset their plans. A burly, florid-faced man with white moustache loomed up before them, and a heavy hand smote Steele on the shoulder with a force that made him wince and bite his lip to restrain a cry of resentment. "Hallo, John, old man!" shouted the stranger, "I am mighty glad to see you. Been searching the town for you; called on that stuck-up Consul of ours, but he pretended he knew nothing about you. I suppose he thought I believed him, but the undersigned wasn't born yesterday, and I had met talented prevaricators before. Oh by Jingo! this you, Consul? I didn't notice you at first. Well, I stick to all I said. You told me this evening that you didn't know where John Steele was, and now I find you sitting here with him. I think, by Jingo! that you owe me an apology."

"I owe you nothing, Colonel, not even my appointment. Every man who drifts in on me appears to think I am indebted to him for my place. I beg to inform you that it is no part of a Consul's duty to bestow addresses upon any stranger who happens to ask for them."

"That's all right, Mr. Stokes," replied the Colonel genially, drawing up a chair and seating himself uninvited at their table. "It isn't the habit of your uncle Ben to get left, and I knew I would find Steele ultimately if he was in town. Say, John, you ought to be in New York nowadays. Things are booming there."

"I have had enough of booms," replied the young man without enthusiasm.

"Nonsense! It's absurd for a capable fellow like you, and a talented man, too, if I may be allowed to say so before your face, to chuck things up the way you've done. And that reminds me, John, did you ever sell that block of Northern Pacific stock you had during the panic?"

"I never did."

"Got it yet, eh? Well, I congratulate you. Now, at the present moment that would form a very nice little nucleus to begin on, and you can count on me to help you till everything's blue."

"The stock wasn't much of a nucleus last time I tendered it to you, Colonel," said Steele dryly.

The Colonel threw back his head and laughed boisterously.

"Oh, you haven't forgotten that episode yet? Well, you bolted from Warmington so quickly that I hadn't any chance of giving you an explanation."

"No explanation was needed, Colonel Beck. You refused me the money I required, and were quite within your right in doing so."

"Yes, but why did I refuse you; why? Answer me that, John."

The Colonel, with great good nature, placed a hand lovingly upon the shoulder of the other.

"Your conundrum is easy enough," replied the young man nonchalantly. "You didn't want to let me have the money, that was all."

"Certainly I didn't; certainly I didn't; and you should be very thankful to me that I refused. I knew Wall Street a great deal better than you did, my dear fellow, and that money would just have followed the rest into the pit."

"I quite believe you."

"Yes; but you didn't believe me then; and you left my house in a huff, without ever giving me a chance to make my position clear."

"If you had been anxious to make it clear, Colonel, there was plenty of time to do it in. That was some years ago, and a letter to Naples costs only five cents."

"True, true," cried the Colonel, in the bluff manner of an honest but misunderstood man. "I might have expended the five cents, as you say, if I had known your address, but you had got on your high horse, and had said things which a younger man should have hesitated before applying to his elder. Now, I don't pretend to be any better than my fellows, and I admit I was offended. Such usage coming from you, John, hurt me, I confess."

The American Consul, finding himself an unneeded third in what was drifting into a private discussion, pushed back his chair and rose to his feet.

"I must bid you good-night, Steele," he said; "I have another appointment. I shall see you at the office tomorrow, I suppose?"

"Don't go, Stokes. The Colonel and I have nothing confidential to discuss," returned his friend, while the Colonel sat silent, as if he thought this was not a true statement of the case. The Consul, however, persisted in his withdrawal, and Colonel Beck heaved a sigh of relief as he watched him disappear.

"Yes, my boy," continued the Colonel, in a tone of tender regret, "I don't think you treated your friends very well. I don't think you should have jumped at the wrong conclusion as quickly as you did. I would willingly have let you have the money if I had not known it was certain to go where the rest of your cash had gone."

"It is quite possible I was mistaken, Colonel; I always was rather hot-headed, and if in this case I made an error, I now offer apology."

"It hurt me, it hurt me at the time," murmured the Colonel in reminiscent tones; "but if only myself were involved, I would never have said a word. I am a man of the world, and am accustomed to the ups and downs of the world. I make no pretence that your silent desertion caused me permanent grief. I resented your impetuous action, but would never have spoken if no one else had been concerned."

"No one else concerned? I do not understand you. Who else was concerned?"

"Well, to speak frankly, as between man and man, I think you treated my niece Sadie rather badly."

"You astonish me, Colonel. I never treated any woman badly."

"I have been all my life a very busy man," rejoined the Colonel, with more of severity in his tone than had hitherto been the case, "and I frankly admit that much went on in my own household of which I was not cognisant. During the first months of our acquaintance you visited us somewhat frequently."

"Well, what of it?"

"What of it? This much of it, that I did not know until you had left that the affections of my niece were centred upon you."

"You are quite mistaken, Colonel."

"Do you mean to say there was never anything between you two but ordinary friendship?"

"I mean to say nothing of the sort. It is not a question for two men to discuss; but since you have broached the subject, I may tell you what you probably know already, that the last interview I had in your house was with your niece. She received me with great coolness and parted from me without visible regret. To put it quite plainly, Colonel Beck, the niece seemed to share the uncle's feelings regarding me. Financially, I was broken, and consequently was of no further use either to man or woman."

The stout Colonel placed the tips of his fingers together over the most corpulent portion of his person, raised his eyes to the ceiling, and drew a deep sigh.

"My hasty young friend, I see exactly what happened. You left me enraged because I refused to lend you money. You said to yourself, 'This man in a crisis declines to befriend me.' That was no state of mind in which to visit a young lady proud and sensitive. Something in your manner must have jarred upon her. Girls are of finer texture than we brutal men. Her seeming coldness was merely offended dignity, and you left her presence under a misapprehension, as, indeed, you left mine. She expected your return, but you never came back. It was long before I even suspected that anything was wrong between you two, but I knew that Sadie had received offer after offer of marriage, some of them most advantageous, but all proposals she rejected. The utmost confidence existed between us. She is to me as if she were my own daughter. I expostulated with her one day, and to my surprise she burst into tears and then confessed her preference for you. I must say that for a time I was filled with resentment against you, but this feeling gave way to sorrow at seeing my girl waste her life through misplaced love. I have spoken to you with the utmost frankness. Sadie is dearer to me than everything else in the world."

For some moments after the Colonel finished his exposition of the case John Steele maintained silence. The Viennese band was playing a lively selection, and he appeared to be listening to the music, but with troubled brow. The place seemed rather unsuited for a confession of love, and the tidings brought no particular joy to the listener. At last the young man spoke.

"Does Miss Beck know—was she aware that you were going to speak to me on this subject?"

"Certainly not. I doubt if she would thank me for my interference, because, as I said before, she is a proud girl. I don't think she knew you were in Naples until she heard me ask the Consul about you. When I was questioning him, she seemed rather eager to hear his answers, but she said nothing until we were outside." This coincided with the account given by Stokes of the visit, and Steele became more and more perplexed.

"What did she say when you were outside?" he asked.

"Oh! she wanted to know why I wished to see you, and I told her it was on a matter of business. This didn't quite satisfy her, so, being pressed, I mentioned that block of Northern Pacific stock which you offered to sell to me once, and said I thought I could dispose of it for you to advantage, if you still possessed it. Sadie knows nothing of Wall Street affairs, so, of course, this explanation seemed quite reasonable. Besides, it is true enough, for I do wish to make a bargain with you about that stock whenever you feel inclined to come down from the clouds and discuss mundane affairs."

"What do you expect me to do? I don't mean about the stock, but about Miss Beck."

"It is not for me to make any suggestions in the premises, my dear fellow. You are a man of honour. You have made a mistake which involves the happiness of an innocent person. I have put the matter before you with a plainness which is, I think, exceptional. The next move must rest with you."

"Where are you stopping?"

"At the Grand Hotel."

"Then, with your permission, I shall have the pleasure of calling upon Miss Beck to-morrow afternoon at four o'clock, if that hour is convenient."

The stout Colonel, with visible emotion, clasped Steele warmly by the hand. "You are a good fellow!" he said. "When you meet my niece, you will let no hint escape you of this conversation?"

"Most assuredly not."

"I came to see you," continued the Colonel, "about the Northern Pacific stock, remember that, and, of course, you call on her for old friendship's sake on learning she is here with me."

"You may rely upon my tact, Colonel."

His mission accomplished, the Colonel seemed to hesitate between going or staying, his attitude that of a man wondering whether it is better to leave well alone or to proceed further. Finally he said: "By the way, Steele, in order that we may make our conference the more legitimate, how about that Northern Pacific stock of yours? I am willing to buy it outright, or to sell it for you, just as you choose."

"I am not quite in a position to sell at the present moment, Colonel."

"I thought you said that you still held the stock?"

"So I do, but I don't care to make any move regarding it just now."

"Delays are dangerous, John."

"I know they are," rejoined the younger man shortly, with a finality of tone which showed the elder that nothing was to be gained by continuing the discussion; so the good man rose and bade farewell to his friend with a cordiality that was almost overdone, and left the other to his thoughts, such as they were.

John Steele enjoyed little sleep that night. The ghost of an almost forgotten love haunted him, and the apparition, as is usually the case, was most unwelcome. He had certainly left the girl with brusque abruptness, thoroughly convinced that she was as mercenary as her uncle, ready to throw him over because he had failed financially. At that time he had possessed the eager confidence of extreme youth; now, it occurred to him that he had often been mistaken in his estimates of people. Might not an error have been committed in this case? The manner of Colonel Beck retained its ancient bluff heartiness, and there was certainly a show of reasonableness in his presentation of the case. Time had long since mitigated the sting of the refusal. At the moment of asking he had supposed that the granting of the loan meant salvation. The continuance of the panic, however, convinced him that the money would have melted ineffectually and vanished like the rest. If his estimate of the situation had been so far astray, might not his judgment of both uncle and niece have been equally erroneous? There was but one thing for a man of honour to do, and that was to stand the brunt of his mistake, no matter what the cost. He was not the first to pay, with interest compounded, an early debt.

Next day the problem presented no more alluring aspect than it had done during the troublesome night. As the hour of the interview approached, Steele's dejection increased. He did not visit the Consul as he had promised. In fact, he had entirely forgotten the appointment made the night before. He walked along the promenade by the sea-wall fronting the fashionable quarter of Naples, with haggard face and bowed head, striving to collect his thoughts, although, so far, those he had succeeded in collecting proved of little comfort to him. However, the hour was set, and, as it approached, he walked resolutely to the Grand Hotel to meet the girl, in a frame of mind almost as greatly perturbed as when he last saw her.

Time had passed lightly over the blonde head of Miss Sadie Beck, who greeted him with subdued sweetness; a touch of melancholy in her voice. As the Consul had very truly said, Miss Beck was an amazingly pretty girl, who dressed with an elegance that suggested Paris.

"Through a chance meeting with your uncle last evening, I learned that you were in Naples, and I asked permission to call."

"Yes, he told me he had met you," replied the girl simply. "It gives me great pleasure to see you again, because, if you remember, we parted rather in anger," and Sadie raised her blue eyes to his, only to sink them again to the carpet with just the slightest possible indication of a little quivering sigh; indeed, the eyes themselves, large and pathetic, gave token of unshed tears.

"Miss Beck—" he began, but she interrupted him in tremulous tones; a crystal drop actually became visible on the long eyelashes.

"In the old days you used to call me Sadie."

"But the old days are gone forever."

These words were his last effort against the silken web which he felt entangling him, and he knew himself to be a brute for uttering them. Their effect upon the girl was instantaneous. She sank down by the table, flung her arms upon it, lowering her face upon them in a storm of weeping.

"Oh! not for me! not for me!" she cried between sobs. "You may forget the old days, and I see you have forgotten them. Leave me, then! leave me to my memories! Why, oh why did you seek to see me again?"

That settled it. He placed his hand upon her heaving shoulders and spoke soothingly to her.

Half an hour later Steele came out of the hotel and went direct to the American Consulate.

"Hullo, old man! what's the matter with you?" cried James Stokes. "You are white as a ghost."

"I'm all right. Didn't sleep very well last night. See here, Stokes! I just called to say that I wish you would forget part of the conversation we had yesterday."

"Easily done! Which part, for instance?"

"What I said with reference to Colonel Beck. I was mistaken about him. He has convinced me of that."

"Oh! has he? You mean, then, he didn't refuse you the twenty thousand?"

"He refused it from the best of motives. I was rather a strenuous fool in those days, and thought everything should come my way. If I didn't see what I wanted, I imagined all I had to do was to ask for it. I left the Colonel in a temper, and I realise now that I did worthy people a great injustice."

"Some one else was involved, then, as well as the Colonel?"

"Yes. I was engaged to his niece, and, as there is no secret about it, I may as well inform you that the engagement has been renewed to-day."

The Consul whistled and then checked himself, as if this indication of surprise were not quite appropriate to so serious an announcement.

"Well, John, I congratulate you. She is a very handsome girl."

"Extremely so," answered the happy man, as he gloomily and abruptly took his departure.

The frivolous Consul was now at liberty to whistle as long as he liked, and he did so. Then he took to muttering to himself.

"I don't admire the position of affairs a little bit. My friend John resembles a man who's just got a life sentence. He was thunderstruck when I mentioned Beck to him last night, and quite evidently didn't wish me to leave him alone with the Colonel. I distrust the Beck contingent. By St. Jonathan, I'll try a little ruse with the gallant Colonel, which at least can do no harm."

The friendly Stokes pondered deeply over the situation, until his meditations were interrupted by the entrance of the Colonel himself. He had come in quest of letters, for the Consulate was post-office-in-ordinary to various tourists from the States.

No letters bearing the name of Beck had arrived, and the inquirer was turning away when Stokes acted with quick heedlessness, which must be the excuse for what followed. In his own defence he used to say afterward that the presence of Colonel Beck so corrupted him with an atmosphere of Wall Street, that he couldn't speak the truth if he tried.

"Oh, Colonel, one moment. You are an old friend of Steele's, aren't you?"

The Colonel turned on his heel.

"Yes. Why?" he asked.

"I'd like to speak with you a moment about him, if you don't mind. I'm an old friend of his, too, but unfortunately I'm poor, and so, however willing, I can't be of much assistance to him. Did he speak to you last night about money matters after I left you?"

"No," said the Colonel, drawing down his brows. "Ah! that's just like him. I came away to give him the opportunity. I owe you an apology for my attitude when you first came to the Consulate. Of course, I knew Steele's address, but I thought you might be a creditor of his, and goodness knows the poor fellow has had enough of them."

"Why, what do you mean? If he owns that Northern Pacific stock, he's a rich man, richer than you have any idea of, if he sells at once. He can realise millions on that stock at the present moment."

"Then he hasn't told you what he did with it?"

The ruddy face of the Colonel seemed to become mottled, and he moistened his lips as he said:

"No. What has he done with it?"

"Well, in spite of all my advice, he sent it over to a friend named Philip Manson in New York. He hasn't even a scrap of writing to show for it. You know Wall Street, so I need say no more."

The Colonel apparently knew Wall Street, for he gasped: "The eternal fool!"

"Exactly. Still, Steele's a good fellow, and we mustn't let him sink. I thought, perhaps, you wouldn't mind stumping up a bit to help him out."

"Hasn't he any other resources?" asked the Colonel. "Not a cent, so far as I know. All his hopes were centred on that Northern Pacific stock, and now that's gone."

"Well, I must say, Mr. Consul, that you have a good deal of cheek to ask me, a complete stranger to you, to spend money on an idiot who doesn't know enough to take care of a fortune when he has got it."

John Steele passed another unrefreshing night, but solace came next morning in the shape of an early letter and an important cablegram.

*Dear Mr. Steele (the letter began).*

*How inscrutable is the human heart! Ever since you left America I have yearned to see you, and at last this desire was gratified. You were the idol of my younger days, and were my first love—my first and only love, I may say; and yet I write these words as calmly as if I were inditing an order to my dressmaker. I find what I should have known before, that we cannot light a fire with a heap of ashes. I know you will think me wayward and changeable, especially after my emotion when you spoke of the olden days. But am I to blame that I find myself changed, and fancy I see a change in you also? There can never be anything between us, John, but that pure friendship which becomes more and more of a solace as we grow older. I give you back your promise of to-day. It will be useless to call upon me, for my uncle and I will have left for Rome before you receive this letter. But believe me,*

*Always your friend and well-wisher,*

*Sadie Beck.*

"Well, by Jove!" cried the astounded man, as he finished the epistle. "The girl is honest, after all, and I have not been able to conceal my real feeling towards her. I am afraid I have kept faith in the letter, but not in the spirit. However, thank God for her decision! Her letter does not betray a broken heart, even if I had conceit enough to think I had caused her suffering."

It was a jubilant man who called upon the Consul in his office that morning.

"Any thing new this morning, Steele? You seem brighter than I have seen you look for a day or two."

"Yes, rather important news. It seems to be my fate to come into this office and contradict what I said the day before, so I am at it again. The Becks have left suddenly for Rome, and the young lady jilts me, so that engagement is off."

"Oh! What is the reason of their change of plan?"

"No reason at all, so far as I can make out. Surely a woman doesn't need to give a reason for preferring Rome to Naples?"

"No; I suppose not," murmured the Consul, wondering how much his hint that John was a ruined man had to do with the sudden withdrawal.

"And I've had a most important cablegram from Philip Manson," continued John jubilantly. "He has sold out my Northern Pacific at a price which more than recoups me for all my losses."

"John, you're a good deal merrier than you were this time yesterday. I expect the next announcement to be that you are returning to the States, to leave me here lamenting."

"That's it exactly. But there's no law compelling you to stay here when there's ten thousand patriotic citizens eager to take your place. Manson has been appointed general manager of the Wheat Belt Line, with offices in Chicago, and he offers me my old position of division superintendent, so I'll be singing that 'Fare-well to Naples' which I've heard so often since I arrived here. Jimmy, I'm going to be a sane and useful citizen hereafter. No more stock exchange for me. I shall plant my money in gilt-edged mortgages where the interest will be as secure as the eternal hills. Then I'll settle down to hard work and show old Philip Manson what an industrious person can do on the Wheat Belt Line."

John Steele arrived in America to learn that it was easier to make good resolutions than to keep them. He settled down in Chicago and found there was little difficulty in placing his money on mortgage at attractive rates of interest. He gave, however, his personal care to the securities offered, trusted no man's word, and always viewed the spot and made close inquiries before he drew a cheque for investment. He divided his money between city and country, not depending on any one lawyer to do the business for him, but seeking local advice and local watchfulness wherever a mortgage was drawn. His eggs were in many baskets, or hatching nests, with a different legal hen to sit on each. The only gentleman of the law he had heretofore known was Beck, and his opinion of the profession seemed to be tinctured by his dislike of the gallant Colonel. He gave work to many legal experts, but never allowed the left-hand lawyer to know what the right-hand lawyer was doing.

He was shocked to find himself so suspicious of everyone except Philip Manson, but even more perturbed to learn that all his old delight in work was gone. Philip Manson was ambitious to make the Wheat Belt Line the model railway of the West, and in his quiet intense purposeful way was accomplishing that object. To John this ambition seemed trivial and above all futile, when it was possible for some speculator in New York or a combination of speculators to make the road a mere pawn in a gamble; to wreck it if its ruin suited the game, to discharge every employee at a week's notice. His liking for Manson, his reluctance to disillusionise the one man on earth who was friend and believed in him, held him for more than a year at his task of division superintendent and the work that was growing more and more irksome to him. Then an incident at Slocum Junction gave the necessary impetus which finally shifted him from a career of usefulness into the predatory class. The faithful watch-dog became the ravenous wolf.

---

## CHAPTER X—BUYING A RAILWAY

THE station-master said nonchalantly that he had nothing to do with it, and from out the telegraph office he brought a stout wooden chair which he set down in the dark strip of shade which ran along the pine platform under the eaves of the station. The back of this chair being tilted against the building, the station-master sat down in it, put his heels on the wooden round, took from his pocket a jack-knife, and began to whittle a stick, an occupation which the momentary pausing of the express seemed to have interrupted. There was nothing of the glass of fashion or the mould of form about the station-master. He was dressed in weather-worn trousers, held to his thin frame by a pair of suspenders quite evidently home-made, which came over his shoulders, and underneath this was a coarse woollen shirt, open at the throat because the button had gone. On top of all this there perched a three-year-old, dilapidated straw hat which had once possessed a wide brim, but was now in a state of disrepair in thorough keeping with the costume. Yet in spite of appearances he was a capable young man who could manipulate a telegraphic machine at reasonable speed, was well up in the business pertaining to Slocum Junction, and had definite opinions regarding the manner in which the affairs of the nation should be carried on. Indeed, at that moment he was an exemplification of the independence for which his country had fought and bled. No one knew better than he that the Greased Lightning Express would never have halted for an instant at Slocum Junction unless it did so to put off a person of some importance. But that important person had begun to give his opinion of the locality in language that was painful and free the moment he realised the situation, and the station-master signified his resentment by sitting down in the chair and assuming a careless attitude, which told the stranger plainer than words that he could go to the devil if he wished. For all he knew, the obstreperous person who had stepped from the express might be his chief, but the station-master made no concession to this possibility.

Opposite him in the blazing sunlight stood a dapper young man grasping a neat handbag. He might have posed as a tailor's model, and he offered a striking contrast to the unkempt station-master. He cast an almost despairing look at the vanishing express, now a mere dot in the horizon, with a trail of smoke, as if it were a comet that had run aground. Then he turned an exasperated face upon the nonchalant station-master.

"You are not responsible for the situation, eh? You don't seem to care much, either."

"Well, to tell the truth, stranger, I don't."

"You mean to tell me there's no train for two hours and a half on the branch line?"

"I never said anything of the sort, because there isn't any branch line."

"No branch line? Why, there it is before my eyes! There's a locomotive, of a kind, and a composite passenger and freight-car that evidently dates from the time of the Deluge. Noah used that car!" cried the angry stranger.

"Well, if Noah was here, he wouldn't use it for two hours and a half," said the station-master complacently.

"I don't understand what you mean," protested the stranger. "Is there, or is there not, a train in two hours and a half?"

"Of course there is."

"You said a minute ago there wasn't."

"I didn't say anything of the kind, and if you weren't adding your own natural heat to the unnatural heat of the day, you'd learn something. You were talking about branch lines; I said there is no branch line. That's all."

"Then what's the meaning of those two lines of rust running to the right?"

"There's five or six thousand people," droned the station-master, "who'd like to know what that object you're referring to really is. Leastways, they used to want to know, but lately they've given up all curiosity on the subject. They're the shareholders, who put up good money to have that road made. We call it the Farmers' Road, and it isn't a branch, but as independent as the main line."

"Or as yourself," hazarded the young man.

"Well, it's independent, anyhow," continued the station-master, "and I've nothing to do with it."

"Haven't the cursed fools who own it the sense to make it connect with anything on the main line?"

"Of course, we're all fools unless we come from Chicago," said the station-master imperturbably.

"I didn't say that," commented the stranger.

"No, *I* did. If your dome of thought was in working order, I shouldn't need to explain these things; but as I've nothing particular to do, I may as well teach a man from Chicago his ABC. You stepped off the express just now owning the whole country, populated with fools, according to you. I've been station-master here for eighteen months, and I never saw that express stop before. I may be an idiot, but still I am aware that a man who steps off the Greased Lightning is one of two things. He is either a bigbug with pull enough on the railway company to get them to stop the Greased Lightning for him, or else he's a tramp who can't pay his fare, and so is put off."

"Oh, you've sized me up, have you? Well, which am I? The millionaire or the tramp?"

"When you stepped off, I thought you were the millionaire; but the moment you opened your mouth, I knew you were the tramp."

John Steele laughed with very good-natured heartiness.

"Say, old man, that's all right. The drinks are on me, if there were a tavern near, which there doesn't seem to be. I suppose there's no place in this God-forsaken hole where on a hot day like this a man can get a cooling beverage?"

"Stranger, you're continually jumping at conclusions and landing at the wrong spot. Allow me to tell you"—here he lowered his voice a bit—"that you don't raise no blush to my cheeks by anything you can say; but there's a lady in the waiting-room, and if I were you I'd talk accordingly."

The change in the cocksure attitude of John Steele was so sudden and complete that it brought a faint smile of gratification to the gaunt face of the station-master.

"Great heavens!" whispered the crestfallen young man, "why didn't you tell me that before?"

"Well, you've been kind of monopolising the conversation, and I haven't had much chance to speak up to now. One would suppose that if a man had a thinking-machine in his head at all, he would know that the little road couldn't connect with a train that never stopped here."

"Of course, of course," said John hurriedly, his mind running on the language he had used in the first moments of chagrin at finding himself marooned at this desolate junction, which might have been heard by the unseen lady in the waiting-room. He hoped his voice hadn't carried through the pine wall.

"Well, station-master, I apologise. And now, if you will kindly tell me what the Farmers' Road *does* connect with, I'll be very much obliged."

"The Farmers' Road runs two trains a day," said the station-master sententiously, as if he were speaking of some mighty empire. "The train consists, as you see, of a locomotive and a mixed car. The first train comes in here at nine o'clock in the morning, connecting with the local going east.

It then returns to Bunkerville, and reaches here in the afternoon at three o'clock, to connect with the local going west. That little train doesn't know there are any flyers on our line; all it knows is that the eastern local comes in somewhere about nine o'clock in the morning, and the western local arrives anywhere between three and five in the afternoon. So a Chicago man can't step jauntily off the express he has managed to stop, and expect to get a train to Bunkerville whenever he chooses."

"Admirably stated," said John Steele. "And if you will condescend further to enlighten a beclouded intellect would you mind explaining what the deuce the little train is doing here at this hour? If I follow your argument, it should have returned to Bunkerville after the nine o'clock local came in, arriving here again just before three o'clock."

"Your befogged brain is waking up," said the station-master encouragingly. "The phenomenon to which you have called attention happens once or twice a week. If you cast your eye to the other end of the platform, you will see piled there an accumulation of miscellaneous freight. The Farmers' Road has just dumped that upon us, and to do so has taken a special trip. That stuff will go east on Number Eight, which is a freight train that will stop here some time in the afternoon when it sees the signal set against it."

"I comprehend," said Steele; "and I venture on my next proposition with great diffidence, caused by increasing admiration of yourself and the lucid mind you bring to bear on Western railway procedure. If I have followed your line of argument as unerringly as the farmers' train follows the Farmers' Road, his nibs the engineer must take the train back to Bunkerville so that he may return here on his regular trip to meet the three o' clock western local. If I am right, what is to prevent him from going now, taking me with him, and giving me an opportunity at Bunkerville to transact my business and catch the regular train back?—for I am going further west, and would like to intercept the local, which would save me spending an unnecessary night at Bunkerville, and wasting most of to-morrow as well."

"The reasons are as follows: His nibs, as you call him, is engineer, conductor, brakeman, and freight handler. When he came in, he had to carry that freight from his car to the platform where you see it. That takes time, even if the day were not so oppressively hot as it is. So, instead of keeping up his fire under the boiler, and burning useless coal, he banks the furnace as soon as he arrives. Then, at his leisure, he removes the boxes to the platform. If he returned to Bunkerville, they would give him something to do there; here he is out of reach; besides, he would have to draw his fires and start anew about two o'clock, and that he doesn't want to do. He has, therefore, curled himself up in the passenger car, put a newspaper over his face to keep off the flies, and has gone to sleep. When the proper moment arrives he will stir up his fire, go to Bunkerville, and then be ready to make the return trip on one expenditure of coal. *Now* do you understand?"

"Yes, thank you, I do; and this has given me an idea."

"That's a good thing, and I can easily guess what your idea is. But before putting it into operation, I should like to mitigate a slight you have put on Slocum Junction. You made a sarcastic remark about cool drinks. Now, I beg to inform you that the nine o'clock local from the west slides off on this here platform every morning a great big square cold chunk of ice. That chunk of ice is growing less and less in a big wooden pail in the telegraph-office, but the water that surrounds it is chilly as the North Pole. If you have anything in your hip pocket or in that natty little valise which mitigates the rigour of cold water, there's no reason why you shouldn't indulge in a refreshing drink."

"Station-master," said John, laughing, "you ought to be superintendent of this road, instead of junction boss. You're the wisest man I've met in two years."

Saying this, he sprang the catch of the handbag and drew forth a bulky, wicker-covered, silver-topped flask.

"I propose we adjourn to the telegraph-office," he added, "and investigate that wooden pail."

The station-master led the way with an alacrity that he had not heretofore exhibited. The result of the conference was cheerful and comforting.

"Now," said the station-master, drawing the back of his hand across his lips, "what you want is a special train to Bunkerville. A man from the city would get that by telegraphing to the superintendent at the terminus and paying twenty dollars. A man from the country who had some sense would go to Joe the engineer and persuade him he ought to wake up and return to Bunkerville at once."

"How much would be required to influence Joe?"

"Oh, a couple of dollars would be wealth. A silver dollar in front of each eye will obscure the whole Western prairie if placed just right."

"Very well, I'll go out and place 'em."

"You are forgetting your flask," said the station-master, as Steele snapped shut his valise.

"No, I'm not. That flask and its contents belong to you, as a reward for being patient and instructive when a darned fool let loose from the city happened your way."

And this showed John Steele to be a reader of his fellow-man; for while the engineer might accept the two dollars, the independent station-master certainly would not have done so. That glib official, however, seemed to have no particular words for this occasion, so he changed the subject and said: "If you persuade Joe to go, I wish you'd remember the lady in the waiting-room. She's a Miss Dorothy Slocum, and a powerful nice girl, that teaches school in Bunkerville. Fact is, this junction was named after her father. Used to be the principal man round these parts; but he lost his money, and now his girl's got to teach school. I never knew him—he was dead long before I came here. She's been visiting relatives. This is vacation time, you know."

"All right. You tell her there's a special leaving in a few minutes, and that she's very welcome to ride upon it."

With that John Steele went out into the furnace of the sun across the dusty road and entered the composite car. The Farmers' Road did not join rails with the main line, and so caused much extra handling of freight. The engine stood there simmering in the heat, both external and internal, a slight murkiness of smoke rising from its funnel, shaped like an inverted bell.

"Hallo, Joe!" cried Steele, as he entered the car. "Don't you yearn for home and friends?"

The man was sprawling on two seats, with a newspaper over his head, as the station-master had predicted.

"Hello!" he echoed, sitting up and shaking away the sheet of paper, "what's the matter?"

"Nothing, except that if the spirit should move you to get over to Bunkerville with this ancient combination, five dollars will be transferred from my pocket into yours."

"'Nough said," cried Joe, rising to his feet. "It'll take me about twenty minutes to get the pot boiling again. You don't happen to have the fiver about you, I suppose? I haven't seen one for a couple of years."

"Here you are," replied Steele, drawing a crisp bill from his purse.

The engineer thrust it into the pocket of his greasy overalls.

"I'll toot the whistle when I'm ready," he said.

This financial operation accomplished, John Steele returned to the station. The station-master was standing by the door of the waiting-room conversing pleasantly with someone within. When Steele entered the room he was amazed to see so pretty a girl sitting on the bench that ran round the bare walls of the uninviting apartment.

"Will you introduce me?" inquired the city man, handing his card to the station-master.

"Miss Dorothy Slocum," said the latter, "this is Mr. John Steele, of Chicago."

The young man removed his fashionable straw hat.

"Miss Slocum," he said, "I desire to apologise to you. I'm afraid that when I found myself stranded on the platform outside, I used language which can hardly be justified, even in the circumstances. But I had no idea at the time that there was a lady within miles of us."

"I was much interested in my book," replied the girl, with a smile, "and was not paying attention to what was going on outside."

She held up the volume, between whose leaves her fore-finger was placed.

"Well, Miss Slocum, it must have been a pretty absorbing story, and I am deeply grateful to it for acting as a non-conductor between my impulsive observations and your hearing. Nothing excuses intemperate language, as the station-master here has taught me through the force of a benign example. Still, if anything could exculpate a man, I should think it would be the exasperating conduct of this Farmers' Railroad, as they call it."

"Indeed," said Miss Dorothy archly, "the book had really no right to interfere, because I am one of the owners of the railway, and so perhaps it was my duty to listen to complaints of a passenger. Not that I have anything to do with the management of the line; I am compelled to pay my fare just like the rest."

"I shall be delighted if you accept a ride on your own road as free as if you carried a superintendent's pass. I am going to Bunkerville in my own private car, as it were, and shall feel honoured if I may extend the courtesies of the same."

"The station-master has just told me you were kind enough to offer a poor vagrant a lift to Bunkerville. I wished to buy a ticket, but this haughty official of the main line so despises our poor little road that he will not sell me one."

"Indeed," said the station-master, "I haven't the power, nor the tickets. They don't entrust me with any business so tremendous. Joe starts his rickety engine going, then leaves it to jog along as it likes, and comes through the car to collect the fares. They have no tickets, and perhaps that's why the road has never paid a dividend."

"Oh, you mustn't say that!" protested the girl. "Poor Joe has not got rich out of his occupation, any more than the shareholders have made money on their shares. If you will permit me to pay my fare to Joe, Mr. Steele I shall be only too happy to take this early opportunity of getting to Bunkerville."

"I couldn't think of it, Miss Slocum; in fact, I must prohibit any communication between Joe and yourself, fearing you, as an owner of the road, may learn by what corrupt practices I induced Joe to make the trip."

The girl laughed, but before she could reply, a wheezy

"Toot-toot!" outside announced that Joe had already got steam up.

"I'll carry your valise across," said the obliging station-master, while Miss Dorothy Slocum picked up her lighter belongings and accompanied Mr. John Steele to the shabby little passenger-car. Joe was leaning out of the cab with a grin on his smeared face, which was there probably because of the five-dollar bill in his trousers' pocket. The station-master placed the valise in the baggage section of the car, and raised his tattered hat as the little train started gingerly out for the open country.

It was a pretty landscape through which they passed, with little to indicate that the prairies were so near at hand. The line ran along a shallow valley, well wooded, especially by the banks of the stream that wandered through it, which even at this parched season of the year was still running its clear-water course, and Miss Slocum informed the Chicago man that it flowed from a never-drying spring some ten miles on the other side of the main line. The little road was as crooked as possible, for the evident object of its constructors had been to avoid bridging the stream, piling up any high embankments or excavating deep cuttings. The pace, therefore, was exceedingly slow; nevertheless John Steele did not find the time hang heavily on his hands. At first the girl seemed somewhat shy and embarrassed to find herself the only passenger except this gallant young business man; but he tactfully put her at her ease by pretending much interest in the history of the railway, with which he soon learned she was unfortunately familiar.

"Yes," she said; "the building of this road was the greatest financial disaster that ever occurred in this section of the country. My father was one of its chief promoters. When the Wheat Belt Line, by which you came here from Chicago, was surveyed through this part of the State, those interested in the neighbourhood expected it to run through Bunkerville, which would thus become a large town. The railway people demanded a large money bonus, which Bunker County refused, because Bunkerville was in the direct line, and they thought the railway must come through there, whether a bonus were paid or not. In fact, the first survey passed just north of Bunkerville. But our poor little village was not so important as its inhabitants imagined, and the next line surveyed was twenty miles away. For once the farmers were too shrewd. They thought, as they put it, that the new line was a bluff, and did not realise their mistake until too late. My father had been in favour of granting the bonus, but he was out-voted. Perhaps that is why the railway people called their station Slocum instead of Bunkerville, which was twenty miles distant. The next nearest railway line was forty-five miles away, and two years after the Wheat Belt Line began operations, it was proposed to organise a local company to construct a railway from Slocum, through Bunkerville to Jamestown, on the other line. Bonuses were granted all along the route, and besides this the State legislature gave a subsidy, and, furthermore, passed a bill to prevent competition, prohibiting any railway to parallel the Farmers' Road for sixty miles on either side."

"Does that law still stand on the statute books of the State?" asked Steele, with increasing interest.

"I think so. It has never been repealed to my knowledge."

"Well, I should doubt its being constitutional. Why, that ties up more than seven thousand square miles of the State into a hard knot, and prevents it from acquiring the privilege of further railway communication."

"In a measure it does," said the girl. "You may run as many lines as you like north and south, but not east and west."

"It's a wonder the Wheat Belt Line didn't contest that law," said Steele.

"Well, I've been told that this law is entirely in the interests of the Wheat Belt Line, although the farmers didn't think so when they voted for the Bill. You see, the Wheat Belt Line was already in operation east and west, and could not be affected by that Act, and, of course, the same Bill which prevented competition to the Farmers' Road also, in a measure, protected the Wheat Belt Line through the same district."

"By Jove!" said Steele, his eyes glistening, "this is a proposition which contains some peculiar points. Well, go on, what happened?"

"Oh, disaster happened. In spite of the legislation and bonuses, the road was a complete failure, and ruined all who were deeply interested in it. The farmers subscribed stock to the amount of something like a hundred thousand dollars, but this money, with the sum of the legislative grant and the bonuses, was all swallowed up in the first twenty miles, and in getting the rolling-stock and equipment, such as it is. The line was never pushed through to Jamestown, and there arose litigation about some of the bonuses that had been paid, and, all in all, it was a most disastrous business. It was hoped that the Wheat Belt Line would come to the rescue and buy the unfinished road, but they would not look at it. This section has never paid a dividend, and is supposed to be doing well when it earns enough money for expenses and repairs. The shares can now be bought for five cents on the dollar, or less."

"How much of it do you possess, Miss Slocum?"

"I own a thousand shares, and my father told me not to part with them, because he was certain that some day they would be valuable."

For a few moments there was silence in the car, and the girl, glancing up at her companion, found his ardent gaze fixed upon her with an intensity that was embarrassing. She flushed slightly and turned her head to look out of the window at the familiar scenery they were passing. It would have surprised the young man could he have read the thoughts that occupied the mind of this extremely pretty and charmingly modest girl who sat opposite him. Here is practically what she said to herself: "I am tired of this deadly dull village in which I live, and here, at last, is a way out. I read in his eyes the beginning of admiration. He shall be the youthful Moses to lead me into the Promised Land. Through this lucky meeting I shall attain the city if I but play my cards rightly."

It would have astonished the girl if she had known what was in the man's mind. The ardent gaze was not for her, as she had supposed. Although he appeared to be looking directly at her, he was in reality almost ignorant of her presence, and saw unfolded before him a scene far beyond her—the whole range of the Eastern States. The power that enabled him to stop the fast express at Slocum Junction gave a hint of Steele's position in the railway world to the station-master, but it conveyed no meaning to the girl. It was his business to be intimately acquainted with the railway situation in northwestern America, and that involved the knowledge of what was going on in the Eastern States. He knew that the Rockervelt system was making for somewhere near this point, and that, ultimately, it would need to cross the State, in spite of the opposition it must meet from the Wheat Belt Line. Whoever possessed the Farmers' bankrupt road held the right of way across the State, so far as a belt of one hundred and twenty miles was concerned. It seemed incredible that Rockervelt, this Napoleon of the railway world, should be ignorant of the obstacle that lay in his path.

Rockervelt was in the habit of buying legislatures and crushing opposition; still, he never spent money where it was not required, and it would be infinitely cheaper to buy the Farmers' Road, and thus secure the privileges pertaining to it, than to purchase the repeal of the obstructing law. At that moment John Steele determined to camp across the path of the conqueror. If Napoleon accepted battle, John was under no delusion as to the result. The name of Steele would disappear from the roll of rising young men in Chicago, and he might be forced to begin at the bottom of the ladder again. However, he knew that Napoleon's eye was fixed on the Pacific coast, and that he never wasted time in a fight if a reasonable expenditure of money would cause the enemy to withdraw. Steele calculated that he could control the road for something under three thousand dollars, which would give him the majority of the stock at the price the girl had named. That was a mere bagatelle. Then he would withdraw from Rockervelt's front for anything between three hundred thousand dollars and half a million. If he succeeded, he would at least recover all the money he had lost in the panic which followed the trickery of Rock-ervelt, Blair and Beck. But success meant more than this. Aside from the joy of relieving Rockervelt of a substantial sum, there would also follow the practical defeat of T. Acton Blair, for the Farmers' Road was situated in that Western district on which the general manager was supposed to keep his eye, in the interests of the Rockervelt system.

A sigh from the girl brought him to a realisation of his neglect of social duties, and the brilliant vision of loot faded from his eyes.

"What pretty scenery we are passing!" he said. "The wooded dell, and the sparkling little rivulet running through it. It is sweet and soothing after the rush and turmoil of a great city. It must be a delight to live here."

"Indeed it isn't!" cried the girl; "it is horrid! Deadly dull, utterly commonplace, with little chance of improving the mind, and none at all for advancing one's material condition. I loathe the life and yearn for the city."

As she said this she bestowed upon him a fascinating glimpse of a pair of lovely eyes, and veiled within them he saw what he took to be a tender appeal for sympathy and, perhaps, for help. After all, he was a young man, and perhaps that glance had carried a hypnotic suggestion to his very soul; and, added to all this, the girl was undoubtedly beautiful.

"Really," he said, leaning forward towards her, "I think that might be managed, you know."

"Do you?" she asked, looking him full in the face.

At this interesting moment the car slowly came to a standstill at a wooden platform, and Joe thrust open the door and shouted: "Here you are! Bunkerville!"

Dorothy Slocum held out her hand shyly to John Steele as she bade him "Good-bye." She thanked him once more for allowing her to ride on the special train, and added: "If you ever come to Bunkerville again, I hope you will not forget me."

"Forget you!" cried the enthusiastic young man. "I think you entirely underrate the attractions of Bunkerville. It seems to me a lovely village. But I shall visit it in the near future—not because of itself, but for the reason that a certain Miss Dorothy lives here."

To this complimentary speech Miss Slocum made no reply, but she laughed and blushed in a manner very becoming to her, and somehow managed to leave an impression on Mr. Steele's mind that she was far from being displeased at the words he had uttered.

When she was gone, the traveller asked Joe where the office of Mr. Hazlett, the lawyer, was situated, and being directed, he was speedily in the presence of the chief legal functionary that Bunkerville possessed. Steele had a considerable amount of money lent upon Bunkerville business property, and his lawyer had written him that, as times were backward, there arose some difficulty in persuading the debtors to meet the requirements of the mortgages. If the mortgages were foreclosed and the property sold, Hazlett did not think it would produce the money that had been borrowed upon it, and so Steele had informed him that he would drop off at Bunkerville on his way west and consult with him.

The lawyer had been looking for him on the regular train, and so was not at the station to meet him. If Hazlett had expected a visit from a hard old skinflint, bent on clutching his pound of financial flesh, he must have been somewhat surprised to greet a smiling young fellow who seemed to be thinking of anything but the property in question.

"We will just walk down the street," said the lawyer, "and I'll show you the buildings."

"All right," assented Steele, "if it doesn't take too long; for I must catch the three o'clock local at Slocum Junction."

During their walk together Steele paid but the scantiest interest to the edifices pointed out to him, and the lawyer soon found he was not even listening to the particulars he recited so circumstantially.

"Do you know anything about the Farmers' Railway?" was the question Steele shot at him in the midst of a score of reasons why it was better not to foreclose at the present moment.

"I know all about it," said the lawyer. "I have done the legal business of the road from its beginning."

"Is there a list of the shareholders in existence?"

"I hold a partial list; but shares have changed hands a good deal, and sometimes no notification has been given me, which is contrary to law."

"I was told to-day that shares can be bought at five cents on the dollar. Is that true?"

"Many shares have been sold at that price; some for less, some for more."

"What is the total number of shares?'

"A hundred thousand."

"Could fifty thousand and an odd share be bought?"

"Do you mean to get control of the road? Yes, I suppose it might be done if you weren't in a hurry, and it was gone about quietly. Some farmers in the outlying districts refuse to sell, thinking the price of the stock will rise, which of course it won't do. Nevertheless, I imagine there should be no difficulty in collecting fifty thousand shares and one more."

"What would it cost?"

"Anywhere between three and five thousand dollars—all depending, as I said, on the thing being done circumspectly, for in these rural communities the wildest rumours get afloat, and so, if it became known that some one was in the market, prices would go up."

"Well, I have in my mind exactly the man to do the trick with discretion, and his name is Hazlett. I will lodge in the bank here five thousand dollars in your name, and I depend on you to get me at least one share over the fifty thousand, although, to be on the safe side, you may purchase at least a thousand in excess. Send the shares to me in Chicago as fast as you secure them, and I'll take care of them."

"Very well, Mr. Steele, I shall do the best I can."

"We will return to your office now, Hazlett, and I'll hand you the cheque. In these matters it's just as well not to lose any time."

"There's another building I want to show you, about five hundred yards down the street."

"We won't mind it to-day. I have determined to take your advice and not foreclose at the present moment. Let's get back to your office, for I mustn't miss Joe's train."

After Steele had returned to Chicago, shares in the Farmers' Railroad began to drop in on him in bulky packages, which he duly noted and placed in a safe. Presently the packages became smaller and smaller, but as the total had already reached forty-nine thousand six hundred and thirty, Steele was not alarmed until he received the following letter from Hazlett:

Dear Mr. Steele:

About two weeks ago I became suspicious that somebody else was buying shares of the Farmers. Road. I came across at that time several people who had sold, although they did not know to whom; and a few days ago a young man called upon me to know if I had any shares for sale. I told him I had none, and as I showed very little interest in the matter, I got some information, and find that a man named T. Acton Blair, of Warmington, is the buyer, and apparently he has agents all over the country trying to purchase shares. I would have telegraphed this information to you were it not for the fact that our telegraph-office is a little leaky, and also because I thought I had the game in my own hands. A young woman in this town, a teacher, Dorothy Slocum by name, possesses a thousand shares, which I felt certain I could purchase for a reasonable figure. I began at ten cents, but she refused, and finally raised to fifty cents, and then a dollar. Higher than that I could not take the responsibility of going without direct authority from you. To my amazement, she has informed me to-day that she has been offered ten thousand dollars for her stock. I obtained her promise that she will not sell for a week. She telegraphed her decision to Blair, and has received an answer from him saying he is on his way to see her. I learn from Miss Slocum that she is acquainted with you, and I surmise, without being certain, that you personally will prove the successful negotiator if you are on the spot. This letter should reach you in time to enable you to arrive here at least as soon as Blair, and I advise prompt action on your part if we are to secure that thousand shares. If you cannot come, telegraph me any one of the following words, and I shall understand I am authorised to offer the amount set down opposite that word.

Yours most sincerely,

James P. Hazlett.

There followed this a dozen words, signifying amounts from ten thousand dollars upwards.

Lawyer Hazlett received a telegram:

*Will reach Slocum Junction at twelve to-morrow. Arrange special train on the Farmers' Road to Bunkerville to be at Junction.*

*Steele.*

The moment Blair's name caught John Steele's eye in the lawyer's letter, he knew that Rockervelt was at last alert and of course could outbid him a thousand to one.

When the Greased Lightning Express stopped at Slocum Junction on this occasion, John Steele had ample time to reach the platform, because the express detached itself from a sumptuous private car before it pursued its journey further west.

"Aha!" said John to himself, "friend Blair travels in style."

The station-master greeted Steele with the cordiality of an old friend.

"Here is a letter which lawyer Hazlett sent out to be handed to you as soon as you arrived, and wished you to read it at once."

Steele tore open the envelope and read:

*I am sorry about the special train, but Blair had telegraphed from Warmington ordering it before your wire came. I have arranged, however, that Joe will return at once for you, as soon as he has landed Blair in Bunkerville. This will make no difference in the negotiations; Miss Slocum has promised to be away from home when Blair calls, and will see you first. I think you've got the inside track, although I surmise the young woman is well aware that she holds the key to the situation. I don't know if she's after all the money she can get, or whether there is something of friendliness in her action. I rather suspect the latter, and I think you can conclude negotiations before she sees Blair at all.*

*Yours most sincerely,*

*James P. Hazlett.*

John Steele gave no expression to the annoyance he felt at missing the special. He distrusted the lawyer's optimism, and like a flash resolved to be in Bunkerville as soon as his antagonist. Blair had stepped down from his private car, asked the station-master where the special was to be found, and quickly ordered his car to be placed on a side track. When he had entered the Bunkerville composition car, and Joe had started up his wheezy engine, Steele darted from the shadow of the station, caught the car and sat down on the rear steps outside, well concealed from the sight of anyone unless that person stood by the end window. All went well until they were about five miles from Bunkerville, when Steele thought he recognised a lady's figure on the highway ahead, and forgetting that he might expose himself to the sharp eyes of Blair, he rose to his feet, clutched the stanchions, and leaned forward. An instant later the rear door was thrown open, a foot was planted energetically in the small of Steele's back, and that young man went hurtling down the embankment, head over heels. There were no half measures with Blair in a crisis like this.

Steele sat up bruised and dazed, not knowing whether he was hurt seriously, or had escaped practically unscathed, which latter proved to be the case. It seemed to him, as he fell through the air, he heard a woman's scream. When he was somewhat stupidly debating whether this was real or imaginary, his doubts were solved by a voice he recognised.

"Oh, Mr. Steele, are you hurt? What a brutal thing for that stout villain to have done!"

"Why, Miss Dorothy, you of all persons! And here was I trying to sneak into Bunkerville to see you first. I thought you were teaching school?"

"Not on Saturdays, Mr. Steele," said the girl, laughing. "I see, after all, you are not injured."

"I'm all right, I think. Fortunately Joe doesn't run sixty miles an hour. Dorothy, I want you to marry me and come to Chicago."

Again the girl laughed.

"Dear me," she said. "I thought you were here to buy my stock. I couldn't think of taking advantage of a proposal that had been literally shaken out of a man. I'm afraid your mind is wandering a bit."

"My mind was never clearer in its life. What is your answer, Dorothy?"

She sat down beside him, still laughing a little. The rivulet was at their feet, the railway embankment behind them, the highway, shrouded by trees, in front.

"Suppose we talk business first, and indulge in sentiment after," said the girl, with a roguish twinkle in her eye. "I have been offered ten thousand dollars for my shares. Are you prepared to pay as much?"

"Yes."

"Cash down?"

"Yes."

"I imagine Mr. Blair would never have come all the way from Warmington to see me if he were not ready to pay a larger sum. I have therefore two further provisos to make. Proviso number one is that you will give me ten per cent, on the profits you make in this transaction. Of course, in spite of Mr. Hazlett's caution, I know there is something very large going on, and naturally I wish to profit by it."

"You are quite right, Miss Slocum, and I agree to the ten per cent, suggestion; in fact, I offered you a hundred per cent, in the beginning, and myself into the bargain, which proposal you have ignored. What is the second proviso?"

"I am told you have a great deal of influence in railway circles in Chicago."

"Yes, I have."

"Can you get a good place for a capable and deserving young man?"

"I think so. Does he understand railroading?"

"Yes, he is the station-master at Slocum Junction."

"Oh, the station-master! Certainly, I should be delighted to offer him a good position. He is a splendid fellow, and I like him exceedingly."

"I am charmed to hear you say so," said Dorothy, with downcast eyes, pulling a flower and picking it to pieces; "for that brings us to the sentiment, and I show my confidence in you and the great esteem in which I hold you, by telling you this strict secret—that I am engaged to be married to the station-master, and am anxious to get to Chicago."

---

# CHAPTER XI—THE TERROR OF WHEAT

ROCKERVELT settled with John Steele by drawing his cheque for three hundred and ninety-eight thousand six hundred dollars, and it was the circumvented Blair himself who carried through the negotiations. Steele asked half a million at the beginning, but had made up his mind to accept three hundred thousand dollars. As he wished to net this sum clear, he added to it the amount he paid for the stock, including Miss Slocum's ten thousand dollars, and the percentage, which came to nearly forty thousand more. Then he informed Blair he was forced to add ten thousand dollars for that kick, which he did. He told Blair that he remembered the kick on an average of once a day, and that this thought humiliated him. Therefore he would be compelled to charge one hundred dollars a day for thinking of the assault while negotiations were pending. Whether this time-penalty hastened negotiations or not will never be known, but it accounts for the odd figures on the Rockervelt cheque, and, after paying all liabilities, Steele found himself with more than his minimum sum in hand.

The station-master of Slocum Junction was given the position of travelling man on the Wheat Belt Line, at a salary of fifty dollars a week, which seemed to him princely. Miss Dorothy Slocum insisted on finishing her year at the Bunkerville school, but during the Christmas holidays she married the station-master, and they set up housekeeping in Chicago with a nice little bank account of nearly fifty thousand dollars. The young lady's dream of life was now realised. She enjoyed the privilege of being an inhabitant of the Western metropolis, in comfortable circumstances, with everything at her disposal that a large city had to bestow. John Steele, in the New Year, had the pleasure of escorting the young woman to a *matinee*, and when he asked her if the few weeks' experience of Chicago had changed her mind regarding the delights of the place, she replied that Chicago was heavenly; which called up a smile to the young man's lips as he remembered the story of a Chicago man who had died and gone to the other place, and told an inmate thereof that his new residence was preferable to Chicago. But John didn't tell the story to his companion. He complained pathetically that she had broken his heart by marrying the station-master, but she laughed and said she had broken his heart no more than Blair had broken his neck by precipitating him down the railway embankment from the running train—which, by the way, was true enough.

As time went on, he saw less and less of his Bunkerville friends. He was rising rapidly in the financial world, had resigned his position on the Wheat Belt Line, important as it was, and had set up an office for himself. The newspapers made a great deal of his encounter with old Rockervelt and his victory over the magnate, but Steele was a clear-headed man who indulged in no delusions on the score of that episode. He had spent some very anxious days while negotiations were pending, and no one knew better than he that if Rockervelt had decided to fight, it might have cost the great railway king more than he had paid, but Steele would have been bankrupt when the battle was ended. He resolved never again to combat a force so many thousand times stronger than himself. He would be content with a smaller game and less risk. John attributed the few grey hairs at his temple to those anxious days while Rockervelt was making up his mind, keeping silent and giving forth no sign.

But grey hairs do not necessarily bring wisdom, and so little does a man suspect what is ahead of him that a few tears from a pretty woman sent him into a contest without knowing who his adversary was, to find himself at last face to face with the most formidable financial foe that the world could offer.

He had almost forgotten his friends from the West, when one day the young woman's card was brought up to him as he sat in his office, planning an aggression which was still further to augment his ever-increasing bank account. He looked up with a smile as Dorothy entered, but it was stricken from his lips when he saw how changed she was. All colour had left her cheeks, and her eyes were red as if with weeping.

"Good gracious!" he cried, springing to his feet, "what is the matter? Have you been ill?"

"No," she said, with a catch in her voice, sinking into the chair he offered, "but I am nearly distracted. Oh, Mr. Steele! you said once that the country was sweet and soothing after the turmoil of the city, and I told you I was tired of the country's dullness. It was a foolish, foolish remark. I wish we were back there, and done with this dreadful town!"

"Why, what has happened? Is it your husband, then, who is ill?"

"No—yes, he is—or, rather, yes and no; for, like myself, he is at his wits' end, and doesn't know what to do; therefore I have come to seek your advice," and with this she broke down and wept.

John thought at first that her husband had been dismissed; and if that were the case, Steele, being no longer connected with the railway, would be powerless to aid. Still, he did not see why such an event should cause so much distress, for a young couple in good health, with fifty thousand dollars in the bank, are not exactly paupers, even in Chicago.

"My husband," sobbed the woman at last, "has invested everything we possess in wheat, and since that time the price of wheat has been falling steadily. Now we are on the verge of ruin."

"What on earth did he meddle with wheat for? It is more dangerous than dynamite."

"I don't know," wept the young woman; "but Tom thought it was sure to rise."

"Yes. They always think that. How much did he purchase?"

"One million bushels."

"Good gracious! Do you happen to know the price?"

"Yes, seventy-eight cents."

"Great Scott! Do you mean to say that you two silly young people took on an obligation of seven hundred and fifty thousand dollars, when you possess less than fifty thousand? When he made the deal, how much of a margin did he put up?"

"You mean the money he gave the broker? Ten thousand dollars."

"Ah, then a decline of a cent a bushel would wipe that out."

"Yes, it did, and ever since wheat has been falling, until now it is seventy-four and a quarter. We have given the brokers so far thirty-seven thousand five hundred dollars, and if wheat drops another cent, we have not the money to meet the call and will lose everything. These last three weeks have been the most anxious time of my life."

"I can well believe it. Now, what do you want me to do?"

"Mr. Steele, I want you to take over this wheat. It can't possibly go much lower, and Tom says it is bound to rise. This time last year it was eighty-nine, and if it went up to that now we would net over a hundred thousand dollars. You see, you would not need to take the risk we have done, for we bought at seventy-eight, and you will be buying at seventy-four and a quarter."

"But I don't see how my taking it over would help you."

"Why if it went up to over eighty—and Tom says it is sure to do that before many weeks are past—you would make a good profit and could give us back our money."

Serious as was the situation John could scarcely refrain from a smile at such a beautiful specimen of feminine logic. Of course, if he wished to dabble in wheat, he could buy at seventy-four now, and if it went to eighty, secure the whole profit without paying anything to anyone.

"Is Tom at home just now?"

"Yes."

"Well, you ask him to call this afternoon, and we will talk the situation over."

The young woman rose and beamed on him through her tears.

"Oh, I am sure you two will hit upon a plan. When I told Tom this morning of the scheme I have just outlined to you he scoffed at me; but you see its feasibility, don't you?"

"Yes, I think I do. Anyhow, Tom and I will consult this afternoon about it, and he'll let you know at what decision we arrive."

He shook hands with his visitor and was very glad to see her depart.

"Good gracious!" he said to himself when the door was shut, "how fatuously silly she is! And to think that a little more than a year ago I proposed to her! Poor girl! Beauty almost gone, too, at the first whiff of trouble. Still, the situation is serious enough; but it is easier to refuse a man than a woman. I'll tell Tom what I think of him when he comes. Imagine the cursed fool marching into Chicago like a hayseed from the backwoods, and losing fifty thousand dollars inside of three weeks. What he needs is a guardian; yet I'd like to help the little woman, too, although I don't see how I can. I wonder if wheat's going any lower. Hold up, Jack, my boy, don't get thinking about the price of wheat. That way madness lies. No, I'll confine myself to giving Tom a piece of my mind when I see him which will make him angry, so we'll quarrel, and then it'll be easy to refuse him."

At three o'clock the ex-station-master of Slocum Junction was shown into John Steele's private office. His face was so gaunt and haggard that for a moment Steele felt sorry for him; but business is business, and sympathy has no place in the wheat-pit. Tom shook hands and sat down without a word; all his old jauntiness had left him.

"Well, my Christian friend," began Steele in his severest manner, "when I was the means of getting you transferred from Slocum Junction to Chicago, and also had something to do towards endowing your wife-that-was-to-be with nearly fifty thousand dollars, hang me if I thought you would act the giddy farmer-come-to-town and blow it all away in the wheat-pit! God bless my soul! haven't you sense enough to know that the biggest men in Chicago have been crumpled up in the grain-market? How could *you* expect to win where the richest and shrewdest dealers in the city have failed? Don't you read the papers? Haven't you any brains in your head at all? Is it only an intellectual bluff that you are putting up before the public, pretending to be a man of sense? Why, a ten-year-old boy born in Chicago would know better! Wheat may be the staff of life when it leaves the flour-mill, but it's the cudgel of death in the speculative market!"

"So I've been told," said Tom quietly.

"Well, you haven't profited much by the telling. What in the name of all the saints made you speculate in wheat?"

"I didn't speculate."

"I understand you bought a million bushels?"

"I did."

"What's that but speculating, then?"

"Look here, Mr. Steele, are you quite done with your abuse of me? Isn't there something more that you could say? That I wear a woollen shirt, and haven't any collar; that my trousers are turned up, and there's mud on my shoes? Do you see any straw out of the farmyard on my hair? If you do, why don't you mention it?"

John Steele laughed.

"Bravo, Tom," he said; "that's quite your Slocum Junction manner. I supposed you were up a tree—that you had bought a million bushels of wheat, spent thirty thousand dollars odd upon margins, and that now you couldn't carry it any longer. Am I right?"

"Quite right. That's exactly the situation. Now, are you in the frame of mind to listen to the biggest thing that there is in America to-day? Are you in a financial position to take advantage of an opportunity that may not recur for years? If you are, I'll talk to you. If not, I'll bid you 'Good-bye,' and go to someone else."

"All right, Tom, I'm ready to listen, and willing to act if you can convince me."

"I can convince you quick enough, but are you able to act, as well as ready?"

"Well, to tell you the truth, Tom, if you mean going in for a big wheat speculation, I'm able, but not willing."

"I told you I wasn't speculating. Wheat will be over a dollar a bushel before three months are past."

"Is there going to be a war?"

"I don't know; but this I do know, that the wheat crop of the entire West is practically a failure—that is to say, late frosts this spring, and the wet weeks we have had since, will knock off anywhere from thirty to forty per cent, of the output. The Chicago wheat-pit is a pretty big thing, but it isn't the Almighty, neither is it the great and growing West. It can do many things, but it can't buck up against nature. Wheat now we'll say, is seventy-five cents a bushel, because of the belief that there's going to be an abundant crop; but if twenty-five per cent, of that crop fails, it means that twenty-five per cent, is going to be added to the present price of wheat. It means dollar wheat, that's what it means, and a man who knows this fact to-day can make unlimited millions of money if he's got the capital behind him. Of course, my mistake was in biting off more than I could chew. If I had gone in modestly, I could have carried it, and would have made a moderate profit; but I was too greedy, and too much afraid Chicago would learn the real state of the crops. I expected the news to be out long before now; but instead of that the papers are blowing about full crops, which either shows that they don't know what they are talking about, or there's a nigger in the fence somewhere."

"What makes you so very sure the crop's a partial failure?"

"Because it's my business to know, for one thing. I have travelled from Chicago clear through to the Pacific coast; south as far as wheat is grown; and up north into Canada. I don't need to ask a farmer what crop he expects; I can see with my own eyes the state of affairs. I was brought up on wheat; I ploughed the fields and sowed the grain, and I may say I was cradled in wheat, if you'll forgive a farmer's pun. Wheat? Why, I know all about wheat on the field, even if I don't recognise it in the Chicago pit. You see, my business is looking after freight, and the chief freight of our road is wheat. Therefore, wherever wheat grows I must visit that spot, and I have done so. I give you my oath that wheat is bound to be a dollar a bushel before two months are past. It's under seventy-five cents now, and it doesn't take much figuring to show the possibilities of the situation. Three things are wanted: knowledge, courage, money. I have given you the knowledge; do you possess the other two requisites?"

"Tom, I esteem you very much—more so now than when you came in; but, after all's said and done, I'd be simply banking on one man's word. Suppose I go in half a million dollars? You say that knowledge is the first requisite. Have I got that knowledge? I have not. I have merely your word that you have the knowledge."

"Yes, that's a good point to make," said Tom imperturbably. "You don't know me well enough to risk it. That's all right. Now, I see on your wall the big map of our road, which I suppose you have kept as a relic of your connection with the Wheat Belt Line. It's a lovely map, with the Wheat Belt Line in heavy black as the great thing, and the United States sort of hung around it as a background. There," continued Tom, waving his hand towards the huge map on the wall, "coloured yellow by Rand, McNally and Co., are the wheat-producing districts of the United States and Canada. Now, I've been all over that yellow ground. I assert that in no part of it is the wheat crop normal. You pick out at random five or six spots in that yellow ground, and I'll tell you just what percentage of failure there'll be in those places you select. Then get on the train and visit them, question the farmers, and find out if they corroborate my statement. If they do, the chances are strong I am right about every other district."

John Steele got up and began pacing the floor, his hands thrust in his trousers pockets, his forehead wrinkled with a frown.

"Tom, that's pretty straight talk," he said at last. "I haven't been following the wheat-market—it's out of my line; but I dimly remember seeing in the papers not very long ago an estimate that we were going to have the most profitable wheat crop of recent years. Of course, that may be newspaper talk; but if recollection serves, it was backed up by telegrams from all over the West. How do you account for that?"

"I don't account for it. I am merely stating what I know. If the papers made such an estimate they were wrong, that's all."

Steele stopped in his walk and touched an electric button on his desk. A young man appeared in response.

"Holmes," said Steele, "there was an account of the wheat crop all over the country in the papers the other day—occupied a page, I think. Go to the nearest newspaper office and get a copy. As you go out, tell Bronson to come in here."

When Bronson appeared, Steele said sharply: "Find out for me, from some reliable source, the lowest price of wheat for the last ten years."

In an amazingly short space of time Holmes reappeared with a newspaper a week old, and laid it on Mr. Steele's desk, and Bronson brought in an array of figures.

"Here we are!" cried Steele, jerking open the crackling sheet. "'Wonderful harvests ahead! Tremendous wheat crops!' Of course, it must be remembered that prophesying prosperity is always popular, and newspapers like that sort of news. Now, I shall select twenty-five places named in this paper. The useful Bronson will find out for me a reliable man in each place, and I will telegraph him. By to-morrow we should have replies from some fifteen or twenty of them; and if the majority say that the wheat crop is a failure, then I think we may rely on your forecast. Now, let us see what Bronson's figures are. Sixty-five, sixty-two and a half, sixty-four and an eighth, fifty-three and five-eighths, forty-eight and three-quarters—gee-whillikins, that's getting down to bedrock!—fifty, fifty-four and nine-eighths, sixty-nine and one-eighth, eighty-five—ah! that's something like—seventy-four and a quarter, and so on. Why, it seems from this that no man is safe in buying for a rise if he pays more than fifty cents a bushel, while you have bought at seventy-eight! Septimus Severus! I admire your nerve, but not your judgment. Well, drop in to-morrow, about two, and we'll see what the telegrams bring us."

"Suppose, meanwhile, wheat falls another cent or two, what am I to do?"

"Oh, they can't hurt you to-day—it's after four o'clock; and to-morrow we'll see what is best to be done. It is useless to conceal from you the fact that there is an unholy gulf between seventy-eight at which you bought, and fifty, to which wheat has on more than one occasion fallen. That means a little deficit of two hundred and eighty thousand dollars on your gentle flutter."

"The truth must come out soon, Mr. Steele, and it may be published any morning. When that happens, wheat will go up like a balloon."

"All right, Tom, I can say nothing further just now. To-morrow you will find me brimful of information, and quite decided as to the course I shall take."

With this the visitor had to be content. Next day he arrived at Steele's office in a more cheerful frame of mind. Wheat had closed the day before one-eighth stronger than it was in the morning. The conference this time was short, sharp, and decisive. Steele was thoroughly the man of business.

"I received seventeen replies," he said, "and they all corroborate your forecast. Now, what do you wish me to do with the little parcel of wheat standing against your name?"

"I thought that in return for the tip you might relieve me of three-quarters of it."

"I'll relieve you of it all. I've given orders to my brokers to buy a pretty large slice of the wheat crop. This purchase may perhaps send up the price to the seventy-eight at which you purchased. If it does, I'll sell out your lot and send you the money, which I advise you to invest in gilt-edged securities and leave wheat alone."

"All right," said Tom. "I know when I've had enough. Nevertheless, it's a sure thing, and I hate to let go."

"If it's a sure thing," said Steele, "I'll hand over to you a percentage of what I win, in return for the information you have given me. You go straight home, taking this newspaper with you. Write out a report similar in length to these Press Alliance telegrams, giving name of locality and the actual state of the crop in each district. Let nobody know what you are doing, and work all night, if necessary, until the report is complete. Then bring it to me, and I'll have it typewritten in this office. Now, this is my busy day. Clear out. Goodbye."

Steele's buying took the market by surprise. No one knew, of course, who the purchaser was, but the price rose rapidly, point by point, until seventy-eight was again reached, and then Steele instantly gave orders for the sale of the million bushels that stood in Tom's name, for the double purpose of getting the man his money, and lowering the price so that his own purchases might be accomplished at a less figure than seventy-eight. The sale took place an hour before the closing of business, and chanced to be just in the nick of time. Orders to sell came in from somewhere—supposedly from New York, and wheat was offered in any quantity at practically any price the buyers liked to pay. Someone was hammering down the market. A fight was on between two unknowns, and pandemonium was let loose in Chicago. The pit went wild, and prices came down with a run. Steele had already stopped his buyers, and he stood from under. Closing prices for wheat were sixty-five, three-eighths. John Steele did some deep thinking and close figuring that night. In spite of his purchases of the day, he had still a million dollars left to gamble with.

"My friend the bear," he said to himself, "is very likely to keep up his antics to-morrow, to frighten the opposition. If he squeezes down prices to sixty, I'll buy five million bushels. Every cent of a drop will mean a loss of fifty thousand dollars. It reached fifty in '94, and next year a cent and a quarter less, but this price has never on any other occasion been touched in the last forty years. Even if it drops to that, I'll have lost half a million or so, but I can still hang on. I'm not trying to corner the market; so, Mr. Bruin, go ahead, and let us see what happens."

Next day the panic and the slump continued. Wheat fell to fifty-nine, and between that price and sixty-one John Steele secured his five million bushels.

Who were the operators? That was what the papers wanted to know. Was it, as surmised, a contest between New York and Chicago? All the well-known dealers were interviewed, but each and every one insisted he was merely an interested spectator, holding an umbrella over his head. There was going to be a blizzard, so everybody had his eye on the cyclone cellar. Experts said it was a good time to seek cover.

Of course, John Steele might have rested on his oars. He was reasonably safe—in fact, he was perfectly safe if he merely held on, which was a good position to be in. But he had a plan of his own, although he resolved not to buy further unless wheat reached the low limit of half a dollar. In that case he feared he would plunge. This night, however, he proceeded to carry out his plan, which led to amazing results. He put Tom's report of the wheat crop's condition, now nicely typewritten, into his inside pocket, and locked up his office.

All the upper windows of a commodious business block were aglow with electric light. It was the home of the Press Alliance, with telegraphic nerves reaching to the furthermost parts of the earth. Its business was to gather news, which it furnished to journals belonging to the Alliance. John Steele was acquainted with Simmonds, the manager, and resolved to pay him an evening call at what was certainly a most inopportune moment. The great hive was a-hum with activity. The wild day on the Stock Exchange was enough of itself to keep it throbbing. Simmonds was a busy man, but he received John Steele, who came in cool and self-possessed, with courtesy and respect.

"Well, Simmonds, I suppose you're just rushed to death, so I'll not detain you a moment. I want to see one of your men who is less busy, if, indeed, he is here to-night."

"We're all here to-night, Steele. I hope you've not been dabbling in wheat?"

"Me? No fear. Wheat's rather out of my line."

"Somebody's going to get badly hurt before the week is out."

"So I understand," said Steele nonchalantly, as if it were none of his affair. "By the way, talking of wheat, you gather statistics of the crops from all over the country, don't you—your company, I mean?"

"Oh, yes, several times a year."

"From what office is that done, New York or Chicago?"

"Chicago, of course."

"Who is in charge of that department?"

"Nicholson. Why?"

"I should like to have a chat with him if he's not too busy."

"Well, you've mentioned the one man who isn't busy to-night. You see, his work is a daylight job."

"What sort of a fellow is he?"

"He's a new man—at least, he's been with us only six months—that is, at this office. He came on from New York. Splendid fellow, though, and well up to his work."

"Good. May I see him?"

"I'll find out if he's in his room."

Simmonds spoke through a telephone, and then said:

"Yes, Mr. Nicholson will see you; but I say, Steele, don't meddle with wheat. If you want any information from him, remember he can't give it out, except to the morning papers."

"Oh, I shan't buy a bushel of wheat; don't be frightened."

"This boy will take you to Mr. Nicholson's room. Good night."

Nicholson proved to be a man of uncertain age. His hair was closely cropped, his face smoothly shaven, bearing a look of determination and power, which one might not have expected to find in a mere subordinate.

"Is this Mr. John Steele," he asked pleasantly, "the Napoleon of finance who stood out against Rockervelt?"

"Well, I don't know about the Napoleon part of it, Mr. Nicholson, but Rockervelt and I had a little negotiation a while ago which I trust ended in our mutual advantage. Now, Mr. Nicholson," continued Steele, sitting down in the chair offered him, "if you are not too busy I should like to ask you a few questions."

"I am not very busy, Mr. Steele, and shall be pleased to answer any question you ask, so long as the information sought belongs to me, and not to my employers."

"Who is your employer, Mr. Nicholson?"

"My employer? Why, the Press Alliance, of course."

"The Press Alliance is one of your employers, I know. Your nominal employer, let us say. It pays you to collect accurate information. Who pays you for disseminating false news in the daily journals of this country?"

If John Steele expected a start of guilty surprise or a flash of anger or a demand for explanation, he was disappointed. The impassive face remained impassive. The piercing eyes narrowed a little, perhaps, but he could have sworn that the faint glimmer of a smile hovered about the firm lips. The voice that spoke was under perfect control.

"They say that all things come to him who waits, and here is an illustration of it. The man for whom every reporter in Chicago is searching, and whom I am most desirous to meet, walks right into my office. How many million bushels of wheat did you buy to-day, Mr. Steele?"

John Steele was a much more genial person than this man from New York. He threw back his head and laughed.

"Mr. Nicholson, I am delighted to have made your acquaintance. Your wild guess that I am the buyer of wheat is really flattering to me. Yet your own reference to my little contest with Rockervelt should have reminded you that I deal in railways, and not in grain."

"The reason I wished to meet you," went on Mr. Nicholson, as if the other had not spoken, "is because I have a message to you from my chiefs."

"Yes, but you have not mentioned who your chiefs are."

"There is no need to mention them, Mr. Steele. When I tell you they own banks in every city in the United States; that the income of the head of our combination is fifty million dollars a year from merely one branch of his activity; that we have employees in the United States Treasury powerful enough to cause the funds of this country to be placed for safety in our banks; that my principals can, if they wish, gamble with the savings of the people of the United States deposited in their keeping; that they have agents in every part of the world, and that there is not a country in Europe, Asia, or Africa which does not pay tribute to them; when I have said all this, Mr. Steele, I think two things may be taken for granted—first: no names need be mentioned; second: you are opposed to a power infinitely greater than that of Mr. Rockervelt or any other financial force which the world contains."

"You are right in both surmises, Mr. Nicholson, and I experience that keen joy which warriors feel with foemen worthy of their steel—if you will excuse the apparent pun on my own name. I am really quoting from Scott, not the railway man of that name, but the poet. And now for your message, Mr. Nicholson."

"You admit, then, that you are the buyer?"

"I'll admit anything in the face of such a formidable rival."

"Very well. My chiefs are the most generous of men."

"Oh, we all know that."

"If you have lost money these last two days, they will refund it. They are even willing to allow you a reasonable profit, and I am empowered to negotiate regarding the figures."

"And all this for pure philanthropy, Mr. Nicholson?"

"All this if you will merely stand aside and not interfere in a market you do not understand, and complicate a situation that is already somewhat delicate."

"And if I refuse to stand aside?"

"If you refuse, they will crush you, as they have crushed many a cleverer man."

"Ah! that's not tactful, Nicholson, and I'm sure it would not meet the approval of your employers. Your last remark is apt to provoke opposition rather than compliance. Would it surprise you to know that I possess a more potent backer than even your distinguished chief?"

"More potent? Yes, it would surprise me. Have you any reluctance in mentioning the name?"

"Not the slightest—it's a lady."

"A lady?"

"Yes. Dame Nature—a charming old woman if you stand in with her; a blue terror if you go against her. The wheat crop in America this year will be only three-quarters of the normal yield, if it is that much. You can juggle with the fact for a little time, but you can't conceal it. Even the great firm on Broadway cannot make a blade of wheat grow where one has been killed by the frost—not in the same year, at least. So you may telegraph to your distinguished principals and tell them that John Steele and Dame Nature are going to dance a minuet with those two Corsican brothers of New York, and your fraternal friends will find some difficulty in keeping pace with the music. And so good-bye, Mr. Nicholson."

"Good-bye, Mr. Steele. I am very sorry we cannot come to terms."

Once outside, Steele hailed a cab and drove to the Chicago Daily Blade building. Here, as at the Press Alliance, everyone was hard at work; but Steele's name was good for entrance almost anywhere in Chicago, and the managing editor did not keep him waiting.

"Good evening, Stoliker," began Steele. "I have got in my pocket the greatest newspaper 'beat' that has ever been let loose on Chicago since the night of the Brooklyn Theatre Fire."

"Then, Steele, you're as welcome as flowers that bloom in the spring. Out with it."

"There's been a gigantic conspiracy to delude the Press and people of the United States."

"Oh, they're always trying that," said Stoliker indifferently.

"Yes, but this time they've succeeded, up to this evening. Just cast your eye over this document."

A managing editor is quick to form an accurate estimate of the proportions of a piece of news submitted to him.

"If anyone else had brought this in," said Stoliker slowly, "do you know what I should have thought?"

"Yes, you would think it an attempt of the bulls to get in out of the rain."

"Exactly. You've hit it the first time. Can you vouch for the accuracy of this?"

"I can."

"You won't be offended, Steele, if I ask you one more question, only one?"

"I know what the question is."

"What is it?"

"You are going to ask if I have been buying wheat?"

"Well, you seem to know exactly what's in my mind. Conversation is rather superfluous with so sharp a man as you are. *Have* you been buying wheat?"

"Yes, I'm the person who caused the flutter in the market these last two days."

"If I publish this, the price of wheat will instantly jump up."

"No, it won't."

"Oh, that's the evident object of the whole thing. If I prove that the wheat crop of America is from twenty-five to thirty per cent, short, up goes the price of wheat."

"My dear Stoliker, your paper will sell like hot cakes, but no one will believe a word you say. Everyone on 'Change will think exactly as you do—that this is a device of the bulls, and so the price of wheat is likely to remain stationary for some hours. But this sensational and categorical statement is bound to make everybody uneasy, and there will be a good deal of telegraphing going on during the forenoon. By the time the evening papers are out, it will begin to dawn on commercial Chicago that you've done the biggest thing that's been done for years. After that, every moment will enhance your reputation."

"Quite so, *if*—and that 'if' is the biggest word in the dictionary just now—if this article is accurate. If it isn't, then the reverse of all you have predicted will happen."

"My dear Stoliker, I was quite prepared for this unbelief, I therefore took the precaution before the bank closed to get a certified cheque for a hundred thousand dollars, and here it is. Pay this into your bank tomorrow, and offer in your paper a hundred thousand dollars to anyone who will prove the report inaccurate. It has been compiled by a man I can vouch for, in the employ of the Wheat Belt Line, who has visited every spot mentioned in the report. Now, time is precious; I give you five minutes in which to make up your mind."

"I don't need them; my mind is made up. I'll print it."

Next day, events proved that Steele was no false prophet. Wheat fluctuated for a time up and down, then began to rise steadily, and at last shot up like a rocket, ending at eighty-three and a quarter. Before the week was out it was well over the dollar mark, and John Steele was richer by more than three millions of dollars. The night of the day in which he sold out he strolled into the Press Alliance offices and visited his perturbed friend Simmonds.

"I would like to see Mr. Nicholson again," he said.

"Oh, curse him!" cried Simmonds, "he's gone to New York; and I wish he had never left there. I suppose you don't know what a hole he put us into, because you're not interested in wheat."

"Really? Why, I was tremendously impressed by Nicholson's manner and appearance!"

"Oh, his manner and appearance were all right. He came here with the very highest recommendations—in fact, he was the one man in our employ of all the hundreds here that I had orders from headquarters not to dismiss on any account. I was as much taken with his looks as you were. I would have sworn he was true to his employers, yet I have not the slightest doubt he sold them as if they were a flock of sheep."

"You are mistaken, Simmonds. He was perfectly true to his employers."

---

# CHAPTER XII
# THE EMBODIMENT OF MAMMON

THERE now projects across these pages the sinister shadow of a man. He was one seldom seen except by his immediate business associates, and yet seldom has a newspaper been issued that did not contain his name. This was Peter Berrington, the greatest financial brain the world had hitherto produced—the modern embodiment of Mammon. In early life there had occurred to him the obvious proposition that if any one man could control the manufacture and sale of some simple article in universal use, he would secure a fortune greater than that of all the monarchs on earth put together. Peter Berrington chose soap as his medium, and the world-renowned trust called Amalgamated Soap has been the outcome. His methods were as simple as his products. He offered what he considered a fair price to a rival for his business and if that rival refused, Peter crushed him by a competition the other could not withstand. Berrington seemed to act on one fixed rule in life, which was to avoid the law courts wherever possible; yet, nevertheless, he was haled to the bar on many occasions, but invariably he escaped unscathed, without a stain on his character, as if the soap he supplied to the universe had removed even the suspicion of dishonesty from himself. It pleases the world to buy soap under different titles, but it is all manufactured by the same company. Berrington's air-tight monopoly finally produced an annual income in excess of the fortune any man on earth possessed twenty-five years ago. With this ever-increasing income he bought banks, first in New York, then in every other great city, and finally in the larger towns. He purchased trust companies and insurance associations. He bought railways and steamship lines, also city councils and State legislators, judges, juries and senators. He was now the guardian and manipulator of the people's savings, and his banks had the handling of all the money the United States Government possessed. Magazines printed vivid articles exhibiting the dark points of his career. Peter never entered a protest. Powerful newspapers hurled vigorous denunciations against him, but Peter never replied. The few who knew him in private life described him as a quiet, timorous man, apparently without opinions of his own, who was withal deeply religious. Yet all the histories printed of him never contained the record of any man who had defeated him.

It was but natural, then, that the Chicago papers should make much of John Steele's encounter with this giant of the financial world. Steele had met him on the battle-ground of the Chicago wheat-pit, and had routed him, horse, foot and dragoons. *The Daily Blade's* exposure of the real wheat situation of the country had been so sudden that the barrels of money which Peter Berrington kept in readiness to buy the whole crop, when he had hammered the price low enough, remained unopened and unexpended.

Berrington would have made billions at one fell swoop had not this man Steele blindly, quite unwittingly, stumbled across his path and tripped him up. The newspapers exaggeratingly credited Steele with making many more millions than he had actually secured, and it was only when the anxious three days of panic had ended that Steele himself realised what a tremendous fortune had been within his grasp if he could have commanded the capital to manipulate the situation, or even if he had risked all he actually possessed. Indeed, Steele perceived when too late that he had blundered into the biggest deal ever projected upon this earth, and while he undoubtedly spoiled the game for its inaugurates, he did not himself profit nearly as much as might have been the case. He began to question his own judgment, and the uneasy thought came to him that if he had made terms that night with Nicholson in the office of the Press Alliance, he might have made from ten to twenty millions instead of three or four. Yet he was consoled by the belief that Peter would have been true to no bargain he might have made, and in the end would have robbed him of the agreed share. In spite of his religious reputation, Peter was accredited with no qualms of conscience in a business transaction.

The Western newspapers re-recited Steele's brief besting of Rockervelt, which was now utterly eclipsed by his victory over Berrington, and they jocularly advised New York rustics to stay at home and not venture into a real city like Chicago. In face of all this ridicule, and in spite of accusations and denunciations levelled against him for his efforts to mislead a free and incorruptible Press, Peter Berrington made no sign, and New York silently swallowed up the mysterious Nicholson. A few wiseacres in Chicago shook their heads as they read the laudations of Mr. John Steele, saying the young man was not yet done with Peter Berrington; and later events proved the correctness of their surmise.

Steele himself was not particularly frightened at the outlook, but neither was he extremely pleased. He was sorry that Fate had brought him into opposition with Peter Berrington, but he had learned that fact too late to withdraw. When he met Nicholson, and became aware that the Great Bear was Amalgamated Soap, he was already committed too deeply for half measures to aid him. He had acted at once, decisively and successfully, and would have been relieved had he merely got out even. It was his usual luck that he came away with large profits, and for that he thanked Fate, because he knew his enemy was ruthless. Success did not turn his head in the least. He was a cool thinker and detested all this newspaper notoriety. He knew fortunes were not made by the beating of drums, and he kept very quiet until the hubbub was over, refusing to see reporters or say anything about the matter, save to his most intimate friends. He hoped that some fresh sensation would speedily drive his name from the columns of the Press, and until that time came he sought shelter, doing nothing. He comforted himself with the thought that Peter Berrington, while merciless to an opponent, was merciless merely to acquire that opponent's business. He believed the great man to be entirely without sentiment, and therefore surmised he would not seek revenge when an act was once completed and done with. Nevertheless, he resolved to keep his weather eye open, which was wise.

The new celebrity he had attained brought all sorts and conditions of men to his offices. He began to think that every wild-cat scheme in the country was placed before him. Letters poured in from various parts of the world, and he was offered gold mines, patents, railways, steamship lines, industrial enterprises and what not. He took larger offices and protected himself from intrusion. He became a much more difficult man to see than even the President of the United States—or perhaps it would be more fitting to say than Mr. Peter Berrington, for Peter allowed no outsider to penetrate to his den.

There was one man, however, who succeeded in reaching the inner room of John Steele, and his card bore the name of William Metcalfe. This card had been preceded, however, by some excellent letters of introduction, and so John Steele made an appointment with him. He was favourably impressed by the appearance of Mr. Metcalfe, who did not look like a city man, but rather a cross between a bluff farmer and a shrewd manufacturer—which, indeed, he turned out to be. After seating himself, William Metcalfe plunged directly into the heart of his business, without preliminary, which also pleased John Steele.

"I know your time is valuable," he said; "so is mine. I have undertaken an operation that proves too big for me, and I want you to help me carry it out."

"I have three rules, Mr. Metcalfe, which I rarely break. In the first place, I never finance anything. If, for instance, you wish to build a factory, or to exploit a patent, it is useless coming to me expecting help."

"I have no factory to build and no patent to exploit," said Metcalfe.

"My second rule is that the man with whom I go in, must be prepared to put up dollar for dollar with me in hard cash, and not in future prospects."

"I am prepared to do that," rejoined Metcalfe.

"My third rule is that I must see for myself and understand the business offered. I do not give a hang for the opinions of experts. If the proposal is complicated beyond my comprehension, I don't go in."

"Quite right," commended Metcalfe. "None of your three rules will be in the least infringed by me. Do you know anything of the beet-sugar business?"

"I do not."

"Did you ever hear of Bradley, of Bay City?'

"I did not."

"Well, what Bradley accomplished may be understood by a ten-year-old boy. He went over to Germany, and came back with a parcel of seeds in his handbag, which seeds he planted. From that parcel has grown the beet root industry of Michigan. There are now factories in that State capitalised at ten millions of dollars. There are nearly a hundred thousand acres of Michigan land in beets. Ten years ago I hadn't a penny; to-day I think I could put as much money on the table as you, and all on account of those seeds Bradley brought from Germany. I own three big factories in Michigan, and four others in States further west. You hinted that you didn't wish to deal in probabilities; but, if you will forgive me for saying it, there is no industry in this country at the present moment which offers greater promise than the manufacture of sugar out of beetroot."

"I dare say," remarked Steele indifferently. "I am quite willing to applaud the excellent Bradley, who made millions of beets grow where none had grown before. I admire such a man exceedingly, even though unprepared to follow in his steps. You see, Mr. Metcalfe, I am not a useful citizen like yourself and Mr. Bradley. I simply make a raid at some project, filch what I can, and get back into my den. As I told you, I am not building factories, not even those that squeeze the succulent beet. I squeeze my opponents on the Stock Exchange. My motto is large profits and quick returns."

"I am here to offer you immense profits and immediate returns. I understand the sugar business down to the ground, and have realised its possibilities for several years past. Therefore I determined to combine all the big sugar factories at present existing in the United States. Rapidly as I myself have acquired wealth, the sugar business has been growing too quickly for me, and at the beginning of this year I saw I had to put my project into action, or else interest a body of financiers, which I did not wish to do, for my ambition is to control the sugar-beet industry of the United States, and ultimately of the world."

"Ah, you hope to become a sort of sweetened Peter Berrington," said Steele, with a smile, and he thought of this remark somewhat grimly later on.

"Exactly," said Metcalfe seriously, without duplicating the other's smile. "As I told you, I own outright seven factories. I secured options on all the rest, and in each case have paid down a forfeit, for I shall be compelled to buy outright within the next month if I am to hold them. Now, the total cost of all the factories in the States at present, built or building, comes to almost double the capital I possess. If you will put up dollar for dollar with me, we will purchase these factories outright. Then we will form the whole into a gigantic company. When this is done, you can withdraw your money, and probably as much more as you put in. If the public does not subscribe the full amount we demand, I will guarantee to relieve you at par of all the shares that may fall to your portion."

"How can you guarantee to do that when at the present moment you have not got more than half the necessary capital for forming the company?"

"I can guarantee it because I am certain the public will subscribe; but even if they do not, the moment the company is formed there is a bank in this city willing to advance me cash to the amount of three-quarters of our capital. Therefore I can guarantee that you will double your money within a month—that is, within a month of your putting it in. You say you care nothing for the opinions of experts; neither do I, therefore I propose that you become my guest for two weeks, and visit most of the factories now under my control. You can see the books and balance-sheets of my own concerns, and from what you learn under my tuition you will be able to form a very good estimate of how the other factories are placed."

"I understand very little about company promoting," said Steele dubiously.

"I understood just as little a short time since, but it was necessary that I should learn, and I have learnt. Besides, I have secured letters of introduction to Far-well Brothers, the most substantial and honest firm connected with that business in Chicago. The same people introduced me to them that introduced me to you. Suppose, for instance, the combined factories were to cost us ten million dollars. With such prospects as there are ahead, we would be quite justified in forming a company for twenty millions. If the public subscribed only half of what we demanded, we would have our factories for nothing, and still control the combination."

"How about your working capital?"

"We don't need working capital. Every factory is making money."

"Well, candidly, Mr. Metcalfe, that project seems too easy and simple to be entirely feasible. There must be something lying in wait to wreck it."

"Nothing so far as I can see," said Metcalfe confidently.

"What if the public do not subscribe a penny?"

"Oh, I've looked out for that. When I got the options, there was, of course, no longer any need for keeping the affair secret, and I have already been promised subscriptions to the new company to the extent of one-third the proposed capital of twenty millions. That one-third will be subscribed in Michigan and Wisconsin alone, without touching the State of Illinois or the capitalists of Chicago."

"Very well, Mr. Metcalfe, you appear to have thought of everything. I'll accept your invitation, so long as it binds me to nothing, and will go wherever you lead me, beginning, let us say, with one of your own factories. I understand figures, and I shall want to see the books and make a somewhat thorough search into the income of at least the principal factories. You have no objection to that, I suppose?"

"No, not in the least. Big as our capitalisation will be, this is a thoroughly sound industrial proposition, and before five years are over I am certain that we will be justified in doubling our normal capital if we wish to do so, and paying a mighty good percentage on the same. Of course, I stand by the business. I suppose you wish to pull out as quickly as possible."

"Yes, that's the idea. I hope you have not offered extravagant prices for these factories?"

"That's just the point. I have not. You see, as I told you, I am thoroughly acquainted with the business. A capitalist from New York or Chicago might have been deluded, but they cannot delude a practical man like myself. Indeed, to convince you of the confidence that others show in the proposed company, I may tell you that the capital promised comes largely from the present owners of those factories, who appreciate the economies to be inaugurated by combination, and who in some instances are putting back into the new company the entire amount I shall pay them."

"Do they know you intend to capitalise for double what the property has cost?"

"Naturally not, Mr. Steele. Of course they understand I am not in this business entirely for my health; but apart from that, anyone conversant with the progress the beet industry has made during the last four or five years is well aware that the developments of the next five or six will be something enormous."

"All right, Mr Metcalfe I'm ready to go with you to-morrow, if that is not too soon for you."

John Steele's visits to the beet-sugar district more than corroborated all that Mr. Metcalfe had told him. Quietly he studied his host and guide during the excursion, and the more he saw of him the better he liked him. If there was an honest man in the country, that man appeared to be William Metcalfe, in spite of his determination to capitalise the properties for double what he paid for them. John's own conscience was not supersensitive on this point, and his private opinion would have been that a man was a fool not to take all he could get. So, before they returned to Chicago, he had quite made up his mind to become a partner with William Metcalfe in forming the Consolidated Beet Sugar Company, Metcalfe having no domicile in Chicago, the headquarters of the new trust was the private office of John Steele and the apartments adjoining. These adjoining apartments were occupied by William Metcalfe, upon whose shoulders naturally fell the bulk of the work. It was he who saw the lawyers to whom he had been introduced; who negotiated with the bank and made such outside arrangements as were necessary in the launching of so gigantic a scheme. Steele was more and more impressed with the business capacity of his new partner as the days went on, and he congratulated himself on being in conjunction with so capable a man. Notwithstanding his increasing confidence he never for a moment relaxed his vigilance, nor was anything done without his sanction and approval, and he allowed no obscure point to pass without thoroughly mastering it. Towards the conclusion of preliminary arrangements, he saw with some apprehension that this project would involve every penny of capital he possessed, and this, of course, was cause for anxiety, though not for alarm, because all the omens were favourable. Yet his vigilance might have been of little avail had not chance played into his hands. Steele was constantly in the office; Metcalfe was frequently called elsewhere, and in one of his absences a telegraph-boy brought in a message.

"Any answer?" asked the lad.

Steele tore open the envelope and gazed at the telegram for a moment, uncomprehending. It was in cipher. Then he looked at the envelope and saw it was addressed to his partner.

"No answer," said Steele to the boy; "but look here, my lad, do you want to earn fifty cents?"

"Sure," replied the messenger.

"Very well, get me another envelope from the nearest telegraph-office. I see this is for my partner, not for me."

He threw half-a-dollar on the table, which the boy grasped eagerly.

"Be as quick as you can," cried Steele, before he reached the door.

The cipher telegram was a long one, but speedily Steele wrote it out on a sheet of paper. When the boy returned with the envelope, Steele placed the telegram within it, sealed it, and addressed it in imitation of the telegraphic clerk. Then he walked into the adjoining office and placed the resealed telegram on Mr. Metcalfe's desk.

"Now, why does honest William Metcalfe receive a long telegram in cipher from New York?" said Steele to himself, knitting his brows. "He has never even mentioned New York to me, yet he is in secret communication with someone there. Lord! one can never tell when the biggest sort of crank will not suddenly loom up as the most useful man in the world!" cried Steele, as he suddenly bethought himself of Billy Brooks, a jocular person who bored all Chicago with his knowledge of cipher, claiming there was nothing he couldn't unravel except the Knock Alphabet cipher of the Russian Nihilists. And Billy had his office in the fifteenth storey of the adjoining block. Steele shoved the copy of the telegram in his trousers' pocket, put on his silk hat, went down one elevator, and up another, in almost less time than it takes to tell about it.

"Say, Billy, I've got a cipher here that you can't decode, and I've got twenty dollars to bet on it."

"Let's see your cipher," cried Billy, his eyes sparkling. "All ciphers fall into seven distinct classes. These classes are then sub-divided into——"

"Yes, I know, I know!" cried Steele impatiently. "Here's the message."

Billy glanced at it.

"Hand over your twenty dollars, Steele."

"What! you haven't solved it already?"

"No, but I see at a glance it falls into division three and into sub-division nineteen. I'll decode it within an hour. Shall I bring it over to your office?"

"No, Billy, I'll sit down right here, even if you are six hours at it. I herewith place two ten-dollar bills on your desk, and if this proves important, which it may or may not, I'll multiply those bills by ten; and for that number of days, at least, I shall require the utmost secrecy."

"All right, John, sit down and keep quiet, and there's the latest evening paper."

There was silence in the room as Billy opened a bookcase and took down one bulky tome, two medium-sized books, and a number of smaller volumes that looked like dictionaries. Turning to his desk, he wrote the message in a variety of different ways, on as many sheets of paper. For nearly three-quarters of an hour no sound was heard but the scratching of a pen now and then, and the rustle of leaves. Then the stillness was broken by a war-whoop.

"Here you are, John, my boy; and I'll take my Bible oath on its accuracy. Couldn't be such a series of coincidences as to run so smoothly otherwise.=

````"Precious greenbacks! Loot divine!

````Twenty dollars, you are mine!"=

Billy jubilantly grasped the currency and shoved it into his pocket, handing the sheet of paper to Steele, who read: "I shall occupy room one hundred and fifty at the Grand Pacific Hotel on Thursday, the twenty-seventh, at eleven a. m. Do not ask for me at the office, nor take the elevator, but come up the stair, and rap twice. Wait two minutes, and rap a third time. Bring all documents with you."

There was no signature.

"Billy," said Steele rather seriously, "we will now burn all your figuring, if you don't mind, and then I wish you to obliterate this from your memory. I cannot tell until after Thursday whether it is important or not. I think, however, if you keep mum, this will be worth an extra two hundred dollars to you."

"You can depend on me, John. We're not all making money as fast as you are. Of course, I know that financial ciphers are usually important. Here's the *débris*; burn it on the oilcloth, near the register."

Steele's investigation of the Grand Pacific Hotel floor occupied by room one hundred and fifty showed him that this apartment was well chosen, for neither of the rooms on either side had a communicating door. However, he engaged room one hundred and forty-nine, on the opposite side of the hall, and before ten o'clock on the twenty-seventh he took up his position inside that apartment. When eleven o'clock approached, he locked his door, shoved the table against it, stood thereon, and looked through the transom into the hall. He darkened his own window so that he could not be observed by anyone glancing up outside. He heard the first knock, then cautiously peered down and recognised William Metcalfe standing there, facing the opposite door, with a bundle under his arm. After the third knock, Metcalfe entered, but opened the door so slightly that Steele could see nothing within, nor did he hear any greeting voice. A full hour passed with not a sound from the closed room, then Metcalfe came out again, with the bundle still under his arm, and walked quietly away, leaving his partner on watch at the transom. Time goes slowly for a man on tip-toe with eyes strained, but at last his patience was rewarded. The door opposite opened, and the head of Nicholson appeared. He glanced quickly up and down the hall, and as the way was apparently clear, stepped out and vanished. John Steele came down from the table, drew aside the curtains, and let the light into the darkened room. He poured some water from the carafe into a tumbler, swallowed the liquid at a gulp, then sank into the arm-chair beside the bed. He gave utterance to an uneasy laugh, then muttered a sentence which might be called unexpected: "Billy Brooks, my boy, you'll get your two hundred dollars!"

Drawing a deep breath, he then concentrated his mind on the crisis with which he was confronted. Metcalfe was probably the owner of the sugar factories, and was, as he had said, a well-known business man in Michigan; but, nevertheless, here was undoubted proof that he was a minion of Amalgamated Soap, a mere pawn in the hands of Peter Berrington and his strong colleague, Nicholson. Every penny John Steele possessed was sunk in Consolidated Sugar, and that these men meant to ruin him he had not the slightest doubt. The question was, How could they do it? Even if Metcalfe's books had been false, even if a hundred per cent, too much had been paid for the factories, there would still be something left for him out of the wreck. Yet from the moment he saw the face of Nicholson at that door, he knew Amalgamated Soap had determined to strip him of every *sou* he possessed. The first obvious suggestion that occurred to him was that here was the occasion for consulting a first-class lawyer, yet what could a lawyer do for him? He had no money to fight. The more he thought of the situation, the worse it appeared. No doubt Farwell Brothers were employees of Amalgamated Soap. No doubt the bank in which his funds were deposited belonged to the same all-embracing combination. There were a hundred perfectly legal methods by which the amount lodged there could be tied up, while, if he appealed to the law, the expense would be tremendous, and he might be dragged from court to court; new trial could follow new trial, and appeal tread on the heels of appeal until his millions had vanished into thin air. He was as entirely in the hands of Amalgamated Soap as if he had been tied in a bundle and presented to that celebrated company. Terror was imported into the situation by his uncertainty as to what method these financial buccaneers would adopt. Yet at that distressful moment his mind wandered to the comic opera of the "Mikado," and a smile came to his lips. Would it be long and lingering, with boiling oil at the end of it, or would it be the short, sharp shock of the executioner's stroke? His resentment turned more against the apparently honest Metcalfe than toward even Nicholson or Peter Berrington. He would have liked to throttle that man, but he knew that, whatever the outcome, he must retain his grip on himself and present an impassive exterior to his colleague and the world.

Next morning John Steele met his partner as usual with a smile on his face.

"Well, Metcalfe, how are things going?"

"Oh, everything's coming our way," said Metcalfe. "This trick will be done so easily that you'll wonder you ever doubted its success."

"Well, I hope so, I hope so," replied Steele, the possible double meaning of his partner's phrase striking him like a blow in the face; but the smile never wavered.

Technically the company had already been formed—that is to say, a number of clerks in Steele's office, together with the brothers Farwell, had constituted themselves the Consolidated Sugar Beet Company, with various powers duly set forth, organised under the laws of the State of New Jersey, and when officers were selected, the beet sugar factories were bought by this company at just double the price Steele and Metcalfe had paid for them. Then the officials resigned in a body, when cheques had been passed and everything done with beautiful legality, while Steele and Metcalfe and their nominees took their places on the board. It was arranged that there should be seven directors. Steele was to nominate two, and Metcalfe was to nominate two, while they were to agree mutually on the chairman. Metcalfe had proposed that the elder Farwell should be chairman, and he nominated the younger as his colleague on the board. Farwell, who knew every intricacy of company law, was accepted by Steele, and there was still one nomination open to Metcalfe, which name he excused himself at this time from proposing, as he was not well enough acquainted with business men in Chicago to fill the place at the moment. He even intimated that he was willing to accept a nominee of Steele's, and this seemingly friendly suggestion had prevented any suspicion of the board being packed against him, arising in Jack Steele's mind. He remembered this now with bitterness, when it was too late for remedy. Steele and his two colleagues could tie the vote of Metcalfe and his colleagues, but the chairman would have the casting vote. Since he had seen the determined face of Nicholson in the corridor of the Grand Pacific, he had no doubt that the Farwell brothers were the minions of Peter Berrington.

At last the trap laid for the public was sprung, and the public, as usual, was nipped. The success of the flotation was immediate, although applications did not come within a million of the sum asked for. After the flotation, Metcalfe's manner changed perceptibly. Steele watched him as a cat watches a mouse, and saw that he was now perturbed and apparently dissatisfied.

"Why!" cried Steele to him, the morning after the figures were known to them, "you don't seem nearly so happy as I expected. You surely did not look for the shares to be subscribed twice over?"

"No," said Metcalfe gloomily, "but the amount that has been subscribed shows what vitality there was in the scheme."

"Vitality!" cried Steele. "Bless my soul! you never doubted it, did you?"

"Oh, no, no," said Metcalfe hastily. "No. I told you we were dead sure of a third, and the actual subscriptions have more than justified my forecast."

"They have indeed!" cried Steele enthusiastically.

"I tell you what it is, Metcalfe, you're one of the first financiers of this country."

"Oh, nonsense!" cried Metcalfe, in no way cheered by the compliment.

"It isn't nonsense," said the genial Steele. "You've taken lessons from a first-rate master, for I look on Nicholson as one of the best men in the business."

When John Steele had plumped a similar pointed remark at Nicholson, not the slightest change of expression had disturbed that individual's calm visage. William Metcalfe kept his countenance under less perfect restraint. Steele's smile was gentle and friendly, but his keen eyes missed no note of the other's face. He watched a ruddy flush mount into his partner's cheeks. He noticed the embarrassed hesitation that accompanied his utterance.

"Mr. Nicholson! Ah, yes, certainly, certainly. He's not a friend of mine, of course, only a slight and recent acquaintance. Not the sort of man, Nicholson, to form friendships easily."

"Really?" asked Steele. "I met him only once, but he seemed rather genial."

"A great business man, a great business man," hurriedly muttered Metcalfe, obviously trying to get himself under control once more, playing for time, and not quite knowing what he was saying.

"So I have been informed," remarked Steele with easy carelessness. "One of the Amalgamated Soap group, I understand."

"Quite so," rejoined Metcalfe, his own man once more. "You see, Mr. Steele, I thought it would strengthen us tremendously if I could get a man like Nicholson to become interested in our project. The mere rumour that

Amalgamated Soap was behind us would have been worth millions to us at the present juncture."

"I quite agree with you, Metcalfe. Amalgamated Soap is a name to conjure with. The public worship success, and there you have success in its most highly developed form. Why didn't you let me know? I might have been of some assistance to you."

"Well, in the first place, I did not wish to mention so important a matter until I was sure of carrying it through. No use of giving promises that you cannot make good. In the second place, I was not aware that you knew Nicholson."

"Oh, you were quite right; it was just a casual meeting, when we were introduced by a mutual friend. I don't flatter myself that my views would have any influence upon a man of Nicholson's standing in the financial world. But there is another part I don't quite understand. I admit the value of Nicholson's name to us, but why wasn't his connection divulged in time to influence subscriptions?"

"You see, it was like this," hesitated Metcalfe, for a liar must be a most agile person, and Steele's questions had a fashion of touching the spot. "It was like this. I did not really conclude my arrangement with Nicholson until this morning. He's a very difficult man to handle, and he knows as well as anyone his own value. I imagine he wished to see which way the cat was going to jump before he committed himself."

"Well, Metcalfe, the cat has jumped entirely our way, even if the leap did not reach the furthest mark we staked out. The success of the subscriptions, then, induced Nicholson to join us?"

"Quite so, quite so, with the proviso that he is to have the vacant seat at the board, unless you have any objection."

"Objection? Certainly not. I am highly delighted with our acquisition. Besides, the seat at the board is entirely in your gift. I have no right to object, even if I wished to do so."

This was said with such an air of childlike simplicity that the perturbed Metcalfe, who seemingly still retained some remnants of conscience, showed confusion.

"True enough," he murmured. "Still, I should not like to nominate anyone who might be personally distasteful to you."

"I cannot imagine, Metcalfe, why you should suppose Nicholson could be distasteful to anyone. He is a tower of strength. I am overjoyed that you have induced him to join us."

"I am very much relieved to hear you say so," rejoined Metcalfe, who seemed bewildered at the turn things had taken.

The preliminary meetings of the company had all been held in Steele's offices. This afternoon, however, the directors were to forgather at the board-room of the bank in which the deposits of the subscribers were lodged. Steele was thus to beard the lion in the lion's own den, for he now no longer doubted that this bank was owned by Peter Berrington, Nicholson and their colleagues. The appointed hour was three o'clock, and John Steele arrived on the stroke, the last man to appear. Nicholson stood in the centre of the group. Metcalfe, who had quite recovered his composure, said with a fine air of good comradeship:

"I think you two gentlemen have met before, so a formal introduction is not necessary between Mr. Steele and Mr. Nicholson."

"I had the somewhat chastened satisfaction of encountering Mr. Steele once under conditions I am not likely to forget," said Nicholson quietly, with impressive geniality. "I count myself one of Mr. Steele's numerous admirers."

"It is kind of you to say that, Mr. Nicholson," replied John, extending his hand, while that winning smile of his played about his lips. "On the occasion to which you refer, I was so unhappy as to be placed in opposition to Amalgamated Soap. I am the more gratified, therefore, to find myself in some measure a colleague of so distinguished a coterie, even if I am admitted into but an outer temple, as it were."

"Your gratification, Mr. Steele, is as nothing compared to my own at seeing you here amongst us."

John Steele bowed his acknowledgment. It was if the lion had begun by complimenting Daniel.

"Gentlemen, I think the hour has struck," said the grave Farwell senior, taking his seat at the head of the long table.

The directors ranged themselves on either side, Nicholson at the right hand of the chairman, Metcalfe next him, and the younger Farwell the third on that side. Opposite Nicholson sat John Steele, and beside him his two nominees. Thus quietly the lines of battle were formed and to all outward appearance the meeting resembled a love-feast. Bunches of papers were heaped before the chairman, while writing-pads, pens and ink were placed in front of each director. Steele, assuming a negligent, unconcerned air that was admirably put on, wondered what particular battery Nicholson would unmask. The latter's eyes were bent on his writing-pad, and he tried one nib after another, as if to find a pen to his satisfaction. The chairman, in droning voice, recited the history of the company up to its going before the public, read documents, and gave various figures which it might be supposed were familiar to all there assembled. There was silence around the table. Nicholson never looked up until the chairman announced the amount of public subscription.

"What's that, Mr. Farwell?" he asked quietly, raising his head. "What are the figures?"

Farwell repeated them.

"And how much do you say is the authorised capital of the company?"

Farwell named the sum.

"Then we are a million short?"

"Nearly so, Mr. Nicholson."

Nicholson's face became set and stern. Slowly he turned towards Metcalfe on his right hand, whose eyes shifted uneasily from one to another without ever resting on John Steele.

"I understood, sir," said Nicholson very slowly, as if weighing his words, "that all the money was in the bank?"

"I told you, sir," replied the hesitating Metcalfe, "that there was in the bank all the capital we thought necessary."

"Necessary?" echoed Nicholson, in cold, even tones. "We make a demand upon the public. We state that the value of our property is so much. The public responds by offering us a million less. Necessary? I have never yet had anything to do with a company whose capital was not over-subscribed. I have never yet sanctioned the sending out of letters of allotment unaccompanied by letters of regret."

John Steele had difficulty in keeping the smile from his lips. The tones of righteous indignation were not in the least overdone. The expression of virtuous disapproval at being tricked, on the splendidly chiselled, clear-cut face, was marvellous in its reserve; in its hint of unlimited power behind. Steele felt, rather than saw, the uneasiness of the two colleagues by his side, who realised, without exactly understanding why, that things were going desperately wrong, like an engineer who sees an open bridge in front of him, and finds the brakes will not work.

"Admirably acted," said Steele to himself. "We pay good money to visit the theatre, and yet there is such histrionic talent as this in the business world."

Then aloud, in a voice mildly protesting, he said: "Nevertheless, Mr. Nicholson, the million shares left on our hands are quite marketable. We have ample capital to go on with, and Mr. Metcalfe will assure you that the factories themselves are all on a paying basis. You cannot surely mean that having arrived at this stage, we are not to proceed to allotment, Mr. Nicholson?"

"That is exactly what I *do* mean," replied Nicholson, speaking as mildly as his opponent had done. "My colleagues would never consent to admit connection with a company formed in the circumstances now before us. Our duty to the public——"

"Mr. Nicholson, I quite appreciate your position, and that of your colleagues, Mr. Peter Berrington and the rest. The public would indeed be shocked to learn that Peter, one of our religious pillars, could be guilty of anything in the least oblique. As cleanliness is next to godliness, we are all aware that Amalgamated Soap stands close to the Pearly Gates, and the only thing we fear about Peter is that when he gets to heaven he shall find another saint of the same name there before him, which may lead to confusion of identity. I take it for granted, Mr. Nicholson, that you are about to move a resolution requiring all this money to be returned to the subscribers. If you will propose such a motion, I shall be very happy to second it."

An electric silence fell on the group, the kind of silence which on a hot summer's night precedes a clap of thunder. Nicholson drew a long breath and squared his shoulders. Metcalfe gazed in fascinated dismay at John Steele. Even the Farwells showed traces of human interest. Nicholson did not venture to challenge a vote. After a few moments of this embarrassing stillness he said gently:

"Perhaps Mr. John Steele has something else to propose?"

"No, I have not," said Steele; "but with the chairman's permission, there being no motion before the house, I should like to make a personal explanation which may save you future trouble."

The chairman nodded permission, and Nicholson said:

"We shall be interested to hear anything you say, Mr. Steele."

"To return the money is, of course, to wreck the company. Hitherto this company has been associated with the names of John Steele and William Metcalfe. Tomorrow the sensation of the daily journals all over the country will be the collapse of the big scheme which those two men undertook to float. Mr. William Metcalfe is unknown in Chicago; is but a stool-pigeon well paid for the part he has enacted, and he disappears from the scene.

John Steele stands the brunt. All the funds he possesses are in Amalgamated Soap's bank. His affairs are in the hands of Amalgamated Soap lawyers. One legal difficulty after another comes up; there is a long fight over the remains, and at last Amalgamated Soap steps in and sweeps up the *débris*. They are in possession of valuable property scattered throughout the West in the beet-sugar line; they announce their possession and the reconstruction of the company, and everything is beautiful, but John Steele is mangled in the collision, with no insurance, even for his relatives.

"When I learned the other week that Mr. Nicholson was interested in this company, I felt like the man who had gone down into a cave and unexpectedly clutched a huge bear at the black bottom of it. That man did not stop to question the intentions of the bear; he simply got out. I followed his example. In the wheat deal Mr. Nicholson knows of, I made several millions, and ever since then certain capitalists in this city have begged me if I fell in with a similar good thing not to hug it all to myself, but allow them to come in on the ground floor, and I promised to do so. The moment I knew Mr. Nicholson was to have something to do with the beet-sugar project, I went directly to these capitalists, pledged them to secrecy, guaranteed that Amalgamated Soap was head and shoulders in this deal, and that no less a person than Mr. Nicholson himself would assume charge of the company. Gentlemen, they bit instantly. I sold out my share to them for the money it had cost me, and fifty per cent, additional; and, furthermore, I got the cash. Now I shall read you a letter which will appear in the Chicago newspapers to-morrow morning."

To the Editor:

Sir—The Consolidated Beet Sugar Company, with which my name has hitherto been associated, and which has been so splendidly supported by Western capital, as indicated by the subscriptions now in the bank, will hereafter be in charge of the eminent financiers associated with Amalgamated Soap. I am pleased to state that this will be almost entirely a Chicago enterprise, and that some of the best men in this city have bought out my interests therein. I have only to add that Mr. Nicholson himself is now a member of the board of directors, and nothing further need be said to assure all concerned of the immense prosperity which awaits this company, and the far-reaching advantages it will offer both to agriculture and manufacture in the West.

Yours sincerely,

John Steele.

"And now, gentlemen," said Steele, as he folded up the copy of this letter and placed it in his inside pocket, "nothing remains for me to do but to resign my seat on the board, as I have no longer the slightest interest in this company. But before handing in my formal resignation, I shall be pleased to second any motion Mr. Nicholson cares to propose."

"Mr. Chairman," said Nicholson, quite unruffled, "I move we now proceed to allotment."

"I have pleasure in seconding the motion," said John Steele, rising, bowing to the company, and leaving the room.

---

# CHAPTER XIII.
# PERSONALLY CONDUCTED BY A GIRL

SUGAR is a fattening product, and the Consolidated Beet Sugar Company waxed fat and prospered. Its shares stood high on the Stock Exchange, and the members of the syndicate to whom John Steele had sold his portion were exuberantly grateful to the young man for the opportunity he had given them. His reputation of possessing a keen financial brain was enhanced by the forming of this company; for it was supposed that it was he who had induced Amalgamated Soap to take it up. It was erroneously surmised that the great Peter Berrington and his colleagues had been so much impressed by Steele's genius in the wheat deal, where he was opposed to them, that they now desired the co-operation of this rising young figure in the commercial world. No hint of the momentary death-struggle in the board-room of the bank had ever leaked out through the solid doors. Steele was now one of the men to be counted with in the large affairs of the Western metropolis. Everything he touched was successful. Personally he was liked, and great social success might have been his had he cared for society, which he did not. He was commonly rated as being worth anywhere from six to ten millions, and the world looked upon him as the most fortunate of men. It did him no harm to be thought to enjoy the backing of the powerful Peter Berrington, and probably not more than half-a-dozen men knew that such was far from being the case. He did not bask in Peter's smile, but, on the contrary, shivered in his shadow.

The one man who had no delusions on the subject was John Steele himself. For the second time he had been entirely victorious over Nicholson and the gigantic coterie behind him; but this, strange as it may appear, gave him no satisfaction. If he had won the determined fight through his own superior skill, or because of some great display of mental power, he might have rested more at ease. Had that been the case, he would have awaited the next onslaught with more equanimity than he at present possessed; but he knew that his victory came to him through chance; chance multiplied again and again. It was chance that his partner had been out of his room when the messenger-boy brought the telegram. It was chance that Steele had opened the envelope. It was chance that he knew a man who could decode the cipher before it was too late for him to take action on the information it carried. After these three lucky throws of the dice, he admitted to himself that he had handled the situation with diplomatic success; but it disturbed him to remember that all his vigilance would have proved unavailing, had not pure luck stood his friend. Yet, after all, the initial mistake was Nicholson's, who should not have sent a cipher telegram to the office of the man he intended to destroy. Nicholson presumably did not know that his agent was actually housed with Steele, and it was a mistake on Metcalfe's part not to have furnished his chief with this information. But even putting the best face upon the matter, he could not conceal from himself the large part that luck had played in compassing his salvation.

This never-lifted shadow of the silent Peter Berrington began to produce its effect upon him. He became timourous—afraid to venture in any large concern. He knew he was wasting time in pottering with small affairs—street railways in outside towns, the installing of electric light here and there, and such enterprises, which furnished only a moderate revenue to an enterprising speculator. Time and again he refused chances involving large amounts which turned out tremendously lucrative to the promoters, but which he had been afraid to touch, fearing the grip of Peter Berrington's unseen hand on his throat. He began to acquire the unexpected reputation of being an over-cautious capitalist, and finally well-known people, who formerly professed much admiration for him, ceased to come to his office with their schemes. Steele laughed uneasily to himself as he thought that Peter Berrington might perhaps accomplish his purpose by the gradual wearing down of his courage. Of course, the fact that a project became successful was no proof that the hand of Nicholson was not concealed somewhere within its intricacies to clutch at John Steele if he had become involved. He tried to shake off this depression, and once or twice plunged rather recklessly, only to become nervous before the climax arrived and sell out, sometimes at a small profit and sometimes at a loss.

At last he came to the conclusion that it was not Peter Berrington at all, or his shadow, that was affecting him, but the usual breakdown which afflicts strenuous business men in the stimulating atmosphere of a great American city.

"My nerve's gone; that's what's the matter with me," he said to himself. "I must go and rough it for a summer in the mountains, or else take a trip to some spa in Europe. If I keep on like this, I shall be utterly useless in a live city like Chicago."

He consulted several of his friends—many of them, in fact—and told them he was feeling far from fit. His complaint was common enough, and every man to whom he spoke suggested a remedy. Some advised the plunging into dissipation at a fashionable health resort, and some recommended various medicinal springs in Europe which would work wonders; but the majority counselled him to take rod and gun, and get into the Rocky Mountains, camp out, and live like an Indian.

"Then," they said jocularly, smiting him on the back, "you'll be all right, and come back yearning for scalps on the Stock Exchange."

The newspapers mentioned the fact that John Steele was going into the Rockies to hunt and fish and camp out for a month or more to recover tone.

It was at this interesting juncture that Alice Fuller called to see him. Now, John Steele was the most susceptible of men, and one reason he shunned society was because he knew he would surely fall a victim to the first designing pretty girl who laid a trap for him—if, indeed, pretty girls ever do lay traps for men said to possess from six to ten millions. His weakness in this line was exemplified by his impetuous proposal to Dorothy Slocum in the environs of Bunkerville, as has already been stated. But Alice Fuller was not the commonplace young person Dorothy Slocum had been. He often thought of his proposal to Dorothy with a shudder, and accounted it a narrow escape, which, indeed, it was not, for Dorothy was thoroughly devoted to her station-master, and never gave even a thought to Mr. John Steele of Chicago.

Alice Fuller was a blonde, and she brought in with her to the conventional private office of John Steele, with its extremely modern fittings of card indices, loose-leaf ledgers, and expanding office furniture, an air of breezy freshness that hinted of the mountainous West. Although dressed as any Chicago woman might be, there was, nevertheless, something about her costume which suggested the riding of mountain ponies and even the expert handling of a rifle.

The glory of a woman is her hair, and in truth Miss Fuller's golden tresses were glorious enough; but her eyes were the most distinguished and captivating features of a face sufficiently beautiful to attract attention anywhere. They were of a deep, translucent blue, darkening now and then into violet, like a pair of those limpid mountain lakes in the Rockies whose depths are said to be unfathomable. It was impossible to look into those honest orbs without trusting the clear purity of the soul behind them, and Steele, whose nerves were unstrung, almost shivered with apprehension when they were turned full upon him.

"Lord save me!" he thought with a gasp. "If this girl wants to sell shares in the most bogus company afloat, I'm her victim. John Steele, if your bank account is to remain intact, now is the time to play St. Anthony."

But aloud he said calmly enough: "Pray be seated, madam," and she sank gracefully into a chair on the opposite side of the flat-topped desk behind which he was entrenched, although small protection the barricade afforded him against such artillery as a handsome young woman might bring to bear upon the position.

"It is so good of you to see me," said the girl. "I have read much of you in the newspapers, and I know that your time is valuable, so I shall take up as little of it as may be necessary to explain my business."

Somehow this remark, although only introductory sparring, disappointed young Mr. Steele. Nearly every stranger he met said the same thing in almost identical words. They all referred to his newspaper reputation, of which he was exceedingly tired, and nearly everyone spoke of the value of his time, promised not to encroach upon it, and then stayed for hours if they were permitted.

"My time is of little value at the present moment, Miss Fuller, because I am doing nothing. For some months past I have been rather out of health, and, in fact, within a few days I expect to leave Chicago."

"Yes," she rejoined, "I saw that also in the papers. I read that you intended to go West among the mountains. Is that true?"

"Such are my present intentions, but they are always liable to change. A man who is fighting his own nerves is rather capricious, you know."

"Like a woman," laughed Miss Alice. "Well, it is on account of the statement in the Press that I am here. I have been thinking of calling upon you for a long time, but it appears we have no mutual friends who could give me an introduction, and so, seeing you were about to leave the city, I said to myself: 'It's now or never.'The reference to the mountains struck me as a lucky omen. You know we women are rather superstitious, Mr. Steele, and I think it was that even more than your impending departure which gave me courage to venture up here."

"I am very glad you came," said John Steele gallantly, "and I shall be more than pleased if there is anything I can do for you."

"My father is the owner of a gold-mine in the Black Hills. Do you know anything of mines, Mr. Steele?"

John slowly shook his head. The mere mention of a gold-mine did something to clarify his brain from the glamour that was befogging it.

"I know nothing whatever about mines, Miss Fuller, excepting the fact that more gold has been sunk in goldmines than has ever been taken out of them."

"Oh, I'm sorry to hear you say that," replied the girl, with a slight tremor of apprehension in her voice, "and, furthermore, I do not in the least believe it to be true. Indeed, it cannot be true, because it is impossible to sink gold without first having mined it. Nothing can be more lucrative than a good gold-mine, for its product is one of the few things taken from the earth which do not fluctuate in value. With copper, or silver, or iron, you are dependent on the market; not so with gold."

"You are a very eloquent advocate, Miss Fuller. Where is your father?"

The girl looked up quickly at this sudden change of subject, and once more John fell under the fascination of those enchanting eyes.

"My father? He is in Chicago."

"Then, Miss Fuller, the best plan will be to have him call upon me, and we can discuss the mine together."

"Alas!" said the young woman, with a mournful droop of the head, "if that had been possible, I should not have been here. My father at the present moment is very ill and quite unable to discuss business with anyone. You are going from the city to the mountains in search of health. He has come from the mountains to the city on the same quest. The gold-mine is at once our hope and our despair. If it can be properly worked, we are certain it will produce riches incalculable; but it takes money to make money, and my father knows no wealthy people nor does he possess the necessary capital for the preliminary outlay. We are somewhat like King Midas, in danger of starving with gold all around us."

"Has the mine been opened, or is it only a prospective claim?"

"At the present moment there are from sixteen to twenty miners working upon it. The shaft, I believe, is something like a hundred feet deep, and one or two short galleries have been run. The ore assay is extremely rich; I have not the figures with me, but can easily bring them; and the reports are better and better as the miners proceed."

"If that be the case, Miss Fuller, I see no reason why you should lack for capital."

"There are a hundred reasons, but one is sufficient. Every capitalist shuns a gold-mine. They speak just as you spoke a moment ago. Then, you see, our lives having been spent in the West, we know very few Eastern people, and those few have no money. The great difficulty is not in proving the wealth of the mine, but in getting a capitalist to listen. If you promise to listen, I shall undertake to prove to you that this is one of the most valuable properties in the world."

"Well, Miss Fuller, I am listening; but, as I told you, I know nothing whatever about gold-mines, and, indeed, am rather afraid of them. If the mine is producing ore in paying quantity, why does not your father have that ore crushed?—I suppose they could do that in the neighbourhood, or at Denver, or wherever the nearest mining town is—and with the product keep himself and pay his men?"

"That is exactly what he has done, Mr. Steele, and a ruinous thing it is to do. If it were not for that, we should have had to give up the struggle long ago. But there are no mines within miles of us, and we are two days and a half's journey from the nearest railway. Ore is bulky and heavy, and the transport alone over those mountain roads, which are not roads at all, and scarcely even paths, is at once slow and expensive. Railway freight is high, and when the ore gets to the reducing-plant, we have to take exactly what is given us, because beggars cannot be choosers. We need machinery at the mouth of the pit, and whoever will furnish the money for that machinery is sure to reap a rich reward."

"Nevertheless—" protested John, but the girl interrupted him, her eyes aglow with fervour.

"You promised to listen, you know. There is another point I wish to put before you. The ore is very rich, and if we ship much of it, there is bound to be inquiry as to where it came from. Now, my father has been able to stake out only a comparatively small claim. If once it becomes known where this ore originates, there will be the usual rush. The rush is ultimately inevitable in any case, but my father is anxious to be fully secure before it comes."

"I'll tell you what I'll do, Miss Fuller," said John in a burst of enthusiasm, "I'll give you a thousand dollars; and if you make money out of your mine, you can repay me at your leisure."

Alice Fuller slowly shook her golden head.

"I could not accept money in that way," she said. "It is like the giving of charity when a pathetic tale is told. Besides, a thousand dollars would be of no particular use; it would not purchase the stamp-mills, or transport them to the mine. In two months, or three, we should be just where we are now, and the thousand dollars would be gone."

"What is it, then, you wish me to do, Miss Fuller?"

"I wish our transaction to be upon a sane business basis, and I don't want you to offer me a thousand dollars or twenty thousand dollars, or two hundred thousand dollars again."

"I beg your pardon. I had no thought of charity or anything of the sort when I made my proposal."

"I am sure you hadn't," said the girl, with a naïve confidence which Steele found very charming. "I'll tell you what I wish to suggest. You are going to the mountains in any case. Very well, go to the Black Hills; there you will find the air pure and bracing; there are wild mountains and sparkling streams, and everything that a tired city man could desire. I want you to camp near our mine and investigate it thoroughly. If you are so satisfied with it as to justify the risk, I ask you to be prepared to buy a half share for three hundred thousand dollars."

John Steele drew a long breath.

"My purpose in going to the mountains is to get away from business, and not to take upon myself a new anxiety; to fish and shoot, not to pore over gold-bearing ore."

"Are you an enthusiastic sportsman, then?"

"Not at all. I was too busy when I was young to indulge in such recreation, and too poor. Since then I have become busier still."

"And too rich?" suggested the girl, with a smile.

"A man is never too rich, I am afraid."

"If you are not an enthusiastic sportsman, a week in the woods will prove more than enough for you. After that comes boredom, and a yearning for the ticker and the morning newspaper."

"I more than half believe you're right," said Steele ruefully.

"Of course I am right. Now, if you camp out beside the mine, you have something to interest you. Don't bother about it for the first week. There is plenty of shooting and fishing in the neighbourhood."

"I hate to put two and a half days between me and a telegraph-wire."

"Then you had better leave mountains alone and stay in Chicago."

John laughed.

"You are a very clever young lady, Miss Fuller, and I wonder you haven't made that gold-mine a success on your own."

"I am doing it now," she said with a flash almost of defiance from her eyes.

Again the young man laughed.

"Are you?" he asked. "You women have us at a disadvantage when you talk business, but I am going to get right down to plain facts, and speak to you as if you were your own brother. You won't be offended?"

"Not in the least."

"Very well. Do you know what a salted mine is?"

"Certainly. I thought you said you knew nothing of mines? A salted mine is one in which rich ore has been planted for the cheating of fools."

"An admirable definition, Miss Fuller. Well, in the matter of mines I'm a fool, and a salted mine would take me in as a gold brick on State Street would delude an Illinois farmer."

"Then induce an expert to go with you—a mining expert who knows pay ore when he sees it."

"I am more distrustful of mining experts than of salted mines."

The girl sighed.

"I suppose all faith has left Chicago?"

"It has—in gold-mines."

"Now, Mr. Steele, I'll talk to you as if you were your own sister. Have you ever done a stroke of useful toil since you were born?"

"Oh, yes; I worked on a railway."

"Very well. Go to the Black Hills and take a miner's outfit with you. Become for the time one of my father's workmen—or, rather, boss of the gang, if you like. Go into that mine, and direct them where they are to run the next level, and follow that level for a month, working with the men and keeping clear of the blasts. After you have penetrated a month in any direction you please, take the ore from the last blast and have it assayed. A mine can't be salted under those conditions. If that whole mountain is salted with gold, you'd better buy it."

"No one can gainsay the honesty of that, Miss Fuller; but, to tell you the truth, I dread the two and a half days' journey from the railway."

"You don't need to. I will be your guide."

"What!" cried John, in amazement.

"I'll take you from the railway to the Hard Luck mine. Will you go?" she demanded with a touch of defiance.

"Go!" he cried, discretion struggling with enthusiasm. "Of course I'll go. Nothing would give me greater pleasure. But, then, on the other hand—you see—well—to speak quite frankly, for a young lady to—to, as one might say, journey across the plains——"

"Yes, I know, I know. You are talking now, not to my brother, as you remarked a while ago, but to my brother's sister. All my life I have had not only to take care of myself, but of my father as well. This project is a matter of vital importance to me, and I cannot allow it to fail merely because the rules of society would frown on what I intend to do. I shall take with me my own tent, and an old man who was in my father's employ long before I was born. This is a cold business deal, and no other consideration is going to enter into it. So let us brush aside every other consideration and come down to plain facts. You offered me a thousand dollars, and I refused it. If you will now give me the necessary money, which may be anything from two hundred dollars upwards, depending on what you want to take with you, I shall go at once to Pickaxe Gulch, which is the nearest railway station to the Hard Luck mine, and will collect what transport we need. There I shall await your coming. Do you intend to take any servants with you?"

"I shall be accompanied by Sam Jackson, a negro man, who is the best cook in this town."

"Very well, you will need a horse for him, and one for yourself; I shall need two horses; that's four. Then if you will give me an idea of the number of tents and boxes you require, I shall secure mules enough to carry them. We shall want two or three men to look after the mules, and you must give me a week at least to get this cavalcade together. Sometimes there are neither animals nor men at Pickaxe Gulch, but I intend to telegraph at once and secure whatever transport is available."

John Steele smiled his appreciation of the capability displayed by the fearless young woman, opened his drawer, and took out a cheque-book.

"Shall we say five hundred dollars?" he asked, looking across the desk at her. "You must leave some money with your father, you know."

"Five hundred will be ample," she replied decidedly, and he wrote a cheque for that amount.

Later on in his life Steele remembered that demand for money with admiration. It was just one of those little points where a less subtle person than Miss Fuller would have made a mistake, deluded by success in getting him to promise to make the trip. But the young woman was evidently shrewd enough to know that after she left he would wonder, she having pleaded poverty, where the money came from to pay for so long a railway journey and at the same time provide for an ailing father at home. He always regarded that request for expenses as the climax of a well-thought-out plan.

# CHAPTER XIV
# AN IMPORTANT CHAMPAGNE LUNCH.

WHEN John Steele stepped down from the sleeping-car in the early morning at Pickaxe Gulch, he found Alice Fuller the sole occupant of the platform. She welcomed him with the cordiality of good comradeship. Her costume differed rather strikingly from the apparel she wore in his office. She reminded him of one of those reckless female riders he had seen at Buffalo Bilks Wild West Show, and he was forced to confess that the outfit suited her to perfection. She was even more attractive than when he had first seen her, and he could hardly have believed that possible. Before he ventured to compliment the young woman on her appearance, she complimented him on his.

"You are already looking very much better than you did in the city."

"Yes!" he cried jubilantly. "Your visit did me ever so much good; and, besides that, I am now out from under Peter's shadow."

"'Peter's shadow?'" she repeated. "What is that? The shadow of a mountain?"

"In a way, yes," laughed Steele, "and a gold-producing mountain at that. I have been a rather anxious person these many months past; but now, whether it is the exhilaration of the air in the West, or the prospect"—he hesitated a moment, then continued—"of this journey, I am quite my own man once more."

Without reply she led the way to the dusty road which ran between two rows of roughly built shanties.

"Did you breakfast on the train?" she asked.

"No."

"I thought you might not have an opportunity to get anything to eat on the train, as it stops here so early, and I have ordered a meal for you at the one tavern in this place, which is far from being first-class. However, possibly, you can endure such a repast for once and then we will get on our way as soon as possible."

"Oh, the cuisine of the West is no surprise to me," said Steele. "I've had a good deal of experience with it in my time."

They walked up the street together, the negro cook following and carrying Steele's valise. At the tavern the caravan was collected, and more than ever the resemblance to the Wild West Show impressed itself upon the young man. The boxes had been sent on some days ahead, and were now securely fastened to the backs of the mules. Four saddle-horses were tied to the rude pillars of the verandah. Steele went inside the building and partook of the breakfast, such as it was, and ten minutes later the procession started north.

Their route lay across the plain, and during the forenoon the party traversed a road of sorts, reasonably well defined. In the horizon loomed low mountains, which did not seem perceptibly nearer when a halt was called by the side of a stream to prepare lunch. Steele was more accustomed to a street-car than to the back of a horse; but the way was level, and the horse developed none of those buck-jumping peculiarities which John, in his Eastern ignorance, had always associated with the steeds of the Far West. His business heretofore had never taken him away from a line of railway, and where it had been necessary to make a road journey, the jaunt was accomplished in some sort of vehicle. However, he soon became accustomed to his new method of locomotion and succeeded better than he had anticipated.

Alice Fuller proved a most expert horse-woman, and her superb attitude in the saddle still further enslaved this ardent young man, who began to think he had never really lived until now. He was rather disappointed, but rendered none the less eager, to find that he was not getting as much of her company as he had hoped. In the beginning they rode side by side in front of the cavalcade, to be out of the dust which the mule train raised. But every now and then she wheeled her horse round and allowed the procession to pass her, scanning each animal and its burden with the eye of an expert, seeing that everything was in order. When Steele expressed admiration of her capability, Miss Fuller told him she had many times been in full charge of a similar expedition going or coming from the mine; and once when he complained of lack of companionship, she informed him that success depended a great deal on the first few hours of the march, and it was her duty to see that none of the animals fell lame, and that no burden shifted, thus causing a mule to lag behind its fellows.

"To-morrow," she said, "we shall be among the foothills, and even this afternoon we shall be free of the road and the dust. Then, if everything is going well, I may find plenty of time to talk to you, for I see you are anxious to learn more about the mine before you reach it."

Steele threw a free-hearted laugh on the echoless air. Any little incident seemed now a fit subject for mirth. The clear atmosphere seemed as exhilarating as wine, and there was the further intoxicant of the girl's alluring presence.

Lunch by the side of the stream more than made amends for the unattractive breakfast. The efficient Jackson had caused each of the numerous boxes to be numbered, and he began with Number One, which his master said was a very good thing to look after. He produced a portable stove, and a handful of coke performed miracles in the desert. It was soon evident that John Steele had no intention of starving while he wandered in the wilderness. He drew from its straw envelope a bottle of prime champagne, a drink which doubtless had never quenched thirst on that particular route before. Miss Fuller partook of the wine but sparingly, and lifted her glass when he proposed the toast of success to the expedition, thrilling him as she did so with those enthralling eyes of hers, and the young man began to wonder whether he actually saw heaven in their depths, or was looking at a desert mirage through an atmosphere of sparkling wine.

He persuaded her to linger after the cavalcade had moved on, saying they would overtake it at a gallop, and the young woman, with scarcely concealed reluctance, acquiesced. He threw himself full length at her feet and gazed up at her, while she watched, with the suggestion of a frown on her smooth brow, the procession lessening in the distance. He lit a cigarette, with her permission; and began the sort of conversation which a young man in the early stages of fascination is prone to indulge in. At first it seemed to him her thoughts were elsewhere, which was not in the least flattering to a person who was doing his best. On his chiding her for this, she drew a sharp breath and cast a glance upon him which he fancied was the reverse of friendly. It was veiled an instant after, and then, with something like a sigh, she appeared to accept the situation.

At this presaging of victory, John Steele's conscience began to trouble him. He guessed why she appeared so changeable. Her father's future and her own depended on the good-will of the young man stretched at her feet. She was anxious not to offend him, and yet her reluctance to remain alone with him, her absent-minded look, and the slight frown that now and then marred her brow, were hints that his attentions proved unwelcome. Steele surmised that any undue compliments or any too palpable indulgence in sentiment at this particular moment might prove disastrous to ultimate success. The resigned air with which she endeavoured to face a *tete-a-tete* not to her liking touched his pride, and also made him rather ashamed of himself for taking advantage of one who in the circumstances was helpless. He wondered if he could put this girl more at ease by telling her he had quite made up his mind to finance the mine, whether it proved all she said or the reverse. Yet she might regard this statement as merely an unblushing bid for her preference, for she knew that until he had examined the mine any such avowal would be made merely because he thought it would please her. While these thoughts ran through his mind, a silence had fallen between them, which, however, the girl appeared not to notice, for her eyes were fixed on the distant mountains. She was quite startled by the suddenness with which he sprang to his feet.

"Miss Fuller," he cried, "I see you are anxious to be off towards the hills, and it is selfish of me to detain you here."

He held out his hand to her and helped her up. She smiled very sweetly and said:

"I think it is time we were on our way again. We have further to go than you suspect, before we reach the regular camping-ground."

He had reason to congratulate himself on his intuition, for during that journey she was kinder to him than she had ever been before, as if anxious to make up for her former coldness.

The sun had gone down ere they reached the halting-station for the night. They were now on an elevated plateau among the hills, and an impetuous torrent near by gave forth the only sound that broke the intense stillness. Tents were pitched, horses and mules tethered, and Jackson set out a dinner which their keen appetites made doubly memorable. Night came down, and the moon rose gloriously in the east. Time and place were ideal for a lovers' meeting, but the adage which intimates that luck with gold does not run parallel with luck in love proved true in this instance. Immediately after partaking of the excellent coffee Jackson had brewed, the young woman rose and held out her hand, pleading fatigue.

"I must bid you 'Good night,'" she said shortly.

"Oh! won't you stay a little while and enjoy this unexampled moonlight? It seems as if I had never seen the moon before."

The young woman smiled wanly, but shook her head.

"I'm really very tired," she explained. "I have had a week of it at that awful hotel in the Gulch. It is fearfully noisy at night with drinking cowboys and miners, and so I have had scarcely any sleep for a long while. If I have proved a dull companion to-day, that is the reason, and I am sure you will excuse me now."

"Miss Fuller, you could not be dull if you tried. I am sorry you should have had so much trouble on my account at that terrible station. I should have sent a man, but I could not guess the horrors of the place before seeing it. Pray forgive my selfishness."

"Oh, that was really nothing. I am quite accustomed to the life; but, somehow, the first night in the mountains always leaves me stupid and drowsy."

"To-morrow night, then," he said very quietly, "we may perhaps view the moonlight together."

"To-morrow night," she murmured and was gone.

Steele threw himself into the canvas camp-chair, and, reclining, gazed on the moonlit plain below and listened to the roar of the torrent. Dreamily he fancied himself floating in the seventh heaven of bliss.

Next morning the camp was early astir, for a long day of mountaineering lay ahead. The party numbered seven, all told, there being three men of peaceable demeanour, but rough aspect, in charge of the pack-train. At no time during that day did Steele secure an opportunity of speaking with Alice Fuller alone. They could not ride together, as the mountain path was too narrow. After dinner, at the final camping-place, a wild spot in a profound valley, where John saw with dismay the moon would not be visible, the girl seemed loth to keep him company as had been the case the night before. She laughed somewhat harshly, he thought, when he complained that she must have known they could not see the moon.

"You can study its rays on the northern peaks," she said. "Who would ever have expected a modern financier to yearn for the moon?"

"A modern financier is but a man, after all," protested Steele.

"I have sometimes doubted it," replied the girl cynically.

"Well, Miss Fuller, if you will sit down again, even in the absence of moonlight, I think I can remove your doubts."

She stood there hesitating for a few moments, but it was too dark to see the expression on her face. Finally she sat down in the chair from which she had risen.

"I am seated," she said; "but not to talk of moonlight, merely to tell you that I intend to go no farther. To-morrow morning we bid 'Good-bye' to each other. You go north, and I go south."

"Oh, I say," cried John reproachfully, "that's contrary to contract. You promised to lead me to the mine."

"I know I did; but it is always a woman's privilege to change her mind. Perhaps you will understand I do not wish to influence you at all in the decision you may come to about the mine."

"Would it make you abjure your cruel resolve if I informed you that I have quite determined to invest in the mine if it gives any show of success, which I am sure it will do from what you have told me about it?"

"The mine must plead its own cause," she said, with an indifference that amazed him. "You have no real need of me as a guide, for the three men I engaged know the route as well as I do. They have been over it often enough. I am really very anxious about my father. He promised to telegraph me at Pickaxe Gulch, but has not done so. I sent a despatch the day before you arrived, but no reply came, and it may be waiting for me now at the office there."

"Why not send back one of the men?"

"Because of my own anxiety. I fear the telegram may call me to his side. I think you will understand now why I have been distraught while in your company."

"Miss Fuller, believe me, I am very sorry to hear that this worry has been hanging over you. If I had known, I should have proposed our remaining at Pickaxe Gulch until you had heard from your father. I fear my own conduct and conversation may have added to your discomfort."

"Oh, no, no," said the girl, quickly rising again.

"Will you accept this trifle from me?"

He spoke hurriedly, and took from his waistcoat pocket something that she knew to be a ring, for even in the dim light it sparkled as if fire were playing from its facets.

"I'd rather not," she replied, stepping back.

"It will bind you to nothing—nothing at all. It is simply to keep me in your memory until we next meet."

"Oh, I shall never forget you!" she cried, in a tone of bitterness that startled him.

"It is a mere trinket," he urged, "and I bought it for you before I left civilisation. If you do not accept it, I shall throw it into the darkness of the valley yonder."

"That would be foolish, even for you."

"Why, Miss Fuller, such a remark has a very dubious sound. What do you mean by it? Do you think I am foolish?"

"Oh, I don't think anything at all of either you or your folly. I tell you I merely want to get away."

"Won't you take the ring with you?"

She stood for a long time with head bowed.

"I don't suppose it makes any difference one way or the other," she said at last.

"Of course it doesn't. I told you it wouldn't."

"Very well, I shall take the ring, if you will accept a much cheaper and more significant present from me in the morning."

"I shall accept gratefully anything you like to give me, Miss Fuller, in the morning or at any future time."

"I wonder," was all her comment, as she took the ring and instantly disappeared.

Somehow this night held none of the glamour that distinguished the previous evening. The depth of the profound shadows surrounding him was merely emphasised by the touch of cold moonlight on the hilltops far away. John wondered if the exhilarating effect of the atmosphere had departed, leaving him sober again. He felt strangely depressed, and although he immediately entered his tent and flung himself, dressed as he was, upon his canvas cot, he found it difficult to sleep. It was after midnight before he dozed off, and then his slumber was troubled and uneasy. Towards morning, however, a kind of stupor descended upon him, leaving him dreamless and lost to the world. This was broken by a sharp and angry voice, whose meaning did not at first reach his consciousness; but the sentence lingered in his awakening mind and at last became clear to him, as an image comes out during the gradual development of a photographic plate.

"I tell you I will not leave until I bid 'good-bye' to Mr. Steele."

It was Alice Fuller's voice, and in an instant the young man was on his feet and out of the tent. Day had just dawned, gray and chill, but already the camp was astir and the young woman in her saddle.

"Did you call me?" he cried.

"No," she answered; but he seemed to detect a tremor of fear in her voice.

"I thought I heard you say you wished to bid 'goodbye' to me!"

"You must have been dreaming. But I do wish to bid you 'good-bye.'"

Two of the muleteers stood near, and the old attendant, mounted, had already started slowly on his way. John sprang to her side, and as he came to a stand by the horse, she stooped and slipped a small box into his coat pocket.

"Good-bye! good-bye!" she cried somewhat boisterously, with an exclamation that seemed to be half sob and half laugh. "Go back to your tent at once and brush your hair. It's enough to frighten anyone," and now she laughed with unnecessary vehemence, the near mountains echoing the peal with a strange mocking cadence that sent a chill up the spine of one listener.

"What does this mean?" he asked himself.

The man at the bridle turned the horse's head towards the distant railway, and the other smote the steed on the flank.

"Let go my horse!" commanded Miss Fuller savagely. The man slouched away. She touched the animal with her heel and galloped off, while Steele stood in a daze watching her. Only once she looked back, then made a quick motion to the pocket of her jacket and disappeared round the ledge of rock. Jack remembered the packet she had dropped into his pocket, and imagining her gesture might have reference to that, walked to his tent to examine the present so surreptitiously given him, remembering that she had said the night before it would prove more significant than the ring she had so reluctantly accepted. It was a little, square parcel, tied in a bit of newspaper with a red string. He whisked this off, and held in his hand a box of white metal. Opening the box he saw within it a simple cake of soap!

Steele held this on his open palm, gazing at it like one hypnotised.

"My God!" he groaned at last, "soap—Amalgamated Soap! Peter Berrington and Nicholson! Trapped, as I am a fool and a sinner! These muleteers are the real chiefs of this expedition. They saw Alice Fuller weakening; but she weakened too late, and now they have sent her away.

What's the object of all this? It is too fantastic to imagine that Nicholson supposes he can exact all I possess as ransom. Even the Black Hills are not the mountains of Greece. What is it, then? Murder? That's equally incredible, and yet possible. Here am I unarmed, rifles in the boxes, no one with me but a cowardly nigger. Walked right into the trap with my eyes open, like a gaping idiot! Well, John Steele, you deserve all you will get! Let's discover what it is."

He strode out of the tent. The negro was preparing breakfast. The three men stood in a group together, talking, but they looked round and became silent as he approached.

"I have changed my mind," said Steele; "we're going back to the railway."

"Oh, no, we're not," said one of the men, stepping forward, and taking a revolver from his hip pocket; "we're going on to the mine."

"Is there a mine?" asked Steele, with a sneering laugh.

"Oh, there's a mine all right enough, and they're waiting for you there."

"Who?"

"You'll find out about twelve o'clock to-day."

"See here, boys," said Steele persuasively, "I'll make you three the richest men in this part of the country if you'll accompany me safely back to the railway."

"We've heard that kind of talk before," replied the man, "and have had enough of it. You tell that to the boss of the gang at the mine; and whatever he says, we'll agree to."

"Yes, but at the mine—How many are there, by the way?"

"You'll see when you reach the spot."

"Well, even if there's one more, he divides the loot with you. You can make better terms with me now than you can at the mine."

"Chuck it, stranger. There ain't no use giving us any more taffy. You're going on to the mine."

"All right," said Steele, turning on his heel. "I'll have breakfast first. Is the coffee ready, Jackson?"

"Yes, sir."

The prisoner sat down at the collapsible table and enjoyed a hearty meal.

At noon they reached the mine, and a dozen, gaunt, wild-eyed men, who were sitting round, stood up when the riders came into sight. They gave no cheer when they saw the captive, nor did their attitude of listless, bored indifference change a particle as Steele stopped his horse and dismounted.

"Here's the goods," said the leader of the muleteers, and the boss of the mining gang nodded, but made no reply.

"Good day, gentlemen," began Steele, a smile coming to his lips in spite of the seriousness of the crisis, as he thought that this sombre, silent gang in the midst of the mountains bore a comical resemblance to the gnomes in Rip Van Winkle when that jovial inebriate appeared amongst them. "I take it, sir, that you are leader here, and I think there has been some mistake. During today's journey I have been forced to travel to this mine against my will. You seem to have been expecting me. Now, what's up?"

"You'll be, in about ten minutes," replied the boss. "Dakota Bill, where's your rope?"

"Here it is," said Bill, stepping forward and exhibiting a slip-noose at the end of about thirty feet of stout line.

"Now, stranger, if you've got any messages to leave your friends, we'll give you ten minutes to write or say them."

"I've no messages, thank you, but I am disturbed by a lively curiosity to know what all this means."

"Oh, of course you've no suspicion about what it means, have you?"

"No, I have not."

"You never saw your mine before, did you?"

"It isn't my mine."

"I knew you'd say that. Well, now, we've been left here for four months without a markee of pay. For the last month we would have starved if it hadn't been for Dakota Bill's good work with a rifle; but even the game has fled from this accursed place and now we *are* starving. You're the man responsible, and you know it. We've sworn to hang you, and we're *going* to hang you."

"My dear sir, your statement is definite and concise, without being as illuminating as I should like. A mistake has been made, of which I am the innocent victim. You are the victims, too, for that matter; because, after all, it is not a mistake, but a conspiracy. I can see, however, that nothing I may say will mitigate the situation in the slightest degree. I shall, therefore, not indulge in useless declamation. Three things are fixed. I am the owner of this mine. I have cheated you out of your pay for four months, therefore I am to be hanged. There comes into my mind at this moment something I have read somewhere about hangings at Newgate prison in England. They drop a man, then all concerned go at once to enjoy what is called the 'hanging breakfast.' The gruesomeness of such a proceeding fastened the item in my mind. Let's have a 'hanging lunch.'"

"Stranger, as I understand your remarks, the person turned off didn't attend that breakfast."

"No, he didn't."

"Very well, stranger, we'll look after the lunch when you're strung up."

"But, excuse me, the victim had a hearty breakfast *before* he was hanged. Now, I beg to point out to you that I drank my coffee just about daybreak this morning, and since then I've travelled over the worst set of mountains it has ever been my privilege to encounter. I'm as hungry as a bear. I therefore insist on your lunching with me, and I shall give you a meal such as you wouldn't better at the Millionaire's Club. Before I left home, six manufacturers of portable stoves insisted on my accepting one each, in the hope of getting an unsolicited testimonial. I shall leave the stoves with you, and trust you will recommend them to your friends. I don't need them where I'm going."

"No," said one of the party, "they'd melt there."

"Now, Jackson," cried Steele enthusiastically, "set up the whole six stoves. You've got to cook dinner for the party. But, meanwhile, open some of those boxes of new sardines with the trimmings on, which they've just sent across to us from Brittany. A little caviare also may be a novelty in this district. I think we've plates enough to go round. If not, use saucers or the tins. Gentlemen, I take it you don't need an appetiser, but what will you drink before we begin?"

"I admit, stranger, you're a mighty plausible cuss, and we expected that; but you don't palaver this crowd. There's no drinking till after the ceremony."

For the first time there was a murmur of disapproval at this, but the leader held up his hand.

"See here, you fellows," he said, "we've got to deal with a pretty slippery customer. You know what them city men are. Now, there's no drinking till after the performance; you hear me. I'd string him up this moment, only we'd scare his cook white, and then we'd have to eat things raw."

Jackson handed round sardines and other tempting extras, while Steele put the collapsible table on its legs and opened various boxes, from one of which he took out a case of champagne, and another of Scotch whisky. Then, getting a large pitcher which had been intended as the water-holder of his tent, he poured two bottles of Scotch whisky into it, followed by bottle after bottle of champagne until the jug was full. Meanwhile the busy negro had got the six stoves ablaze, and the appetising smell that came from the utensils over the fires made the starving miners oblivious to everything else. The first course was devoured in silence.

"Although you may not care to consume intoxicating liquors, and I quite agree with you that it is best to keep sober, I hope you have no objection to temperance drinks. Who'll have some cider?"

"Cider?" said the leader. "Have you got any?"

"Here's a pitcher full."

"That's all right. Pour it out. I wish you had brought beer instead. We'd risk beer."

"Oh, well, you can risk the cider. I'm sorry I haven't any beer," and, hungry as he was, the young man himself poured out full glasses to each.

"By jiminy crickets!" cried the leader, "that's the best cider I ever tasted."

"It's the very best cider made in this country," said Steele earnestly, "and thank goodness, I've got plenty of it."

As course after course was served, and bumper after bumper was drunk, the geniality of the crowd rose and rose, until Steele at last saw he could possibly make terms with them, but he resolved not to chance that. He determined to leave them so drunk that none could move; then he would depart at his leisure. Under the exhilarating effects of the mixture he poured out, all objections to intoxicating liquor fled from the jovial assemblage, and Jackson now opened whisky bottle after whisky bottle. The miners were laughing, singing, weeping on one another's necks, utterly oblivious of mine owners, lack of pay, lynching, or anything else, when Steele and Jackson mounted their horses, the coloured cook leading one of the mules laden with provisions ample for a week's journey.

When Steele reached Pickaxe Gulch, he thought he never should be so glad to see a pair of rails again. He felt like throwing his arms round the neck of the station-master, but instead asked that rough diamond if there were any news.

"No, not much," replied the station-master, "except that Peter Berrington, the billionaire, is dead."

"Thank God!" fervently ejaculated Steele, to the astonishment of the station-master.

"Yes," said the official, "he's gone where his money won't do him no good. Found dead in his chair in his office in New York, two days ago. There's the paper, if you want to read about it."

Steele went in and possessed himself of the paper.

"By Jove!" he muttered, as he gazed at the big, black headlines. "He or his system sent a man to death when he ought to have been preparing for death himself. That's as it should be. Thank goodness the shadow has lifted!"

John Steele forgot the words of Shakespeare:=

````"The evil that men do lives after them."=

````

CHAPTER XV
AN ATTEMPT AT AN ARMISTICE.

JOHN STEELE'S friends were amazed to find him back in town almost within a week after he had left with such lavish preparations for a long stay in the wilderness. It was difficult for him to offer an adequate explanation, and it grew to be most annoying, once he had constructed his excuses, to be compelled to repeat them to every friend he met, and listen without cursing to the inane advice given by people who didn't in the least know what they were talking about.

"What! back already?" cried Philip Manson, who had offered to place a private car at his disposal if he would keep close to the railway. Manson held that camping out in a private car was the right way to do it, and that a canvas tent was a delusion and a snare. "Back already?" exclaimed the general manager. "Why, John, you look as haggard as if you'd been through a panic in the wheat market. Didn't the Black Hills agree with you?"

"No," said John shortly and truthfully; "threatened to develop throat trouble," and he tapped his neck significantly.

"How long were you in the mountains?"

"Five days."

"Oh, well, I told you how it would be before you left. That's what comes of sleeping in a cot-bed, over damp ground, under thin canvas. You should have taken both my advice and my private car then you could have carried all the comforts of town with you."

Now that the immediate tension of the crisis had relaxed, John Steele found himself very close to a mental and physical collapse. It was true that the great Peter Berrington was dead, but the elation which that startling piece of news had first caused subsided long before he reached the city. Men die, but systems remain. Had the shadow of Peter Berrington been lifted, after all, even though Peter himself was now a shadow? The grotesque uncertainty of the situation was making rags of John Steele's nerves. Even as he walked through the crowded streets he had to fight down an impulse to shriek aloud, raising his hands to heaven and crying: "In God's name, if you're going to do anything, do it *now*, and let's have it over!"

It was not that he shrank from ruin, or even from death, both of which he had faced within the past year. It was the uncertainty of when and how the blow was to fall. He began to fear that something worse than either ruin or death would overtake him. In the privacy of his own room he would sometimes march up and down with set teeth and clenched fists, saying to himself: "You must quit thinking of this, or you'll go mad," and yet with all his strength of mind he could not stop his planning to circumvent the unseen danger which threatened him.

The fantastic nature of the peril that surrounded him was such that if it were made public, he would be laughed at from one end of the country to the other. In a busy, practical, work-a-day world, it was incredible that a group of men, only one of whom he had ever seen, and that most casually, should sit in a sky-scraper in New York and actually plan the murder of a young man in Chicago; for this group of men were churchgoers, Sunday-school teachers, philanthropists who had founded colleges; bestowers of charity on a scale of munificence hitherto unexampled. And yet more potent than all these things was the fact that they were hard-headed business men, the most successful business men in the world, intent on their own affairs, and naturally far removed from any thought of revenge, for the simple reason that revenge is not business, and there is no money in it. It was quite true that this same group, in early days, had been accused of burning rival factories, of inciting riots, and of many other crimes against the peace and security of the commonwealth, but these things had never been legally proven or brought home to the group by irrefutable evidence. Where investigation had followed crime, and the inquiry was not quashed, it had always been shown that the rash acts were the work of over-zealous employees exceeding their instructions. The hands of the financial group in the tall building on Broadway were clean. No band of Quakers were more set against violence than these mild-mannered men in New York. If John Steele had told the story of the attempted lynching among the Black Hills, the incredulous public would have looked upon the affair as a practical joke played by humourous mountaineers on a tenderfoot from the East. No one knew better than John Steele that to connect Dakota Bill of the Black Hills with Nicholson of New York was an impossibility. He was certain the miners knew nothing of Nicholson; that they held a genuine lynching grievance against the owner of the mine, whoever he was, and that they were acting quite naturally according to their instincts when this supposed owner had fallen into their hands.

Alice Fuller, who led him so easily into the trap, as the tame animal in the stockyards leads its fellows to the slaughter-pen—she, of course, knew for whom she was acting, but John doubted if this knowledge led by any followable clue to Nicholson. When he thought of the handsome girl, he shuddered; and, for ten thousand reasons, that episode must never become public. To be hoodwinked by a pretty woman was merely to join the procession of fools that extended from the time of Adam to the year 1905.

It was difficult for Steele to cease his thoughts of the Amalgamated Soap combination, for the papers continued full of Peter Berrington and the financial upheaval which his sudden death was certain to cause. The imagination of the world was touched by the fact that this tremendous power which Peter Berrington had wielded in ever-increasing force for nearly half a century now lapsed into the hands of a girl, Constance Berrington, aged twenty-four, the only child of the billionaire. The newspapers printed column after column about this young lady, who appeared to be even more of a recluse than her father was. They published portraits of her, no two alike—pictures ranging from the most beautiful woman in Christendom to the most gaunt and ugly hag; which seemed to indicate that photographs of Miss Constance were unobtainable, and that the artists drew on their imagination as well as on their Whatman pads. She avoided society, was never seen at such resorts as Newport or Lenox; she took no part in the festivities of a great city, and believed that the door of a theatre was the gate of hell. Gossip said she was haunted by a fear of being married for her money, and so at this early age had become a man-hater. It was also alleged that she kept a conscience, a possession with which her father had never been credited even by the wildest imaginative writer. She was going to devote her life and her billions as far as possible to the undoing of the harm which her parent had accomplished.

"She is fanatically religious," proclaimed one newspaper.

"She is a plain, commonplace girl," said another, "whose father has bequeathed her his cash, but not his brains."

When John Steele found he could not cease thinking over his paralysing situation, which had entirely emasculated his initiative and wrecked his business career; when he feared lunacy awaited him, he resolved to meet this girl, and persuade her, if he could, to stop the huge, golden Juggernaut which threatened to crush the life or reason out or him. Yet it seemed cowardly for a grown man to make such an appeal to a young girl who was an entire stranger to him, and who, if he actually succeeded in reaching her presence, would most likely consider herself insulted that such crimes as he placed before her without the slightest proof, should be attributed to her father. Thus the interview would doubtless end with his being turned out of the house by the servants. Then again, even if she believed him—and the chances were only as one in ten thousand—did she possess the actual as well as the nominal power to stop the persecution? Was she like the Czar of Russia, helplessly at the head of an organisation over whose movements the supposed chief had no control?

Yet, after all, Steele had not gone so far towards insanity as to be in any error regarding the real mover in the conspiracies of which he was the victim. Nicholson was the man; there could be no doubt of that. Twice Steele had beaten Nicholson to the ground. In the great wheat deal he had exposed his treachery and dishonesty; had publicly shown him to be an unscrupulous scoundrel; had prevented him from making millions in a single coup, which was all prepared and certain to succeed had not Steele disarranged the machinery. He had humiliated the man personally, wounding his pride and crushing his self-esteem. Was it possible, then, ever to make terms with one naturally so embittered? Steele braced himself and resolved to try. Twice he had defeated him, and there remained in John's hand the powerful weapon of publicity. After all, could Amalgamated Soap risk such an exposure as it was in Steele's power to cast forth to the eager Press of the country? Was it so certain that the public would not believe the story he might tell regarding Amalgamated Soap? Even though Nicholson was imbued with malice, his colleagues would be more reasonable, more amenable to persuasion. They would undoubtedly try to induce this angry man to refrain from tempting the avalanche. He resolved to propose a treaty of peace with Nicholson. Then came the doubt. Should Nicholson agree to such a pact, would he keep it? Would he merely use it as a sedative to lull his intended victim into false security? Such an outcome was very likely; still, a frank talk with Nicholson could do no harm, and Steele had not the slightest intention of being lulled into security by anything Nicholson might say. Recalling to his mind the stony countenance of that human sphinx, Steele could not delude himself that any appeal to conscience or any plea for mercy would have the least chance of success. Nicholson was as unemotional as the Pyramids; Steele could make no bargain with such a man unless he had something to offer. Therefore he did not go impetuously to New York and fling himself at the feet of Nemesis, the divinity of chastisement and vengeance. He set about the preparation of the goods he would trade with, this white Indian. It gratified him to think that after all these months of doubt and uncertainty he could at last come to a definite decision about anything.

There were no women in John Steele's office. His confidential stenographer was a quiet man, a little older than himself, named Henry Russell. Steele touched an electric button on his desk, and Russell came in, notebook in hand.

"Sit down, Russell. If I remember rightly, you were connected with a newspaper in your early days?"

"In a very humble capacity, sir; I was merely a reporter."

"Oh, don't say 'merely.' A reporter is ever so much more important than an editorial writer. Have you ever attempted a novel?"

"No, sir."

"Still, you know something of literary form and the way a book is put together, I suppose?"

"I know nothing about the writing of books, sir. I think I have a fair knowledge of how a sentence should read."

"Well, that's the main thing. Still, as a reporter you must have seen a good deal of the seamy side of life, and later you have had to do with important business affairs, ever since you came into my employ."

"That is very true, Mr. Steele."

"Don't you think you could concoct the plot of a novel? A novel of every-day business life, let us say, like one of those that have been so successful lately—a book pulsating with the greed of gold, and all that sort of thing, you know? Unscrupulous men, and perhaps an adventuress here and there, of perfectly stunning beauty. For instance, someone resembling that girl who came in to see me a fortnight ago."

"Y es, I remember her. She was good looking."

"An amazing beauty, I thought her," said Steele, thrusting his hands into his trousers pockets and marching up and down the room. "Well, couldn't such a belle of the markets as that inspire you towards the writing of a great work of fiction?"

Russell shook his head. "I'm afraid not, Mr. Steele."

"There's nothing much doing just now," continued the promenading man. "At this present moment I intended to be off on my vacation, but I found the mountains too exciting—er—too dull I mean—and so you see I am back among you earlier than I expected. Now, Russell, between ourselves, there is nothing more absurd than for a successful business man to attempt the writing of a novel. Yet I'm the sort of person who cannot remain idle, and there is nothing in sight to do for a month or two. I'm going to while away the time by composing a business novel, and I want you to assist me. I'll dictate the thing straight off to you, and you must invent the names and kick the sentences into shape."

"I'll do my best, sir."

"And remember, Russell, of all the confidential transactions you've been called upon to perform, this is the one in which I demand the utmost secrecy. I should be the laughing stock of the town if it once got out that I were plunging into fiction instead of into wheat."

"I'll never breathe a whisper of it, sir."

"I am sure you won't, and that is why I trust you. Now, we'll just lock the doors and refuse ourselves to all comers. If a novel is to be a success nowadays, when people have so much to read and so little time for reading, it must be as sensational as possible, and I think I can do the trick. Anyhow, if it fails, there's no great harm done, and for a time we two will court that seclusion with which, I read in the papers, all true literary men surround themselves."

The two men worked together day after day, until the first draft of the history was completed and typed; then they revised this copy very thoroughly, and Steele directed that duplicates should be made, with blanks left for all proper names. He professed himself dissatisfied with the titles they had invented, and said that while the final manuscript was being prepared, he would concoct more suitable appellations for his main characters, and insert them with his own hand. This final revision was accomplished by John Steele alone, when he inserted the real names; then with his own hand he wrote the following letter to Stoliker, editor of the *Daily Blade*:

My dear Stoliker:

If the accompanying manuscript ever comes into your possession, I want you first of all to remember that on a certain night I brought to you a most remarkable article regarding the wheat situation in this country, the truth of which you quite legitimately doubted. After-events proved the accuracy of my statement, and you were thus enabled to score a great triumph for your paper. Believe me, then, when I tell you that every word here typed is true; for when you read the accompanying pages, I shall not be by your side to use arguments in favour of its publication. I shall either have disappeared, or, more probably, I shall be dead. In either case, this manuscript, every name in which is real, will give you a clue to the disaster which has overtaken me. In the meantime I remain, Your friend,

John Steele.

This letter and the manuscript he wrapped up into a parcel, which he securely sealed. On the outside he wrote instructions that in the case of his death or disappearance the package was to be handed intact to Stoliker, of the *Daily Blade*. The other package, with a duplicate of the letter to Stoliker, was placed in the vault of a depository, supposed to be the greatest strong-room in the city, which, he afterwards learned with some amusement, belonged to Amalgamated Soap. The thin key and the code word which opened this receptacle he placed in a sealed envelope which he left in the hands of his legal advisers, with instructions to forward the envelope to Stoliker in case of his death or disappearance.

All this accomplished to his satisfaction, he took the Limited to New York, and entered the tall building on Broadway which was body to the brain that directed the activities of Amalgamated Soap. Asking that his card should be taken to Mr. Nicholson, and replying to an inquiry that he had no appointment, he was taken into a small but richly furnished waiting-room, which he saw to be one of many on the eleventh floor, and there he rested for nearly half an hour before a messenger entered and announced that Mr. Nicholson would be pleased to see him.

Nicholson's room was large and sumptuous, with several windows opening on Broadway. The two financiers, big and little, met on the plane of ordinary politeness, without any effusion of mutual regard on the one hand, or evidence of mutual distrust on the other.

"I have called," said Steele, "to see if we can come to any workable arrangement."

"In what line of activity?" asked Nicholson.

"In a line of passivity rather than of activity," explained Steele, with a smile. "When I was a youngster, and engaged in a fight, it was etiquette that as soon as the under boy hollered 'Enough!' the fellow on top ceased pummelling him. I have come all the way from Chicago to cry 'Enough!'"

Nicholson's eyebrows raised very slightly.

"I fear I do not understand you, Mr. Steele."

"Oh, yes, you do. It will save time and talk, if we take certain things for granted. When we first met, I was so unfortunate as to find myself opposed to you. I admit frankly that I entirely underestimated your genius and your power. Since then, on one occasion you came within an ace of ruining me. On a second and more recent occasion you came within an ace of causing my death. Now, I have called at the captain's office to settle. In the language of the wild and woolly West, my hands are up, and you have the drop on me. What are your terms?"

For a few moments Nicholson regarded his visitor with an expression in which mild surprise was mingled with equally mild anxiety. When at last he spoke, his voice was perceptibly lowered, as if he addressed an invalid in a sick-room.

"You are not looking very well, Mr. Steele?"

"No, nor feeling well, either, Mr. Nicholson."

"I am sorry to hear it. What is the trouble?"

"Amalgamated Soap, I should say," said John, with a dreary laugh. "Excellent for the complexion, but mighty bad for the nerves."

"I shall make no pretence of misunderstanding your meaning, Mr. Steele," Nicholson went on with the patient enunciation one uses towards an unreasonable child. "You are hinting that in revenge for fancied opposition on your part, either I personally or the company with which I am associated, or both, have entered into a conspiracy, first to rob, and secondly to murder you. I hesitate to speak so bluntly, but, as you quite sensibly remark, we should be frank with each other."

"Your bluntness is more than compensated for by your accuracy, Mr. Nicholson. What you describe is exactly what you have done. Mere accident saved me from ruin in the Consolidated Beet Sugar formation. Less than a month ago I was led across the plains by one of your minions—a most charming, beautiful, and fascinating young woman—into a death-trap, from which I escaped largely through my own ingenuity. Now, I have written down a rather vivid and strictly accurate account of these doings. I have put in your name, and that of Amalgamated Soap, and my own, and there are three copies of this narrative in existence, two of them with a slow match attached which you can very easily light."

"Meaning that this interesting account will appear in print, Mr. Steele?"

"Quite so. Now, I ask you, Mr. Nicholson, is it worth while going any further with this feud? We're not illicit distillers in the mountains trying to pot-shot each other, but two supposedly sane men; and the world is amply wide enough for both. What do you say?"

"Really, Mr. Steele, it's rather difficult to know what to say without seeming impolite. Many things have been printed about Amalgamated Soap during the last twenty years, and so far they have never been replied to, nor have our dividends been adversely affected. A few of the articles I have read. Some were largely statistical, others of a defamatory character, others, again, contained the two qualities combined. But you, Mr. Steele, threaten to inject a most unusual and interesting quality—namely, that of an attractive young man journeying across the prairies with a beautiful and mysterious young woman. If I raised a finger to prevent the publication of a human document so well calculated to touch the better and more sentimental parts of our nature, I should consider that I was depriving my fellow-creatures of a source of pure enjoyment. I believe we sometimes unite beauty and soap in our advertisements. Attractive pictures they are. But this romance of the Black Hills——"

"How do you know it was the Black Hills?" asked Steele quickly.

"Didn't you mention that locality?"

"I said the plains."

"Then I beg pardon—this romance of the plains——"

"Now, stop a moment, Nicholson; just stop where you are. Do you see what a blunder you've made? For your own purpose, whatever it may be, you have been pretending that this human document of mine, as you call it, is a myth. Yet, in the calm and choice language with which you are describing it, you have suddenly given yourself away. You know the mine was in the Black Hills, and, of course, I knew you knew from the very first. Now, let us quit sparring. I asked you what your terms were. I am not using threats at all. I am merely trying to come to an arrangement. Suppose, on the third attack, you succeed in driving me to the wall. What good will it do you?"

"None at all, Mr. Steele, and I assure you I have not the least desire to interfere even in the remotest degree with your affairs. You evidently attribute to me more-power than I possess. The undertakings of our association are all matters of mutual arrangement between the directors, of whom I happen to be one. We meet each day at eleven o'clock, and I trust you will believe me when I say that if I proposed to my colleagues either the robbery or murder of Mr. John Steele, I should be very promptly asked to resign my position, and deservedly so. Really, Mr. Steele, if I may make an appeal to your own common sense, you must admit that the building up of the prestige of this company, its successful carrying on, its increase of business in all parts of the world, are not accomplished by such bizarre devices as you ascribe to us."

"Do you mean to say that you did not, in my own presence, attempt to wreck the Consolidated Beet Sugar Company when you thought I would be ruined by it, and immediately go to allotment when you learned I had escaped the trap?"

"I am very glad you mentioned that, Mr. Steele, because a few simple words will show you that I am not the Machiavelli you suppose me to be. To wreck you I should have been compelled to wreck ourselves to at least an equal amount, and it is not the custom of Amalgamated Soap to purchase revenge at so excessive a price. It is one of our principles never to enter into any company put before the public unless the capital is fully subscribed. To my surprise I learned that we were a million short, therefore I could not agree to go to allotment."

"But you went to allotment all the same when you learned I was out."

"Pardon me, it was not learning that you were out of it which caused me to change my mind. It was knowing you had sent a letter to the papers informing the public that we were interested in the Consolidated Beet Sugar Company. The moment our good name was involved I proposed going to allotment; but before doing so I myself drew my cheque for a million dollars and bought the unsold shares. Your being in or out of the Company had nothing to do with my action."

"You will not come to terms, then?"

"There are no terms to come to."

"Is this your last word, Mr. Nicholson?"

"If you will pardon the liberty I take, Mr. Steele, I shall venture some last words on another subject. As I said when you came in, you are not looking well. Do you know what paranoea means?"

"I do not."

"Then, if you take my advice, you will consult a physician and ask him about it."

"I'll ask you, to save the physician's fee. What is paranoea?"

"It is a disease of the brain, and its symptom is fear. The victim imagines that someone, or everyone, is plotting against him. All the energies he possesses are directed towards the circumvention of conspiracies that are wholly imaginary. This disease, if not checked, leads to insanity or suicide."

John Steele rose to his feet.

"Does paranoea ever lead to murder, Mr. Nicholson?"

"Quite frequently."

"Then as I have been told that the directors of Amalgamated Soap are a most piously inclined body, please solicit their prayers that I may not be afflicted with the malady you mention. I thank you for giving me so much of your time, and now bid you 'Good day.'"

"Good-bye, Mr. Steele," said Nicholson, rising; then speaking in his suavest manner, he said: "If ever you entertain any project that requires more capital than you can command, I shall be most pleased to submit it to Mr. John Berrington, and perhaps we may be of assistance to you. As I told you before, I have the utmost admiration for your financial ability."

"Thank you, Mr. Nicholson; I shall bear your kind invitation in mind. However, I may inform you that I have entirely dropped out of all speculative business. I am one of the few men who know when they have had enough. I have accumulated all the money I shall need during my lifetime, and I intend to take care of it."

"A most sensible resolution, Mr. Steele; and once more good-bye, with many thanks for the visit."

John Steele walked up Broadway the most depressed man in New York. His attempted compromise had proven a complete failure; his journey East a loss of time. And yet of what value was time to him, who dared not undertake the most innocent project through fear of the developments that might follow? Nicholson had said that fear was the symptom of the malady he had so graphically depicted. Could it be possible, Steele asked himself, that he was actually the victim of a disease, every indication of which he seemed to possess? Nicholson had evidently planted that thought in his brain to his further disquietude. That man, who rarely allowed a smile to lighten his face, had inwardly laughed at him, flouted him, defied him! and all done with soothing, contemptuous insults.

Steele walked slowly up Broadway until he came to its intersection with Fifth Avenue, and then he followed the latter street, aimlessly making for his hotel. Nevertheless, when he came opposite the hotel he wandered past it and on up the Avenue. Suddenly he shook himself together and denied the cowardliness which he had hitherto attributed to the design forming in his mind. He would appeal to a woman, and if he could not thus circumvent the demoniac Nicholson, he would go out of business entirely, as he had threatened, and either travel or take up some interesting recreative occupation. He made inquiries, was directed to the Berrington residence, walked up the steps of that palace, and rang the bell. A servant in gorgeous livery opened the door.

"I wish to speak with Miss Berrington," he said.

"Not at 'ome, sir," was the curt answer.

Steele put his hand in his pocket and drew forth a twenty-dollar bill.

"I think the lady is in," he said quietly, handing this legal tender to the man in plush. Even in the residences of millionaires tips of this size are unusual, and the haughty menial at once melted. He pocketed the money.

"No, sir," he said, "she is not in town at all. Speaking confidentially, sir, Miss Berrington's that peculiar she don't like New York. Her ladyship—I beg your pardon, sir—Miss Berrington is at her country 'ome some distance out of town, sir."

"How far? Where is it?"

"On a lake, sir. I don't quite remember its name. Begins with a h'S, I think, sir."

"Lake Saratoga?" suggested Steele.

"It begins with a h'S, sir," repeated the man thoughtfully; then with a sudden burst of inspiration: "Oh, yes, sir, Superior—Lake Superior, sir."

"Great Heavens!" cried Steele, unable to repress a smile, "that isn't just exactly in the environs of New York. I suppose you couldn't tell me whether the house is on the Canadian or the United States side?"

"No, sir, I couldn't say, sir, being it's in Michigan, sir."

"Oh, well, that's near enough; I can guess the rest." The man in plush pronounced the name of the State as if the first syllable were spelt M-i-t-c-h.

"Yes, sir, her ladyship—beg your pardon—Miss Berrington owns a large estate there, so they tell me—thousands and thousands of acres, all covered with forests, and there's a big 'ouse full of servants; but her lady—but Miss Berrington receives nobody, sir. Not if you brought a letter from the King of Hengland, sir."

"Ha! rather exclusive, isn't she?"

"Yes, sir."

Thanking the man, Steele turned away and walked down the Avenue to his hotel, resolved to let the Berring-tons or the Nicholsons do their worst. He would attempt no further parley with any of the gang, and—probably inspired by the accent of the servitor in plush—gave serious thought to the investing of all his money in British Consols, small as was the percentage granted by that celebrated security. He took it for granted that the

Government of Britain was probably free from the influence of the Berrington crowd, and he was rapidly coming to the conclusion that no other sphere of human activity was.

Arriving at his hotel, he found a telegram waiting for him. It proved to be from Philip Manson, and it ran:

Congratulate me. Have just been appointed president of the Wheat Belt System. Important development. Great opening here that just suits you. Must see you immediately. If you cannot come here, telegraph me, and I will go to New York.

"Ye Gods!" cried Steele, bracing back his shoulders, while the chronic look of anxiety vanished like mist before the sun, "just at the point when I don't know what to do, here comes my chance. I'll bet a farm Manson is going to offer me the vice-presidency of the road. I'll take it like a shot, and raise the freight rates on soap if Philip will let me."

He seized a telegraph blank and wrote:

Heartiest congratulations. The right man in right place. You need not come to New York, as I am leaving for home to-night. I shall accept your opening, whatever it is.

Before two days were past, John Steele was closeted with Manson in the president's room of the huge Wheat Belt building. The great, flat table in the centre was covered with broad maps taken from the civil engineer's department, maps unknown to the general public.

"Now, John," said his friend, "I'm in a position to offer you the absolute surety of doubling, trebling, or even quadrupling your money."

"Thunder!" cried Steele in a tone of disappointment, "I thought you were going to present me with the vice-presidency of the road."

Manson glanced up at him in surprise.

"Would you take it?" he asked.

"Take it? Of course. That's what I thought I was engaging to do when I telegraphed from New York."

"Why, no sooner said than done, John. I'd no idea you wished to get back into the railway business. I should think a man who can make millions outside wouldn't be content to sit here at a salary of ten or fifteen thousand a year."

"I am tired of making millions," said Steele.

"You don't mean to say," protested Manson with something like dismay in his words, "you don't mean to say you won't go in with us? I took your telegram as consent, and because I could thus guarantee the bringing in of a big capitalist, I have induced others to join and secured an extra slice for myself."

"Where there are millions to be made," said Steele dubiously, "there is always a risk, and I had determined not to accept any more chances."

"There is no chance about this, John; it is a sure thing, and the development of it rests entirely in my hands. You can double your money and pull out within ten days after I give the word, and I'll give the word whenever you say so."

"What's your project, Mr. Manson?"

"Well, you see, the Wheat Belt Line, which has been one of the most prosperous roads in the country for some years past, is going to build a branch running two hundred and seventy miles northwest until it taps the Wisconsin Pacific. This red line shows you where the road will run. The Wheat Belt Line has secured all the timber land on each side, but the former president, whose place I have taken, and myself have an option on the prairie and the stump-lands where timber has been cut. The president resigned simply to give his whole time to this land company, and that's why I am in his place. Now, we can get the property at prairie value just now; but the minute we begin surveying, up it will jump. You can trust me to keep my word. If you join us, I shall give the order for surveying the line the moment deeds of the land are in our possession."

"How much money do you expect me to put up, Mr. Manson?"

"You couldn't invest twenty millions, I suppose?"

"Twenty millions! Heavens and earth, no! It would practically clean me out to furnish nine."

"I mentioned the bigger amount simply because I am sure you will double your money within a month, and the more you put in, the more you're going to take out. You see, this is not a speculation, but a certainty."

For a few minutes Steele walked up and down the room, hands deep in his pockets, as was his custom, brow wrinkled and head bent. At last he said, with the old ring of decision in his voice:

"All right, Mr. Manson, I'll go in; but if I fail, you must give me the vice-presidency, as a sort of consolation prize."

"I'll give it to you now," said Manson. "But it can't fail. I tell you everything is in my hands. It is not as if this were any bluff. The proposed line is a road that is becoming more and more needed every day, and the land is good for the money, even if the road were never built. It's as safe as government bonds."

It would be going over ground already sufficiently covered to recount the history of the Western Land Syndicate. Steele had resolved not to invest more than half his fortune; but once a man is involved in an important enterprise, he rarely can predict where he will stop. A scheme grows and grows, and often the financier is compelled to involve himself more and more deeply in order to protect the money already ventured, and finally it becomes all or nothing. Besides this, every speculator is something of the gambler, and once the game has begun, the betting fever has him in its clutch. Before a month was past, Steele had not only paid over every dollar he possessed, but had also become deeply indebted to his bank. In borrowing from the bank he made his irretrievable mistake. As the president had said, the land was intrinsically worth the money paid for it; and if John Steele had merely risked his own assets, he might have been penniless for ten years, but he would ultimately have been sure of getting back what he paid, and probably a good deal more. But to borrow hundreds of thousands at sixty days, in the expectation that he would take profits enough to pay the loan before that time expired, was an action he himself, in less feverish moments, would have been the first to condemn. He felt the utmost confidence in his old friend, the new president, and it may be said at once that Manson throughout the history of what was known as the Great Land Bubble, was perfectly honest and sincere. He was merely a pawn on the board, moved by an unseen force of which he knew nothing.

On the afternoon of the day when the final payment on the land was made, the president of the Wheat Belt Line entered the room of his subordinate with a piece of paper in his hand. His face was white as chalk and he could not speak. He dropped into a chair, before John Steele's desk, and the latter, with a premonition of what was coming, took the paper from his trembling hand. It was a telegram from New York, and ran as follows:

The Peter Berrington Estate has acquired control of the Wheat Belt system. The new Board of Directors yesterday resolved to abandon the Wisconsin Pacific Branch. If the branch is built at all, which is doubtful, it will begin a hundred and seventy miles West of the point formerly selected. You will, therefore, countermand at once any instructions previously given regarding the Wisconsin Pacific connection. The board also refuses to ratify the nomination of John Steele as vice-president of the road.—Nicholson.

"Cheer up!" said John, with a laugh that sounded just a trifle hollow. "Cheer up, old man. I know all about this, and you're not in the least to blame. You acted in good faith throughout."

"It's horrible, John, horrible; but still, you know, you have the land, and before long that will realise all you've put in."

"Yes, Mr. Manson, I've got the land; that's one consolation."

But he knew perfectly well he hadn't. He knew that when the sixty days were up the bank would foreclose, which was exactly what happened. There were practically no bidders for so large a plot, and Nicholson purchased the property for the exact amount owing to the bank.

The ruin of John Steele was complete.

CHAPTER XVI
THE RICHEST WOMAN IN THE WORLD

THE clearing in the primeval forest had been only partial, for several tall trees were left standing here and there, grouped around a log-house. The house itself, to a casual observer, resembled the dwelling of an ordinary pioneer, except that it was much larger than any residence a poor woodman ever erected. It was built of great pine logs, the ends roughly dovetailed together with a lumberman's axe. Where log lay on log, the interstices were plastered with clay. A broad verandah ran completely round the oblong building, a luxury which the pioneer usually denied himself. A settler would also have been contented to cover his roof with split oak clapboards, but here the refinement of yellow pine shingles was used, which not only kept out the weather better than the pioneer's economical device, but caused the tone of the broad roof to harmonise well with the hue of the bark on the logs; and as one approached the edifice from the forest, the whole structure standing out against the background of deep blue afforded by the lake and sky, formed a more pleasing colour scheme than might have been expected where contrasts were so vivid in that translucent air. Around the large log-house were grouped many other log-buildings, with no attempt at regulation and order. Each one appeared to have been put up as needed, and these ranged from an ordinary outhouse or shed to complete residences. A few hundred yards away from the verandah of the house, down a sloping lawn, lay sand of dazzling whiteness, and along these sands rippled the smallest waves of the largest lake in the world.

No such body of fresh water as Lake Superior exists anywhere else on earth. The water in bulk is blue; taken in detail, it is almost invisible; and this was strikingly illustrated by an adjunct of civilisation which no stretch of the imagination could attach to pioneer days. Anchored in the bay floated a large white steam-yacht, with two funnels and two slender, sloping masts. It seemed resting, not on the surface of the lake, but in mid-air, for the details of the twin screws, the long, level keel, and submerged part from prow to stern were as plain to the eye as the upper works or the funnels or the masts.

To the south and east and west, this little oasis of civilisation was walled in by the eternal forest. To the north, blue lake and blue sky blended together. On this day in late summer the place was a paradise of solitude. The great lake, which on occasion could raise a storm that might swamp an Atlantic liner, was now placid and on its good behaviour. The only sound was the gentle whisper of the leaves in the forest and the impatient pawing of a horse, which a groom held, saddled, by the southern verandah.

Through the open doorway there presently emerged a young woman, in a tight-fitting riding-habit, so short in the skirt that it looked like a walking dress rather than a costume for an equestrienne. The girl seemed very slight, and not as tall as the average woman. In spite of the frown on her brow, the face was redeemed from lack of amiability by some indescribable spiritual intellectuality which beamed from it. The whole figure gave an impression of gloom. The hair was black; the complexion almost that of an Italian woman. The eyes of velvet midnight could sparkle with dark anger, but at times they melted into a glance of appeal that was strangely pathetic, which partially redeemed the austerity of the other features. The costume was of unrelieved black, but the attention of a stranger invariably returned again and again to the face, puzzled by it. It seemed to stamp its owner as querulous, selfish perhaps, caring little for the feelings of others, yet nevertheless there sometimes fitted across it an expression indicating true nobility of character, that seemed to account for those many deeds of kindness, with which even a critical world credited the young woman.

She spoke with cutting sharpness to her groom, who had not placed the horse to please her. The man did his best, but the animal was restive from its long wait, and with a curt word of impatience at what she called the stupidity of the groom, the girl sprang with great dexterity into her saddle, gathered the reins in her left hand, and flecked the animal a stinging stroke on the flank with her whip. The horse snorted and reared, pawing the air, and again the whip descended. Now he tried to bolt, but she held him firmly, in spite of her apparently slight physique, and at last the frightened horse stood there trembling, but mastered.

"Shall I follow you, madam?" inquired the groom.

"Don't ask unnecessary questions!" snapped the girl, scowling at him as if she were in half a mind to hit him as well as the horse with the whip. "If I wished you to follow me, I should have told you so."

The cringing groom raised his forefinger to the peak of his cap and slunk away. The horse would have cantered, feeling the exhilaration of the air and the delight of the day in its supple limbs, but the girl appeared to take a grim pleasure in restraining the ardour of her steed and forcing him to a slow walk. The horsewoman certainly rode well and looked well in the saddle, but her face was marred by an expression of chronic discontent, which perhaps had a right to be there, for she was accounted the richest woman in the world, living what she supposed to be the simple life.

Constance Berrington was one of those unhappy persons whose every wish had been gratified almost before it could be expressed. Slight as she appeared, her health was excellent, and she had never yet come upon a crisis in life which money could not smooth away. It would have done her a world of good to be compelled to earn her living for a year, and meet a section of humanity she had never yet encountered, who cared not a rap whether she lived or died. But at this moment, when her ill-temper caused her to curb the eager horse to a slow walk, she was playing into the hands of the enemy in a manner that would have startled her had she but known.

Parallel with her course, a stooping man dodged from tree to tree. There was something of the stealthiness of the savage about him, and he took all the precautions of a savage to avoid observation—precautions that were unnecessary in this case, for the girl was absorbed in the conquering of her horse, and the horse's own hoofs in the pine needles made noise enough to render inaudible the footsteps of the pursuer. For more than a mile the conscious hunter and the unconscious hunted kept their course. The ground rose perceptibly all the way, but at last became tolerably level, and then the girl shook out the reins and settled herself for a gallop. But at that instant, the wary pursuer, who day after day during the past month had been baffled by the speed of the horse, sprang out from behind a tree and seized the bridle near the bit. The complexion of the woman became a shade less swarthy with the sudden fright of this assault, and although she did not cry out or scream, her inward panic was in no way lessened by the sight of the countenance turned upon her. It was the face of one in despair, and the fierce, vengeful light of the eyes betokened a mind perilously near to insanity.

"Let go my horse!" she said in a low, tense voice.

The man tightened his grip.

"Keep quiet!" he retorted.

She raised her arm and struck the animal with all the force at her command, then with both hands jerked the reins and tried to ride down her obstructor. The horse reared and for a brief second lifted the man off his feet; but he held on, and horse and man came to the ground together.

"If you try to do a trick like that again," he cried, "I'll throw both you and the horse! Drop that whip!"

Instead of dropping it she raised it again, leaning forward this time to strike the man; but he sprang towards her, holding the rein in his right hand, and with his left caught the whip as it descended and wrenched it rudely from her grasp. For a moment she thought he was about to strike her, and her arm rose waveringly to protect her face.

"*Will* you keep still?" he demanded.

"If you want money," she said in the quiet, semi-contemptuous tone with which she would have addressed a beggar, "you might have the sense to know that I carry none with me in the forest."

"I want money," he replied, "and I *have* the sense to know you carry none with you."

"Then how do you expect to obtain it by this violence?"

"That I shall have the pleasure of explaining to you a little further on."

She folded her empty hands on her knee, now that he was possessed of both whip and rein.

"I advise you, sir, to turn my horse's head in the other direction, and warn you that you will make less by threats than by trusting to my good will."

"I reject your advice, Miss Berrington. The philanthropy of your family is well-known and widely advertised. Your good deeds rise up and call you blessed; but I am not an object of charity, although I may look it. The sum which I demand I shall exact by coercion."

"Oh, very well. Set about it, then. Pray do not allow me to hinder you in the least."

"Thank you, Miss Berrington; you shall not." Placing the riding rein over his arm, he turned his back upon her and led the horse along the level towards the west for perhaps half a mile further, when he deflected to the right until they arrived at the top of a high cliff overlooking the lake. Neither had spoken a word during the journey, and Constance Berrington sat very rigidly on her led horse, like a clothed Lady Godiva, *sans* the beauty. The look of discontent, however, had vanished from her face, and the expression which took its place was not unpleasing.

At the cliff her leader stopped, swung round, and said gruffly, "Get down!" without, however, making any offer to assist her.

She sprang lightly from the saddle to the ground and stood there, as if awaiting further commands.

"Seat yourself on that log."

A fallen tree which one of the winter storms had uprooted lay with its branches far out over the chasm. The girl sat down on the trunk as she had been directed. "I am John Steele, of Chicago," he said.

"That does not interest me," replied the young woman. "Have you ever heard the name before?"

"No, and don't wish to hear it again."

"Six months ago I was worth ten millions."

"That does not interest me, either."

"You need not reiterate the statement, madam; I shall interest you before I am done with you."

"I wish you were not so slow about it, then."

"Do you know a man named Nicholson?"

"Yes."

"Nicholson tried first to ruin me and then to murder me."

The young man paused, as if to allow this startling sentence to produce its effect. The young woman's eyes were upon the ground, but after a few moments of silence she glanced up at him with a languid air of indifference and said: "Is this the interesting part? Is any comment expected of me? If so, I can only say that Mr. Nicholson is usually successful in what he attempts, and I deeply regret the failure of his second project. It would have saved me from a most unpleasant encounter."

"Quite so," said Steele, tightening his lips. "I am glad you take it that way. Nicholson, as, of course, you know, was acting for the organisation which, I understand, contributes some fifty millions a year towards your support. In spite of your humane wish, he failed in his two attempts, but his third conspiracy succeeded."

"Ah! you were right, Mr. Steele, you *do* interest me. What did he endeavour to do on the third occasion? Consign you to a lunatic asylum?"

"No. To tell you the truth, madam, I feared that would come of itself. The fact that I have not gone mad under the silent persecution I was called upon to endure leads me to suppose that I shall hereafter be proof against any malady of the mind."

"I do not in the least doubt that. Nothing can damage a sanity already destroyed. If you are not a lunatic, you are worse—a cowardly hound who dares to offer violence to an unprotected woman."

Slowly the colour mounted in John Steele's pale face, and a glint of admiration came into his eyes. The little woman was absolutely at his mercy, yet she said these words with perfect serenity and turned upon him a gaze that was quite fearless. He noticed now for the first time the gloomy depths of those dark eyes, and thought how much more steadfast and beautiful they were than the blue orbs which had crazed his brain on the plains.

"Not such a coward as you think me, madam. Now that we are entirely free from any chance of molestation, when you must recognise your own helplessness, I beg to assure you that I shall treat you with the utmost courtesy."

"Thank you. But let us get to the point. You are John Steele. You were worth ten millions. Nicholson plotted against you and ruined you. Nicholson is one of the combination in New York from which I draw my money. In spite of what you say, you are too much of a coward to face Nicholson; therefore you have endeavoured to kidnap me and terrorise me into giving you a cheque for ten million dollars. How near am I right?"

"You are exactly right, madam."

"Very well. Although I am no admirer of Mr. Nicholson, nevertheless, it is easy to see why he defeated you. A man who takes so long to reach the kernel of his business may be all very well in Chicago, but he has no right to pit himself against a citizen of New York. I refuse to give you one penny."

"Don't say 'give,' madam, I beg of you. 'Restore' is the word. As I told you, I am making no appeal to the renowned philanthropy of the Berringtons. My ten millions, although lost to me, have gone into the coffers of your company. You have no more right to the money than I have to this horse. I own that amount because I made it without cheating anybody. I made it legitimately. I demand it back."

"I have already refused. What is your next move?"

"My next move will take some little time to tell, and you are so impatient of my loquacity that I almost fear to venture——"

"Oh, pray go on!" she cried wearily.

"Does the height make you dizzy? I should like to have you look over this cliff."

"It doesn't make me in the least dizzy. I know the cliff very well, and have been here many times. There are five or six hundred feet of sheer precipice, then a ledge of rock, then the lake."

"You have described it admirably, madam. Well, what I shall do is this. I possess, within a mile and a half of this place, a log cabin not so large or comfortable as your house. I intend to take you there and to hold you prisoner until I receive back what is mine."

"Mr. Nicholson would have mapped out a more feasible plan. How long do you think I shall remain captive without being found? To-morrow there will be a hue and cry after me—to-night, indeed, if I do not return. I shall be tracked by dogs, or an Indian will be got and put on the trail. Your scheme is absurd, Mr. Steele."

"You have forgotten the cliff, madam. I shall lead your horse to the edge of the cliff, strike him with your whip, and send him over. He will lie dashed to death on the ledge six hundred feet below. The Indian or the dog will trace the horse to this cliff. It will be naturally supposed that you have been flung into the waters of the lake, which are another six hundred feet deep. Then the search will end, madam. Lake Superior never gives up its dead, and to dredge at that depth is impossible."

"I beg your pardon," she said; "your plan is better than I thought. There is just the risk that the horse, poor creature, may bound from the ledge into the lake, and in that case the search would not end at the cliff."

Saying this, she rose and walked bravely to the very brink, looking over.

"Don't go so near!" cried John Steele, taking a step towards her. She paid no heed to him, and for a moment he held his breath in alarm as she walked along the extreme edge of the precipice. Then she turned listlessly.

"Alas!" she said, "the ledge is quite wide enough for your purpose."

"Oh, I have planned it all out," replied John, relief coming to his voice as she turned away from danger with her head lowered as if in deep thought. Then she took him entirely unawares. With a spring forward like that of a lynx, she jerked the reins from his unprepared hand. Striking the horse sharply with the loose leather, making him snort and shy with fear, she then smote him with her open palms on the flank, and away he galloped in a panic of fright. The face she turned to the astonished man seemed transformed. The black eyes danced with delight. She sank to the log again, shaking with laughter.

"Oh! I was wrong, Mr. Steele, when I said you didn't interest me! You do, you do! I have never met so interesting a man before. In twenty minutes, or thereabout, the riderless horse will gallop into my courtyard. Now, Mr. John Steele, of Chicago, what is the next move?"

"Well, logically," said John Steele, unable to repress a smile, grave as was his situation and quick his recognition of its seriousness, "logically the next move should be for me to throw you over the cliff."

"No, that wouldn't be logical. It seems, to the poor reason that a woman possesses, Mr. Nicholson is the man who should be thrown over."

"I am rather inclined to agree with you, Miss Berrington; but, alas! Nicholson is in New York, and you are the only member of the company now in my power."

"Are you quite sure I am in your power?" she asked, looking up at him.

"Frankly, I'm inclined to doubt it."

"I haven't laughed for years," she said, "not since I was a girl."

"Oh, you're nothing more than a girl now."

"I'm afraid I act like it," she replied, flushing slightly, and that evidently not from displeasure. "You are mistaken about Mr. Nicholson being in New York. Did you see that white yacht in front of my house?"

"Yes."

"Well, it belongs to Mr. Nicholson."

"Is he your guest?" asked John, the light of battle coming into his eyes.

"No, he is in Duluth. He went there a few days ago in his yacht, and sent the vessel back, in case I should wish a sail on the lake. Shall I arrange a meeting between you?"

"I suppose you will not credit me, Miss Berrington, when I tell you that I do not wish to meet Mr. Nicholson, and it is not cowardice which keeps me from the encounter. If I met him, I should kill him; then the law would hang me, and I have no desire to be executed."

"Oh, you are quite safe in Michigan," said the girl encouragingly; "there is no capital punishment in this State."

"I had forgotten about that, if I ever knew it. You see, I live in Illinois, and Nicholson lives in New York. In the one State they hang, and in the other they electrocute. It may be weak in me, but I shrink from either of those ordeals, much as I detest Nicholson."

The girl rose to her feet, put up both hands to her hair, and arranged the black tresses that had gone astray.

"How long have you possessed your log cabin, Mr. Steele?"

"About two months. One month I have spent round your house watching for you; but you have always left on a canter, or else that confounded groom of yours was following you, and I didn't want to hurt him. In truth, I didn't wish to hurt anybody."

"Poor man! have you been lingering in the forest all that time? No wonder you look like an escaped convict."

"Do I?" asked John in alarm, glancing down at his ragged garments. "I suppose I do. Since I came into the forest I have paid no attention to my personal appearance. Pray accept my apologies."

"Oh, don't mention it. I imagine you didn't expect to meet a lady."

"Well, I've been frustrated so often that I suppose I did not."

"You are, then, my nearest neighbour? By the rights of etiquette I should have made the first call, being the older resident. I think, however, Mr. Steele, that your methods of teaching me politeness to a new-comer were somewhat rough. So, if you will excuse me, I shall not go with you to your log-cabin this evening. It is getting late; see how low the sun has sunk, and how gloriously he lights up the lake."

"Yes," said Steele dolefully, "it reminds me of the copper situation here."

"It is copper that brings Mr. Nicholson to this district," she replied brightly, "although I suppose I should not tell that to an opposing speculator."

"Oh, damn Nicholson!" cried John hastily; then: "Really, I beg your pardon, madam. I have been a savage these two months past, as you very rightly remarked."

"I was going to say," she went on, "that if you will waive etiquette and come and dine with me to-night, I shall be very glad of your company."

"Ah, Miss Berrington, that is heaping coals of fire on this tousled head of mine. I could not venture into a civilised household in these rags. I am sure you will excuse me."

"Indeed I shall not. I make a bold appeal to your gallantry. I do not know my way; I am certain to get lost in the forest. You see, my horse has always been my guide, and, entirely through your fault, my horse is no longer here to lead me through the woods, so please be my pathfinder."

"Certainly, certainly, I'll lead you to the gates, but don't ask me to come in. I'm very much ashamed of myself, and I assure you that if your horse were here, I should help you to mount, and allow you to depart unscathed."

"You didn't help me to dismount," said the girl, glancing at him with eyes brimful of mischief, and laughing again.

With something of his old-time heartiness, Jack laughed at her readiness of repartee.

"You should not hold that against me. We were not acquainted then. It seems years ago, instead of minutes. I think if you and I had met when I first called on you, my later troubles would all have been averted."

"Oh, they did not tell me you had called."

"My visit was to your palace on Fifth Avenue, where I was received by a gorgeous individual with a cockney accent, whose knowledge of geography was such that he supposed Lake Saratoga and Lake Superior were neighbours and about of a size."

"Really? You met Fletcher then? Poor man, he is quite lost now, for I have him here with me in the woods. Nicholson brought him in the yacht. I rather suspect that the quiet Mr. Nicholson wishes to acquire this man's services; but, thank goodness, I can always outbid him, and Fletcher is peculiarly susceptible to the charms of money."

"Fletcher seems to be in demand, then?"

"Oh, he is most useful, but I fancy—which is a word he is very fond of—that he is very unhappy, for I have compelled him to abandon the gorgeous raiment you mentioned and dress as a northern farmer. I fear I shall need to restore his plumage, for he seems to think he has lost caste entirely. I am unable to convince him that he has gained it; but perhaps when he sees you in such raiment, and learns you were worth ten millions six months ago, he will be reconciled."

They were walking homeward through the forest, but at this remark John stopped and said ruefully: "Look here, Miss Berrington, if you are merely taking me with you to show Fletcher how badly a man may be costumed, I shall at once return to my cabin, for I have another suit there. I think that allusion to my clothes was most unkind, just as I was trying to forget them."

"Indeed I am going to turn you over to Fletcher, who will see that you are clothed, now that you are in your right mind. I think this is the spot where I first had the pleasure of meeting you, Mr. Steele."

"Now, that's another subject you are not to refer to."

"Dear me, I must get you to write out a list of them," and the sprightly little woman looked up at him with merriment sparkling in her fine eyes. No one would have recognised her as the Tartar who a short time before had browbeaten her servant and lashed her horse.

A cry rang out through the forest.

"They are looking for me," she said. "Answer the call."

John Steele lifted up his voice and gave utterance to a piercing scream that rent the silence like the soul-scattering screech of a locomotive.

"Bless us and keep us!" cried Constance Berrington, covering her small ears with her small hands, "is that an Indian war-whoop, that once used to resound in this wilderness?'

"No, it's the acme of civilisation; merely a college yell. If any of your people are graduates of Chicago University they'll recognise it."

The people who were not graduates of anything, except the college of hard labour, hurried to meet them with anxious faces.

"No, I am not in the least hurt," said Constance Berrington quite composedly. "I was merely compelled to dismount more rapidly than I usually do. Did the horse get home all right?"

"Yes, miss."

"Oh, then everything is as it should be. Luckily this gentleman was near by, and I came to no harm. Fletcher!"

The dejected, crestfallen man came slowly to the front, while she advanced a few rapid steps toward him, gave him some instructions in an undertone, and the search-party left under his leadership for the house, Steele and the girl following them at their leisure.

"How true it is that fine feathers make fine birds!" said John. "I should never have recognised Fletcher, whom I once took to be the finest specimen of our race."

"It's a poor rule that doesn't work both ways," laughed the girl. "Did you notice that Fletcher failed to recognise you?"

"Oh, I *will* go back and get that other suit!" cried John, coming to a standstill. "Don't wait dinner for me."

"Nonsense!" she said, letting her hand rest for one brief moment on his arm. "I didn't think men were so vain."

"I'm afraid you don't know much about them, Miss Berrington."

"I didn't until to-day. I've had my eyes opened."

"Well, I must make one proviso. You are to return my visit."

"Will you wear the other suit, then?"

"Yes, I will; and besides that, I have a negro cook who can prepare a meal that will surprise you, in our neck of the woods."

"A negro cook? Dear me, I thought you were ruined!"

"Oh, well, in a manner of speaking, so I am, now you mention it; but still, let us live by the way, you know."

When they reached the clearing, Fletcher was awaiting them on the verandah.

"If you will come with me, sir," he said, "I shall take you to the guest-house."

"Dinner at seven. Fletcher will show you the way to the dining-room. Until then, *au revoir!*" and the girl disappeared into the log-house, while Fletcher escorted Steele to a building near by and ushered him into a sumptuous bedroom facing the lake. On the bed was laid out a suit of evening clothes and all that pertained to it.

"I think you will find this about your size, sir. If not, I can get you one larger or smaller, as you wish."

"Good gracious!" said Steele, "do you keep a clothing store out here in the backwoods?"

"Well sir, for a country 'ouse situated as this is——"

"So far from London, eh?"

"Why, yes, sir, we are very well stocked, sir. And now sir, if you'd like a hair-cut, or your beard trimmed——"

"What! do you employ a barber, too? Thank Heaven!"

"Well, sir, you see, I used to be servant to General Sir Grundy Whitcombe, of the British Army, sir, and they do be particular."

"Do you mean to hint you can shave me, Fletcher, and cut my hair?"

"Oh, yes, sir."

"Well now, Fletcher, you don't like look an angel, but that's exactly what you are. I'll have the beard cut away entirely, but leave the moustache where it is; and if you give me the hair-crop of a British general, why, I've nothing more to ask in this life."

"Very good, sir," consented the admirable Fletcher.

When the task was finished, and John looked at the result in the mirror, he absent-mindedly thrust his hand into his pocket, but brought it forth empty. Fletcher was regarding him with admiration.

"By Jove!" cried the young man, "I haven't got a sou markee on me; but I won't forget you, Fletcher. I'll see you later, as we say out West, and you won't lose by it."

"Well, sir, I think I remember you now, sir; and if I may make so bold as to say it, sir, I'm already in your debt. Her Ladyship—I mean, Miss Berrington—being as she was thrown from her horse, sir, and you 'andy to 'elp 'er, you got the right kind of introduction, after all, sir."

"Ah, Fletcher, it seems like it, doesn't it?"

CHAPTER XVII
TO THE SOUND OF THE SILVER CHIME

A GREAT deal of nonsense has been written about the inartistic qualities of the modern man's evening clothes. The truth is that no other costume so befits a stalwart, good-looking young fellow. It is in plain black and white, and affects none of the effeminacy of lace and ruffles and colour which made a fop of the dandy centuries ago. There is a manly dignity about dinner-dress which nothing else can give, except perhaps a suit of armour, but armour, unless it be chain mail, develops inconveniences at table.

When Miss Berrington entered the dining-room, and found her guest standing by the huge open log-fire, awaiting her, she stopped still for a moment in amazement, and then an expression of unqualified admiration came over her ever-changing face.

"Why—why—" she hesitated, as he came eagerly forward with a smile to meet her, "is this really Mr. Steele?"

"It is Fletcher's Mr. Steele, madam. You have tamed the bear, Miss Berrington, and Fletcher has groomed him, that's all."

"I remember, Mr. Steele, that you interdicted the topic of costume; but may I be permitted the vanity of congratulating Fletcher and myself on our collaboration?"

John laughed as he led her to the head of the table.

"In my youth I read once of an enchanted land, presided over by a fairy princess so gracious and so good that when outside barbarians wandered into her realm, they became what we would call civilised; but I never knew this land and this princess existed until to-day."

In the soft glow of the shaded candles the expressive face of the girl seemed almost handsome. She wore no jewels, but even the young man's uncritical eye could not mistake the richness and exquisite design of her evening gown, which indicated that if this young woman shunned society, she had nevertheless chosen an artist for her dressmaker.

The dinner was so excellent that Steele regretted he had mentioned his negro cook. White-fish from the icy waters of Lake Superior is unequalled by anything that swims, unless it be the brook-trout which the northern streams that enter Lake Superior produce. Wild turkey of the Michigan woods is world-renowned as the choicest of game.

Although Steele's hostess drank nothing but cold spring water, an ancient and renowned vintage sparkled at his right hand. It is little wonder that Jack, healthily hungry, was brilliant that evening as even he had never been before, and this poor, rich girl who listened, delighted and amazed, began to wonder if, after all, she had not missed a good deal in life by flouting smart society which she considered frivolous.

After dinner, Constance Berrington put a shawl over her shoulders and asked her guest if he would come outside and see the lake glittering in the moonlight. On the verandah he found the unique arrangement of an out-of-doors fireplace facing the platform, and in its depths roared a hickory fire, which burns with a flame bright as electric light, and leaves an ash white as flour. Two screens of sailcloth drawn like curtains along the roof of the verandah partially fenced in this snug spot, leaving it open only towards the lake. The pale yacht lay like a liner's ghost on the silver sea, bathed in the light of the moon, and now and then the phantom ship gave forth melodious sounds as it chimed the hours in nautical fashion, the peal sweetly mellowed by the intervening water. John laughed in boyish glee to find himself in such a Paradise.

"I never saw anything so beautiful," he said; "nor have I ever known so ambitious a fireplace, trying to warm all outdoors."

Two rocking-chairs awaited them, and between these chairs stood a round table, on which the silent servant placed coffee and liqueurs. The hickory fire kindled a gleam of ineffable satisfaction in the young man's eyes when a box of prime cigars was placed before him.

"May I really smoke?" he asked, taking one between his fingers.

"I believe that is what they are for," replied the girl, with a smile, rocking gently to and fro. Then, when they were alone she said seriously: "Mr. Steele, I want you to tell me the particulars of the conspiracies you referred to, that proved so disastrous to you."

"Dear princess," he answered earnestly, "do you think I am going to talk finance in the land of enchantment? Not likely. Do monetary centres exist in the world? I don't believe it. Are people struggling anywhere to defeat one another? This silver silence denies it."

"But the silence is not going to deny me," she persisted. "I must know. You said I was responsible."

"I said such a thing? Never! That is a mistake in identity. You are thinking of the barbarian whom you quite justly tried to ride down in the forest. He said many stupid and false things, for which I refuse to assume responsibility. Reluctantly I admit that that barbarian was my ancestor, but a thousand years have passed since he lived, and I say the race has improved."

He blew a whiff of smoke into the still air and, watching it waft upward, murmured softly:

"And yet those wretched comic papers say a woman cannot choose cigars."

"I am glad they are good. It was not I who selected them, but Mr. Nicholson."

If some of the icy water of Lake Superior had unexpectedly dropped upon him, he could not have appeared more startled than at the mention of this name.

"Ye gods!" he whispered huskily, "I had forgotten that man existed! For years he has never been out of my mind before."

The girl's eloquent eyes were fixed upon him.

"The smoke has disappeared into the blue," she said, "but that name has brought you to earth again. Now tell me what he did."

"Miss Berrington," he said solemnly, "you are no more responsible for what Nicholson did, than I am for the actions of the savage who seized your horse. Let me forget again that either the white Indian or the savage ever lived."

"No," she persisted, "you must tell me." And so he told her, sometimes puffing at his cigar like a steam-engine, again almost allowing it to go out. The narration was vivid, but possibly it might have been more interesting if he had not substituted the father for the daughter in the case of Miss Alice Fuller. When the recital was finished the girl shivered a little; and seeing that he noticed it she said: "I think it is getting cold, in spite of our fire. And now I shall bid you 'Good night.' I must thank you for the most interesting day and evening I ever spent in my life. Good night, and I hope you will not dream of Mr. Nicholson."

He rose and took the hand she offered, raising it, before she was aware, to his lips.

"Princess," he said, "I know of whom I shall dream."

She laughed a little and was gone.

When the maid had girded round her the soft and trailing dressing-gown, bidding her mistress "Good night," Constance Berrington opened the window, knelt down before it, placed her elbows on the low sill, with her chin on her open palms, and remained thus gazing at the moonlit lake. The ship of mist tolled the unheeded hours as on a silver chime. At last, with a sigh that seemed to end in a sob, she murmured: "Oh, how beautiful the world is, and yet I never appreciated it before!"

Then she closed her window.

The informative Fletcher told Steele that the breakfast hour was nine, and the grandfather clock was striking as he entered the dining-room next morning. The fragrance of the coffee-urn was stimulating to a man from the keen outer air, and the girl who presided over it turned towards him a smiling face, radiant as the dawn. Steele spread out his arms.

"What do you think of this?" he cried, jovial as a lad with a holiday. "This is the other suit."

"Dear me!" replied Constance Berrington. "How came it here?"

"I was up this morning before five, donned my rags, tramped to my hut, comforted my negro, who was nearly white with panic at my absence, put on the other suit, and here I am."

"Well, if you do not enjoy your breakfast after that, I shall admit my cook inferior to your negro. Why didn't you take one of the horses?"

"Never thought of it. I seemed to be walking in midair."

"Then come down to earth, and buckwheat pancakes and maple syrup. Do you prefer tea or coffee?"

"Oh, coffee, of course. The aroma excels all the perfumes of Araby."

The breakfast was even more intimate and delightful than the dinner had been. Daylight had not removed the glamour of the moon from the land of enchantment. When the meal was finished, Constance Berrington rose and said: "Before you go, I wish to show you my library."

He followed her into this attractive room, its walls lined with books. Here and there were cosy alcoves and recesses, with leather-covered easy-chairs that might have graced a metropolitan club. A very solid table of carved oak occupied the centre of the room, and beside this the girl came to a stand, while he glanced around him in admiration.

"I never had much time for reading," he said, "and I do envy you this room. My own library is small, consisting mainly of books by friends of mine who kindly presented me with some of their writings."

"Then I wish you to accept a specimen of my works. My writings may not be very literary, but they are concise and to the point."

Here she placed a slip of paper before him, and glancing at it he saw it was a cheque for ten millions. Then he looked up at her, a slow smile coming to his lips, and shook his head.

"Princess, this is for the savage, not for me. The savage is dead."

"You are his heir, remember."

"No, we are too far removed from each other, the savage and I. Remember the centuries between us, and less than ten years outlaws all claim."

"You must accept it. It is mere transference, as you quite rightly pointed out. It does not belong to me, but to you."

The young woman spoke with tense eagerness, and the former frown came into her brow before she had finished. He picked up the cheque.

"That's right," she said, with a sigh of relief; but the smile broadened on his face as he slowly tore the signature from the cheque and placed her autograph in his pocket-book.

"Give me the hope that this may prove my return ticket to Paradise, and I am satisfied. Miss Berrington, you called me a coward yesterday, and you spoke the truth. I was, but I hope I am one no longer. I am young and reasonably ambitious. The world is before me. I shall begin where I began half-a-dozen years ago. I do not need your money."

"I shall write you another cheque—you must accept it."

"You dare not."

"Why?"

"Because I am your guest, and I forbid you. The rules of hospitality, madam, extend even to the land of enchantment."

"Is the guest so cruel, then"—there was a pathetic quaver in the voice—"as to leave his hostess to brood over this weight of obligation? Will he not thus, in the only possible way, lift that weight from her shoulders?"

"No!" cried John, coming swiftly round the table to her, "I shall lift her and the obligation together," and, suiting the action to the word, he picked her up as if she were a child and seated her on the table before him. "I'll not accept your cheque, but I ask you to accept me."

For an instant her eyes blazed up as if lighted from within, then dulled again. She did not in the least resent his boisterous action, but she shook her head and said:

"I shall never marry a man who is not in love with me, and I am too insignificant a woman for any man to love me for myself."

"Insignificant! Magnificent is the word! Why, Constance Berrington, you are the most beautiful woman I have ever seen. Your face makes every other in the world insipid. I'm not going to try and persuade you that I love you, because you know it. You knew it last night. You saw it in my eyes, and I saw the knowledge in yours. Curse the money! I'll make all the money I need if I have you by my side. What is money, anyhow? I've made it and lost it, and I can make it again and lose it again. Constance, let us take that yacht, go to Duluth, and be married before a magistrate for ten dollars, like a lumberman and his girl."

She looked up at him and smiled, then down again, then up once more, and he kissed her.

"Oh, don't!" she cried. "There is some one coming!" A knock sounded at the door, and Miss Berrington sprang down from the table.

"Your foot has touched the electric bell that is under the carpet," she whispered quickly, with a nervous laugh; then "Come in!" she cried, and the servant entered.

Steele was turning the pages of a magazine; Constance Berrington stood in the middle of the floor.

"Did you ring, miss?"

"Yes, tell the captain to get the yacht ready. I am going to Duluth."

THE END

Milton Keynes UK
Ingram Content Group UK Ltd.
UKHW010803110624
444053UK00004B/440